DEATH ECHO

ALSO BY JANUARY BAIN

City of Lies

No Good Deed

No Ordinary Man

Anna Hale, PI Thrillers

Death Secrets

Death Trap

DEATH ECHO

AN ANNE HALE PI THRILLER
BOOK 3

JANUARY BAIN

ROUGH
EDGES
PRESS

Rough Edges Press
An Imprint of Wolfpack Publishing
1707 E. Diana Street
Tampa, FL 33610

roughedgespress.com

Paperback ISBN 978-1-68549-514-5
eBook ISBN 978-1-68549-513-8
LCCN 2024942622

For Don

DEATH ECHO

ONE

A myth of creeping fog
and pouring rain
The scourge of alleyways
and darkest night
A will o' the wisp,
are they real or insane?

SATURDAY, AUGUST 31, 1888—WHITECHAPEL, LONDON, ENGLAND

"You can't stay until you pay. Thems the posted rules, Polly. No blaming me," the housekeeper reminded, hands on hips, her eyes bearing no sympathy for the likes of her. She stood in the middle of the kitchen, having sleuthed her out and interrupting a good chin wag Mary Ann Nichols, a.k.a. Polly, felt the better for.

"Don't let my bed. I'll soon get my doss money. See what a jolly bonnet I've got now," Polly said, pointing at her head with a smug smile, slurring her words. One of the other women seated at the table hooted her agreement.

Polly got to her feet and stumbled away from her chair, righted herself, and then opened the lodging house back door leading off the kitchen, venturing out into the night. The comforting warmth was replaced by a chilly dampness making her hunker down inside her clothes, wishing for a warm shawl. *Damn, I had it three times tonight. I could be sound in my bed if I cared. No matter, I'll soon make it again. I shouldn't have stolen those clothes and that bit of money, not that they couldn't afford it, those pompous people. It would be nice though, to still have a proper roof over my head. But I'm nobody's good servant.*

There were few people out at this hour and she worked to bolster her courage while she walked along the cobblestones, her footsteps echoing in the stillness of the night. She decided to venture over to Osborne Street, keeping an eye out for punters. A quick tiff and she'd soon be in her warm bed

"Ellen," she called out, catching a glimpse of her friend walking toward her. Ellen crossed the street and joined her, her expression tight with worry. Polly slumped against the wall, thinking she should have skipped that last drink. She swallowed hard and pressed a fist against her chest, keeping herself upright with some difficulty. *I need a moment or two and all will be fine.*

"Polly, are you daft? Come, I'll take you to mine." Ellen liked the lodgings on Thrawl Street, same as her, but Polly didn't have her money yet. Her new bonnet needed to be her lucky charm one last time tonight, then she'd be all set.

"You go on. I'll find the money. Had it already three times tonight, but I was too thirsty."

"It's quiet, but I pray you find it soon. Don't be drinking it away this time."

She watched Ellen walk on, then pushed herself off the grocer's wall, wishing it was open and she had the doss for a proper meal. She slowly made her way down the street, her spirits rising as she walked toward Whitechapel Road. She'd check out a spot where she'd often found her money, Bucks Row.

She stumbled against a doorway a short while later, then stood leaning against it while she checked out the side spring boot bothering her foot. Darn things fit so poorly. And her always on her feet too, turned out to make a bit of doss to keep body and soul together. She had a maudlin moment, thinking of her children. The life left she'd behind when she'd been paid the princely sum of thirty shillings a week in a printer's shop. Those were the good times, before it all fell away. *The cheating bastard took it all. Him and that damn whore. Worse than I am—taking my man from me.*

The sound caught her unaware. She hadn't heard anyone walking nearby in some time. She dropped her offended foot to the ground and began to turn toward the person if indeed it was a person coming up to behind her, their barely discernible footfalls quietlike as if they wore well-fitted shoes. Her breath quickened. This might be him, the punter she needed.

But she didn't get to see who or what it was. They grabbed her from behind, by her throat, dragging her to the ground as their hands squeezed tightly on her neck. No time to scream. Fear struck hard, and she struggled madly for her life even as the edges of her vision darkened. Then everything went black. She never felt the blade against her throat, shining dully under the streetlamp.

TWO

AUGUST 31—ANCHOR, ALASKA

Dear Boss, this is the letter Saucy Jack would write if he lived again in the twenty-first century. And low and behold he does! He arises, his spirit lives in in yours truly. Reincarnation's a fine, fine thing. Oh, and my knife's so nice and sharp I want to go to work right away if I get the chance, but alas, I must wait until the proper due date to begin. August 31st. Catch me if you can.

Jack the Ripper

"You looking for a good time?" Julie asked through the open vehicle window. The driver had lowered it down on the passenger side and she'd taken the cue. She'd spotted the John circling the block earlier. When he'd stopped his black SUV on the street next to the curb his second time around close to where she stood, she'd sauntered over in her new high heels, leaning forward to catch a glimpse of his face. It was summer in Anchor and so much easier to hustle up a few bucks for necessities. She swiped at her nose. It had begun to drip, a reminder that one of those "necessities" was soon to rear its ugly head. She decided the man looked respectable enough, the front seat clean of debris and no disgusting odors wafting through the opening. Anyone with manure on their boots was out, even if she needed a fix in the worst way.

"As it happens, I am. A *very* good time. What's it going to cost?" The tone of his voice was off-putting. Cold. Not heated or nervous like most of her dates.

But his asking about price relaxed her a little, even though she was smart enough to stay on guard. Cops never inquired about cost first, wanting to trap her into listing her prices and services without actually asking, otherwise they'd be soliciting for sex.

"Depends on what you want and for how long?" She'd need to find Benny soon. He had the good stuff. She shifted from one leg to the other, the shoes pinching her toes. How much could she get off the guy in the shortest time possible was always the question.

Thunder rumbled across the dark, moonless night sky heralding a bright flash of chain lightning a second or two later. The rip in the atmosphere lit up an entire section of Whitechapel in an unholy glow while making the hair on her arms dance with static. The press of time knowing Benny would close up shop and go home when the rain started forced her to get a move on. It was getting late, even for a Saturday night. Or, more rightly, Sunday morning.

"Don't have a lot of time tonight. How about a quick blow job? Forty bucks up front, of course."

"Is there any other way?" She opened the passenger door and slid inside, grateful for the chance to get off her feet for ten minutes; a blister was blooming on her right heel. One of the few perks of the profession, calling her own hours being the other advantage. The need for a fix loomed heavy in her mind. Choices were slim for dates at this time of the morning, and most of her friends were long gone, leaving Julie on her lonesome. If only she hadn't had to buy baby food earlier, she'd have been long gone too. But the food bank had been out of formula today, leaving her scrambling for cash for her six-month-old grandson. Not like her daughter would be on the hook for it—no, she left it to her sorry ass to provide. At least Julie had the strength to throw out her cheating husband a few weeks back after he'd fucked her best friend, leaving one less mouth to feed.

She turned in her seat to study the man driving. It was hard to get a real good look at the guy. He wore a baseball cap common to Anchor, Alaska, hiding much of his face. But he didn't give off any obvious vibes of wanting to do her harm.

"Pull into the alley over there," she said, pointing out the spot through the front windshield. The SUV smelled like wintergreen, not unpleasant. It was a reminder of her favorite mint and she reached into the pocket of her short dress to feel for the roll of candy she'd bought earlier. She'd have one later after the deed was done. She didn't focus on what she had to do, only a way to a means. She should have gotten a better education, not started drinking and doing drugs in her teens. She'd been smart in school too, but she'd drifted after her mom was arrested and thrown in jail. The pleas for her to get a part-time job to put some money in her mom's prison account had led her to dropping out early, one semester shy of graduating.

She glanced in the back, noting a pile of clothing

bunched up on the seat that didn't fit the tidiness of the rest of the vehicle.

"Would you mind changing your clothes?" the man asked. "I'll pay you extra."

"Why? You into doing a scene or something? Like Cosplay?" She'd never been asked to do it before. Most guys couldn't care less what she was wearing as long as it didn't interfere with their pleasure. Pigs, all the damn lot of them.

"Yeah, it's my thing."

She shrugged. "How much more cash we talking?"

"Double your money." He reached into his pocket and drew out the folded bills, handing them to her.

Should she be worried? But then she thought of how much the extra money could buy. Maybe she'd not even feel the need to go out tomorrow night but could stay in and soak in a nice warm bubble bath. Forget everything else. She tucked the precious resource in her bra.

"Okay, I'm game."

"Excellent."

He parked halfway down the alley next to a storage shed, well out of sight of the street. Most the buildings back here were abandoned, giving them the privacy to conclude their business in secrecy. She didn't need another arrest on her rap sheet, she had enough for shoplifting offenses as it was.

When he turned off the motor, he reached around and picked up the bundle of clothing, handing it off to her.

"Get dressed in the shed. It's open."

"But how am I going to see what I'm doing?"

"There's a light on inside. I've seen to it." The guy looked a bit too pleased with his planning. Odd, to say the least. Who the hell goes to such trouble for a blow job? Another rumble of thunder roared followed by a flash of intense light gave her a quick sense of disquiet.

"I don't know about this," she started to protest.

"Nothing to know. You can even keep the clothes after."

She looked down at the pile of fabric in her lap and read the label stitched into the one on top. Lambeth Workhouse PR by the light emitted by the dash display. Was it an old-fashioned petticoat? Odder still.

"What could I do with them? No one wears stuff like this anymore." Then she remembered the Anchor Community Players were hosting a play at the Elks Hall, Doctor Jekyll and Mr. Hyde. Maybe they could make use of them?

"You could donate them to the museum. The Lambeth Workhouse one is authentic. All I ask, is please take off your dress first. You know, to make the scene real."

"Yeah? Okay, then. Give me five minutes to change." She opened the SUV passenger door and scooted out, carrying the bundle the few feet to the shed. The door was unlocked and when she opened it, she found she could see fine, even though the light didn't show from outside. The one window had been covered with a blanket, keeping all the light inside.

She quickly lay the clothing on the single wooden bench, the only item inside the shed other than the battery-powered light attached to the metal wall. Hell, he'd even included an old-fashioned black straw bonnet with a velvet band wrapped inside the petticoat. Guy must love history, she mused, tugging on the stays that acted like a shelf for her breasts. She left her dress on. No way was she going to take a chance on losing it. The John wouldn't notice it anyway, covered up as she'd be. She pulled on the two petticoats, then the drab brown dress, feeling too weird for words. The pair of woolen stockings were the worst, scratchy and filled with what looked like moth-eaten holes. Most men wanted less clothing, not more. Finally, she was dressed. She sat down on the bench to wait for him, her knees jiggling up and down. She had his money, if he decided to leave now, she'd be none the worse for wear. She chewed on a thumbnail. *Please, don't close up shop, Benny.* All this damn preparation was eating into her timeline.

The door to the shed opened and closed as quickly. *Good, let's get this over with.*

"We need to do it outside," he said, gesturing with a quick nod of his head. "And put on the bonnet."

"More privacy here," she suggested, frowning, doing as he asked. The guy must have a screw loose she thought while tying the velvet ribbon under her chin. "There's even a bench." She patted it for emphasis. Five minutes and this would be all over, she reassured herself, then she'd be making a quick dash for Benny's place.

"No." He shook his head, his tone adamant. "This won't work. Outside."

She sighed and got to her feet. Why were the specialists always such a pain? At least they paid more. She didn't like the bonnet perched on her head, finding it obstructed her view. She pushed it back further from her face before stepping out, careful not to trip on the long skirts. A breeze had come up, the atmosphere heralding rain at any second. The cumbersome clothing at least was warm, maybe a little too warm as she felt a trickle of sweat escape under her arm pits.

"This work for you?" she asked, careful to stay out of view of the road. She didn't need to get caught in this getup by the cops and have her ass hauled into jail for a mug shot, she'd never live it down.

She was in the process of turning around to face him, when she was grabbed from behind around the throat. She went to scream, but she couldn't make a sound, his hands squeezing so hard her face felt on fire. Her vision darkened, spots appearing in front of her eyes as she was pulled to the ground, unable to utter even a single word. But one echoed in her brain. *Why?*

THREE

"I've met someone," Zoe said, studiously studying her glass of white wine. Anna had sprung for a decent bottle tonight. Not that she wouldn't be drinking boxed wine anymore, but it was a special occasion.

"Someone I know?" Anna asked, her interest growing as her sister took a sip of the liquor. They were celebrating moving in day for Anna, after her home had been deliberately exploded to smithereens this past winter. She'd rebuilt, refurnished, and outfitted her new place with every modern bit of technology and safety features the internet and town provided, though it would never bring the precious mementos of her former life back from the ashes.

Friday, her protective wolfdog she'd rescued six months ago, was even settled into his new bed near a warm furnace duct on the kitchen floor. He'd given it a jaundice eye earlier in the evening, too busy sleuthing through all the rooms checking out the strange scents

11

left by the builders. His whiskey-colored eyes opened every time someone spoke a bit louder or walked close to him, still on high alert from his close brush with death. Thankfully he'd escaped the fire caused by the deliberate gas leak. Anger replaced her sadness at losing everything for a second time in her life, thinking about the callousness of psychopaths. It had never been determined who had caused the explosion, but Anna was certain she knew. Either the three members of the Order of Blood and Bone who had been hunting women with bows and arrows or the duplicitous Dr. Molly, still MIA. Well at least the three murderers had been dispatched to hell where they belonged.

"So, what's his name?"

Her sister tucked a lock of her golden hair behind her ear, a becoming blush creeping across her smooth cheeks. "You know him. Cullen Cross."

"The medical examiner, Cross?"

Zoe nodded. Anna didn't hadn't known his first name, having always called him Cross. The forensic specialist was a man she respected for his careful attention to detail in his meticulous work, but dating her sister? An entirely different matter.

"When did you meet him?" The pair of them didn't move in similar circles. Her sister was a social worker, helping mostly teens and young adults get back on their feet, while Cross dealt with the other end of the human spectrum.

"By happenstance at the Anchor Inn. I was buying donuts for the crew—my turn being the last Friday of the month—and he'd gotten there ahead of me. Bought all they had. Three dozen. I was so mad that I'd been outmaneuvered, and running late because my car needed a new battery, I could have been a bit nicer. I mean, I only needed a dozen. But Cullen took sympathy on me and handed over a boxful. Said they were a gift, to make up for my lousy morning."

"Really?" It didn't sound like the Cross she knew, always talking about the importance of eating right while he dissected bodies, explaining the health issues that could be avoided with the proper diet. Not to mention his office was comprised of himself and one part-time assistant. "Who was he buying all the donuts for anyway? Did he say?"

"What? I don't know." Zoe shrugged off her question. "Maybe he was hosting a group or something? Or taking them to the hospital for the staff? But the point is, he was so darn nice about it. Ignored my sour lemon face and handed over the treats so I wouldn't feel bad heading into the office."

Was it a setup? Maybe the guy had been interested in Zoe for some time and he wanted to trick her into going out with him? Zoe was beautiful and kind-hearted, deserving of a really great guy. Was Cross the right kind of man for her? Anna took a large gulp of her wine, considering the question.

"And, well, he asked me out, and I said yes, you know, to thank him and all."

"When was this?" She checked up on the date, wanting to see if indeed Cross would have needed all those donuts.

Zoe narrowed her eyes at her. "Why does it matter? What are you getting at? Can't you be happy for me?"

"Of course, if he makes you happy?"

"He does. He's got a quirky sense of humor, always making me laugh about something."

Cross was funny? Maybe he was only serious in the office. Truth was, at work was the only place she ran into the man. Detective Josh Pace, their brother, though not Anna's sibling by blood but by the fact the Pace family had adopted her, had taken her into the coroner's office on more than one occasion to hear autopsy results or let her ask a question or two. He was a serious man, never smiled, and only laid out the facts in a monotone, dead serious voice, no pun intended. Anna had great respect for the dead, long as they weren't killers.

"How long have you been dating?"

Zoe blushed again. "Two months."

"And you're just telling me now?" Hurt filled her. She thought they were closer than this.

"Well, you've been so busy rebuilding the house, and well, I didn't want to say anything if it wasn't going anywhere."

"I want to host a barbeque and have him over. Invite a few friends. Does he have any allergies?" She needed to see them together. Because if he didn't treat her sister like she deserved, Anna needed to know right now. In her mind, they were too different to be as compatible as Zoe was suggesting.

"Sure. If I don't have to cook, count me in."

"What? I was expecting you to bring your famous cloverleaf rolls." Anna wasn't much of a cook beyond the basics. Maybe she'd get it catered? Her skill set ran more to boxing, weaponry, and sleuthing out the bad guys. Her PI business, Lone Wolf Investigations, though the moniker was out of date since she'd joined up with Josh and his friend Tom Jackson to become Wolf Pack Justice, was back on strong financial footing. The three siblings had been left millionaires by her deceased adopted parents. The reminder of losing her kind, adopted mom a few months back made her throat ache. She took a swallow of wine to ease it.

Anna pulled out her phone to check her calendar while Zoe poured them more wine, finishing off the bottle. "How about Friday night? September seventh."

It was then she realized what today was: August thirty-first. The digital reading on her phone duly pointed out it was also well past midnight, remembering the clock in the hall bonging out the time a short while ago. This was the infamous day in history from 1888. The Mary Ann Nichols murder. The beginning of a murder spree the likes no one had seen before. Her pulse quickened. The Anchor Police had stepped up patrols in the Whitechapel area after the ominous letter was published by the Anchor Free Press back in late March. It contained information about Jack the Ripper being reincarnated this century. Since then, nothing. Most people considered it fake, a set up by a writer in town looking for publicity for his fantasy novel. She'd been so busy these past few weeks, dealing with trade persons and contractors, she'd forgotten for the most part other than reading a few books on the case by noted historians. *Please, please let it be a hoax.*

Wolf howls erupted too close to the house for comfort, sending chills down her spine. Zoe shuddered, also aware the pack had become more brazen this summer, venturing closer to the town's perimeter. Why? Most wolves were shy of humans and stayed clear, and wisely so, aware of the harm humans could do them. Friday whined, his head cocked at an angle, listening to the ongoing chorus.

Listen to them, the children of the night. A remembered line from Bram Stoker's *Dracula* didn't dispel her unease.

"Cosmo Chapman has a book signing event for *I know Jack* scheduled this week," Zoe said after taking a last gulp of her wine, polishing it off.

Anna had no comment. Chapman rubbed her the wrong way. From his pompous byline in the Anchor Free Press reporting on town council business to using it as a platform to shill his book under the guise of bringing in the tourists.

"Have you read it?" Zoe asked.

"Hardly. I don't need more speculative theories about the Ripper bouncing around in my head," Anna scoffed. "Have you?"

"No, but my friend Ainsley has. Apparently, he's hot on the suspect being Charles Lechmere a.k.a. Charles Cross. You know, the first guy on the scene who found the poor woman brutalized by the monster. He says there wasn't time for it to be anyone else, that the Ripper pretended to find her right after killing her. Plausible if it wasn't for the fact the crimes stopped so abruptly and yet I read in one of the books I've perused that Lechmere remained in the area for years after. I'd think it's more likely to be someone who died soon after the last crime or was incarcerated or housed in an insane asylum or moved away from the area. Someone like Druitt, Kosminski, Tumblety, Maybrick, Sickert, Chapman, Levy, or an unknown."

Anna knew the story well enough, but only the proven facts interested her, and those were few and far between. She understood on an intellectual level that the gruesome crimes were one of the biggest mysteries in history. A whodunit that had kept multitudes obsessed with who the suspect was for over a century. Oddly, she hadn't realized her sister was so interested in the case.

"Every suspect known or brought forward from that time onward is a case built around circumstantial evidence. And a case from a hundred and thirty-six years ago when the police didn't have access to fingerprinting,

DNA testing, and profiling. Well, suffice to say, the chances of it being solved now are less than a thousand to one. Do you want some whiskey?" Anna got up to prepare the drinks after a nod from her sister. She felt a need for more of a bracer than the wine. Something to drive away the chill that had crept over her.

Zoe pushed her hair back again, her expression animated. "Don't call it just yet. There have been some new finds in the last few decades. Like the diary, even though it's mostly been proven a hoax, but there was DNA found on a shawl thought to be Catherine Eddowes. And the mitochondrial genetic material matched closely to that of a living relative of Kosminski."

Anna stared at her sister. "Okay, that was unexpected." She handed her off the heavy-bottomed tumbler of whiskey and sat back down across from Zoe. "You don't give any credence to it being a Freemason connection, or even a royal one?"

"Ha! So you do know more than you're letting on."

"Maybe a little," Anna admitted after taking another sip of the seductive liquor, enjoying the bite of the liquor and the bracing heat.

The new grandmother clock in the hall began to strike the hour, giving off a single bong. "I didn't realize it was getting so late," Zoe said, covering a yawn.

"Stay over." Anna was enjoying the special time with her sister and didn't want it to end. She'd made sure to have extra guest suites incorporated into the floor plans for her new home to make sure to always have a place for friends or family to stay over on any given whim.

"Nah, can't. My turn to bring donuts again." When Zoe got to her feet, she swayed a bit. The reminder made Anna think of Cross again. She'd soon know his deal. Sleuthing was her business.

"Sorry, sis, can't allow you to drive home in good conscience." Anna got up to support her sister who looked annoyed by the intervention. Guilt struck. She shouldn't have offered that last drink. But she had been enjoying a rare moment with Zoe, something she wished she had done more of in the past.

"What? I came on a snow machine. Nothing could be safer."

"Yeah, what if you don't see something strung out on the road. Remember what happened to Sherry McMillian? Almost decapitated in the middle of the night by a hydro line that had gone down. No. I insist you stay here, at least until daylight."

"Fine. But it's only a couple of miles. Not at the end of the world."

Anna assisted her sister into one of the four ready guest rooms, taking off her shoes, and tucking her into bed. She'd even bought a quilt at the craft fair in town, liking the idea of the log cabin design and the roots it suggested to the past.

"Where do you think our fascination with serial killers comes from?" Zoe asked. She didn't wait for an answer but continued on. "I think mine stems from back when you came to live with us when we lived in Lexington. I never understood why your stepfather did what he did. It sucked, big time, but I'm so proud of you for overcoming it and becoming who you are today, Anna. Damn proud to call you my sister."

The final half of Zoe's diatribe was more like her, positive and upbeat, and Anna blinked away a rush of tears.

"I'm proud of you too. I know this past year has been the toughest one of all. And yet you picked yourself up after Tia, and then Mom died, and went on to help others in need. Not everyone can manage that."

But Zoe was already snoring lightly. Anna turned off the light and crept from the room.

She headed upstairs and quickly prepared for bed, then slipped under the covers, Friday at her feet.

"Fingers crossed, buddy, tonight's just a normal Friday night in Anchor." Friday looked less convinced of the fact than she would have liked. Maybe he was picking up on her apprehension? But he soon settled down and she drifted off to sleep, comforted knowing her sister slept safe and sound under her roof.

Her cell phone buzzing woke her sometime later and she clumsily picked it up off the night table to stare at the message.

The text was from Josh, a detective on the Anchor Police Department.

A body's been found in Whitechapel.

FOUR

"Look who showed up," Detective Browne said to Detective Josh Pace, his mouth twisted into a sneer. "Mr., *I Know Jack*, himself."

The pair of them stood near the back of the shed where the body of Julie Ann Johnson, or JJ as she was known in the area, had been found, collecting evidence while waiting for the medical examiner to show up. Her ID gave her age as forty-one. It had been discovered a short while ago by an old man walking his dog, the shock of what he'd witnessed sending the man to the hospital with a suspected heart attack. No surprise there. It was a brutal slaying. They'd have to leave off questioning the man until later. But dressing the woman in period costume, leaving her like a bundle of rags, the initials M.A.N. carved into her forehead, what the hell kind of monster did that?

Detective Josh Pace glanced over at the councilman, the insufferable Cosmo Chapman. Careful to keep his expression neutral, Josh replaced his cell phone in his jacket pocket. He'd second-guessed sending the message to Anna, but knew she had to know as soon as possible for him to avoid any throwback. This was going to hit her hard and he wished he could be there to somehow soften the blow. His adopted sister was a crusader all the way to her righteous, beautiful core. She was on a mission bigger than anyone he knew, set on a path few would tread. Or want to. But Josh knew he'd follow her into hell if necessary.

"Crap. Just what we needed. I swear, this has all the hallmarks of being only the beginning of the worst chapter in Anchor's history. And that's saying something," Josh said, watching Chapman talk to the constable in charge of keeping the crime scene secure. The young officer, newly sworn into the force, was shaking his head no. Obviously the guy was pressuring him to let him by.

"Chapman has managed to put himself at the top of my suspect list," Browne said with a grimace. "Writes a book then shows up at the crime scene. Probably did it for the free publicity. Wouldn't put it past that asshat."

A twisting in his guts spoke the bald truth. Bad as the last year had been, what with the Black Rose Killer, then those damn outsiders, which couldn't be blamed on anyone from Anchor, a trio of movie assholes dispatched to their proper reward, this current crime hit him hardest of all. Innocent women slain to create copycat crimes from the 1888s? Something less than sub-human, something on par with the likes of that psycho Ted Bundy, Edmund Kemper, or a Jeffrey Dahmer. If only the monster would turn himself in like Edmund did? Hopeless wish. The original Ripper got away with his crimes, something the current asshole was most likely also trying to achieve. He'd bet his new ulcer on it. But he had to set all his anger aside and focus on the here and now, using it to fuel the investigation, not get waylaid by fury.

"What the hell is keeping Cross?" Browne asked.

"Don't sweat it. The time of death has already been pre-arranged by the first Ripper. No one goes to such trouble to stage a crime, then ignores the obvious," Josh said. He watched a young constable set up the lighting around the body to give a better view of the crime scene within the yellow crime scene border tape. High intensity LED lamps dispersed around the area were essential. Dawn was two hours off, it now being 0500 hours. Both he and Browne had suited up a few minutes ago to avoid contaminating the crime scene. They'd observed all they could without disturbing the body and were now in the process, with the help of the newly installed lighting, to get a good look at the blood splatter. And not surprising, there wasn't much of it. Meaning the victim had been dead before their throat had been cut. Nothing on the shed or the fence nearby either because most of it had soaked into her clothing.

"Pre-arranged?" Browne asked, deepening the permanent frown marring his forehead.

"The original murder happened shortly before 3:40 a.m. when her body was found. In fact, one of the men who found her thought she maybe she was still alive. Her body was warm to the touch. In the dark, they couldn't see the extent of her injuries, which explained it." Josh shook his head slowly. "Only a fucking madman would attempt to recreate such atrocities."

"There he is," Browne said, followed by a curt head nod in the direction of the man they'd both been expecting parking his car alongside the others in the alley. Most of the force was already on scene. This had all the hallmarks of a big case. He expected the chief of police to show up at any moment as well.

"Good. Time for forensics to weigh in on this shit."

Cross came striding over, medical kit in hand. He was suited up, his expression grim. "Sorry. Bit of food poisoning."

"That sucks," Browne said. They both watched the tall, lean man in his late thirties crouch down and begin his inspection of the body. He went about his business with his usual attention to meticulousness, using a liver probe to check for time of death. Cross's recent bout of illness didn't appear to be hampering him, which was a relief. Dark hair combed slickly back from a broad forehead, the guy had the look of the serious librarian or scholar about him, his black tie visible above the white paper suit. They needed answers. Now. Everyone on the force would be working round the clock until this case was solved. How was it even possible that this town had bred a second serial killer? The outside movie people didn't count, being from LA. The Black Rose Killer had been born into the Ironwood cult COFA or Circle of Friends Anchor, located north of the town, though he was technically from the catchment area. Unless there was a recent increase in population, someone drawn to the town due to the notoriety of Chapman's book and the renaming of the area to Whitechapel? Hell, there was even a play being performed by the Anchor Community Players that echoed the crimes from 1888: *Doctor Jekyll and Mr. Hyde*. Josh made a mental note. Maybe someone in the cast or crew knew something?

"How long has she been dead?" Browne asked.

"Taking all things into consideration, being as the lowest temperature in the past few hours only hit sixty-two degrees, and the fact of organs being removed from her stomach cavity that would speed it up some, though there has been the addition of extra clothing covering her chest, I'd say roughly between shortly after three o'clock and before three-forty-five. Probably closest to three-thirty. She hasn't been dead long. She was strangled before her throat was cut, the petechia in the whites of her eyes and the surrounding area prove it, which is why there is little blood splatter."

"Just like you said," Browne said, glancing over at Josh with speculation riding high in his eyes. "Same time of the morning as the victim in 1888."

"Which means we have eight days to solve the case before the next victim." September eighth was the next infamous date in the Ripper cannon of five.

FIVE

"Why are you here, Chapman?" Anna demanded. She held back the surge of intense white-hot anger at seeing the councilman badger the much younger constable to let him inside the yellow police tape. Nothing more she'd like than to bitch slap the bastard. First, he writes an obviously biased speculative book on a crime that had as much chance to be solved now as getting everyone to agree on how best to combat climate change, and now he was trying to interject himself into the crime scene? No way in hell.

"Morning, Anna," he said, pushing out his fleshy lips and giving her a once over with his roving eyes. Now she needed another shower, damn it. The guy was a few inches taller than her, dressed all in black as if that would help others see him for the serious writer he considered himself to be. It would take a hell of a lot more than clothing for that to happen. "I'm surprised to see you here." He made a point of looking over at Josh who at the moment was speaking with Cross. "But then I guess I shouldn't be. Since you two are related."

"You have anything to do with this?" She narrowed her eyes at him, enjoying the outrage that sparked behind his slimy expression. The constable gave her a grateful look before walking a short distance away to get away from Chapman's constant pushing for answers no one could provide yet. Except for the killer.

"Looking to get hit with a libel charge? You breathe one word of that accusation and I'll have your ass in a sling before you can say Jack Daniels."

"More like Jack the Ripper." She shook her head, catching a pair of gestures from Josh in telling her to back off and meet him at her vehicle. The pair of them shared an interest in sign language, developing their own as teenagers. It came in handy.

"I'll give you twenty to one that I'll be the first one to solve this case," Chapman boasted.

She ground her teeth together before managing to speak again without screaming at him. He thinks this is the kind of situation where bets are placed? The idea disgusted her beyond measure. "Then do it before another woman is slaughtered."

He had the grace to at least look taken aback at her words, finally clamming up and stalking off. She stood there for a few minutes and took in the crime scene. The body was lying next to the shed wall, legs spread as expected, skirts raised above her groin. She was in period costume, a fact that further revolted Anna. Blood pooled on the victim's forehead. That was different than in 1888. Who was the poor woman?

She noted Josh making a move toward her and she retreated to her truck parked at the end of the alley and out of view of the crime scene, getting in and waiting for him to join her.

Thirty seconds later he opened the door and slid into the passenger seat.

"What do you know? Who was it?" she asked, not bothering with a greeting.

"Julie Johnson, JJ, forty-one, lives over on Ring Road with her daughter and grandson. Cross pegged the time of death around the same time as in 1888. Sometime after 0300 hours and before 0400. A known prostitute, arrested numerous times for drug offenses. But you can't breathe a word of this until next of kin is notified. I'm on my way there shortly."

"Of course. I saw blood on her forehead which doesn't match up with the original crime," she ventured, staring at him. Josh looked pale, his eyes shadowed from lack of sleep and what he'd witnessed this morning.

"He left a signature. Carved the initials M.A.N. which I'm assuming stands for Mary Ann Nichols into her face. Fucking bastard!" Josh punched the dash.

"She went by the name Polly as well. You need to take up boxing. That will help." Every time Anna hit the heavy bag, a face she loathed was the intended target. It used to be her stepfather before he was executed by the state. Now it was overlaid by Strobel's, the monster who'd murdered their sister Tia in cold blood.

"Need a sparring partner?"

"Sure. I didn't have a ring built into my new place though maybe I should have, but we can head on over to Jimmy's and rent a ring."

"Right. Maybe after this case is solved."

"In my experience, you need it more now than later."

"Probably. Okay, I'll keep you in the loop. Soon as I know anything, I'll text or call you. This thing..." Josh raked a hand through his short fair hair, disheveling it further. Not that it could take away from his handsomeness, no matter how rugged he got. He looked like the kind of guy a photographer would pay good money for him to pose on the cover of a romance novel with his chiseled jawline and deep-blue eyes. She'd had a crush on Josh all her life. One she'd never act on even though it had reached forever status. In spite of what was going on, a moment with him brought on an inner peace.

"It's going to be an upset to the town. All the crazies will be climbing out of the woodwork wanting a piece of it," Josh said.

"If it's anything like what happened in history, expect a barrage of letters and postcards, maybe even packages in the mail containing a piece of human anatomy. How can I help?" Anna asked.

"After Browne and I canvass the neighborhood, I want to talk to the community theater people putting on the play *Doctor Jekyll and Mr. Hyde*. Maybe the costume was stolen from them?"

"I'll talk to the director. Sam Fields's in charge. He owes me one." She'd helped his daughter Raylene erase the naked photos of herself when an ex-boyfriend had posted them online in hopes of embarrassing her. Not the first client who'd come to her with the exact same problem and she'd not be the last. Always pro bono. Thanks to her adopted parents, far more diverse cases could be solved or fixed for free going ahead.

"Also, Fast Eddie's is only two blocks from here." *Here* being what could be rightly called crack house alley aligned with Anchor's Redlight district, a few square blocks not far from the downtown core. Yeah, why not rename it Whitechapel and invite all the crazies to town? Chapman had a lot to answer for. But the truck stop held possibilities. Who knew what manner of person was driving their cargo through town? Easy enough to park their vehicle at the large lot provided for truckers, then under guise of needing a few hours sleep, slip out and find a hooker who frequented the area. Such a pre-meditated crime was beyond understanding, but maybe they'd get lucky and a security camera would pick up something.

"Right. Could be a trucker hauling his load up north. This time of year, the highway's a constant stream of big rigs trying to get all the supplies into smaller communities before the snow flies," Josh agreed.

Anchor was on a major trucking artery, a business hub for a number of smaller towns and communities dotting Alaska's landscape with plenty of space to spare. Geography was the challenge of the north. It was a disadvantage to be located such vast distances from manufacturing. Everything needed to be trucked or flown in. "Robert Rembert comes to mind. Then there was that sick vampire bastard that kept the women trapped in his truck for months." Anna shuddered in horror. He'd even sharpened their teeth to make them appear more like a vampire. What kind of monsters lurked among us? She'd long given up on ever finding the bottom of the pit of depravity that existed.

"There's been a few. The ease of escaping the scene in a truck has made them more difficult to find." Maybe he too was hoping the murderer wasn't from Anchor. Or maybe a recent import was a possibility? Somebody drawn to the town with enough similarities to the Ripper's 1888 to make him think this was the ideal spot to recreate the terrible crimes? The idea of someone that devious and depraved in Anchor. It made her sick to her stomach thinking of it.

Josh patted her shoulder with concern riding high in his blue eyes. "You okay?"

"Yeah. But it sucks pretty bad."

"Lots of overtime going ahead. Patrols will be stepped up. No doubt, the chief will call in help from surrounding towns to put more boots on the ground per shift. I'll come by your place later. We haven't even toasted it yet." Josh opened the passenger door and stepped out, headed back toward his police vehicle.

Anna shook her head as she cranked over the GMC's starter, firing the motor to a powerful purr that satisfied her inner child on a normal day. But this was no regular morning. And to think she was considering having Cross over for a meet and greet barbeque before this shit hit the fan? She decided to pick up her wolfdog Friday on the way to the Elks Hall where the community players were in dress rehearsal. The play was scheduled for production later in the week. Then she realized it was too early in the morning for anyone to be around. Fast Eddie's first then.

As she drove out onto the street that ran past the crime scene, she glanced up at the full moon hanging in the sky to the south. In her experience, nothing good happened on full moon nights. Human beings were stirred up by the ancient light it threw down, especially in the summer when blood's up anyway. But this crime, this was no spur of the moment murder brought on by passion or a desperate need for money or revenge. No, this had all the hallmarks of an intelligent psychopath looking for immortality. Anna couldn't imagine a worst-case scenario.

SIX

Fast Eddie's parking lot was packed with idling trucks keeping their cargo cold for delivery for Northern grocery stores. Anna pulled up close to the entrance to the large family restaurant and gas bar reserved for smaller vehicles. She and Friday disembarked in tandem. She noted several cameras pointing at the parking lot and gas pumps before she headed inside. The heady fragrance of fresh coffee and fried food greeted her, making her stomach rumble.

"Morning, Ed," she said as the owner came striding right over to greet. You'd be hard pressed not to run into the man no matter what time you visited. There were even bets in town on if he ever slept at all.

"Anna! Good to see you. It's been too long." He took both her hands in his, encasing hers with his meaty paws. Ed Wheeler was a big man, at least six four and three hundred pounds. Unmarried, he fancied himself a ladies' man. She began to ease herself out of his grasp, finding the sense of being trapped a bit off-putting, though she knew that was just Ed being friendly. Friday gave a low growl speeding up the transaction.

"It has. Been busy rebuilding my house. But it's nice to be done now."

"Aww, an unfortunate thing," Ed said, shaking his head in sympathy. "You and Friday here for breakfast?"

"Actually, I was hoping to check your camera feed for the last few hours?"

His open expression darkened. "What's happened?"

"I'm investigating an incident than happened early this morning. I'm looking for anything suspicious going on in your parking lot. Someone walking away from their truck instead of sleeping?" Long-haul truckers had extended cabs with sleeper compartments and even small kitchenettes to make living on the road more comfortable.

"Come into the back." A few customers had turned to watch us, mostly men, though a couple of women sat together at one of the tables looking as ready to drive the big rigs as any other employee.

The three of us went behind the counter and through the short swinging doors leading to the kitchen. Ed's office was right off the cooking area, a small space made even more claustrophobic by a collection of memorabilia heralding his twenty-odd years in business. Even plaques from sport teams he'd sponsored and the funniest addition, a trout that sung and danced when movement alerted it to a presence.

He pushed aside a stack of assorted red T-shirts the staff wore with the famous Fast Eddie's logo stitched into the fabric in white thread and several pizza takeout boxes not yet folded into a familiar square shape, making room on a straight-backed armless chair for her to sit down beside him at his cramped desk. Friday whimpered, trying to find the space to lie down comfortably, finally settling on sitting and staring at us from the doorway.

The desk housed a monitor with the feed from eight cameras. Not large enough to catch anything more than movement, but each image could be brought up separately for viewing.

"What time did the incident happen?" Ed asked. His alert eyes bore into hers for a split-second. She was grateful for his discretion, calling it an incident.

"Around three-thirty. I'd like to start watching before midnight."

"Sure." He pointed out the keyboard as he plunked himself down beside her, squeezing her in place with his considerable bulk. "Take all the time you need. I always wanted to watch a pro at work."

About the last thing she needed was Ed pressing her tight against the wall for the next couple of hours or however long this would take.

"Could I trouble you for a cup of coffee?" she asked after a few tedious minutes of his peering over her shoulder at the computer screen like it held all the secrets of the Valley of the Kings in Egypt as she worked the camera feed offering the best view of the trucks parked along the fence.

"Sure." He snapped his fingers and a waitress appeared in the doorway, unable to get past Friday standing guard.

"Two cups of coffee, one heavy on the cream and three sugars, one black for our Miss Anna here, right?" He beamed, pleased to know her preference.

She nodded, praying desperately that someone out in the restaurant would need him and he'd be called away.

Guilt struck. Ed was trying to help. But did he need to be *this* helpful?

A sweat-inducing hour later of peering at the feed being fast-forwarded on the monitor, two cups of coffee —each—and no one had needed Ed for anything. But nothing out of the ordinary had occurred on screen either and the time read 03:11 hours. No one walked from their truck onto the sidewalk that would lead down the street to Deerhorn Street and the back alley where JJ had been found. Frustrated, Anna pushed back a limp strand of dark hair that kept releasing from the haphazard bun she'd tugged her hair into earlier. Lots of surveillance work is difficult. Hours sitting in vehicles waiting for some action to occur. At least they'd been able to watch the view in quick time.

Then when she thought it was all a waste of time a man with a fair-sized gut got out of the cab of his truck, and pulling his ball cap down low, strode away from his rig toward Deerhorn Street instead of toward the restaurant.

She stopped the feed and backed it up to show him getting out of the truck cab and froze the screen.

"Do you know this trucking company or the guy?"

Ed peered at the screen. The diagonal angle of the trucks made it difficult to read the insignia on the doors of the company's name most trucks used in advertising. "Looks like one of the Northern Star trucks. Most of theirs are Peterbilt and white. Couldn't swear to it though. And the guy—no idea. I guess I need to upgrade my equipment. The picture's a bit grainy and his hat's obscuring most of his face, but dark curly hair is clearly visible sticking out beneath it. Unless it's a wig?"

"Could you print this out for me?" She also needed to check on the time he arrived back at his truck and left the parking lot. She kept fast forwarding until she found what she needed. He got back in his truck and left the parking lot just after 0400 hours.

"Sure. Take a sec."

"And could I have a copy of this feed? I have some video equipment at my place, brand new, and it should be able to sharpen the resolution."

"Of course."

"Thanks, Ed, this was very helpful." She gestured she wanted to get up as he handed her the items she'd asked for.

"How about breakfast on me?"

"Thanks, but I need to be somewhere." She'd head over to the Elks Hall and check in with Sam Fields next.

"Aww, before you go. Maybe you could give me a clue as to what happened last night? I know it's confidential, but my lips are sealed."

"Ed—"

"Nod your head or say nothing if I'm right. But does this have something to do with the threat in the paper from a few months ago? That guy saying all that crazy stuff about being reincarnated?" Ed kept his voice low, his expression one of concern.

She pressed her lips together.

Ed nodded sagely. "Yeah, I thought so."

"You can't say *anything* until the family is notified."

Ed had the grace to look horrified. "It won't come from me, Anna, you have my word on it."

"Thanks for your help, Ed."

"Anytime, pretty lady."

SEVEN

"Northern Star Trucking," a bored voice said over the phone. Anna sat in her GMC outside the Elks Hall, deciding to give the company a quick call on her cell before heading in. She'd spotted Sam Fields's red Mustang in the parking lot among others involved in acting and putting on the production.

Anna introduced herself to the young sounding female and explained the situation. Then asked her question, "Do you keep a manifest of all your drivers?"

"Of course, it's the law."

"Would you be able to tell me which of your drivers was in Anchor, Alaska last night between midnight and 0400 hours?"

"That's not in my job description. You'll have to talk to the boss."

"Fine. Could you put him on?"

"He's not in yet. I'm the only one in the office at the moment." The young person sighed like it was a big imposition. "You'll have to call back after nine."

Before she could say another word, the individual hung up on her.

"Thanks for nothing," Anna muttered, checking the time. 0800 hours. "Okay, let's roll."

Friday wagged his tail and followed Anna out the driver's door.

The side door to the Elks needed some maintenance, squawking on rusting hinges as Anna pulled it open. She strode across the wide-board wooden floor toward the rows of chairs empty except for Sam Fields. The stage-hands were working on the set while Sam had his head down, writing in a spiral notebook. She slipped into a seat beside him.

He looked over at her with surprise followed by a quick smile. "Anna Hale. Good to see you."

They shook hands and Friday extended his paw in greeting. Sam did likewise, a wider smile lighting his rough-hewn middle-aged face at the unexpected invitation. "We need this guy on stage. He's a natural."

Anna snorted. "He's just hamming it up for you. He's had a tedious morning lounging in doorways and waiting for me to finish my business." She gave Friday a loving pat. "He needs a good run more than anything, which he'll get soon as I've finished here."

"Something on your mind, Anna?"

"Yes. Something has happened. An incident early this morning involving a woman dressed in period pieces of clothing. I can't give specifics until next of kin are notified, but it's a bad one, Sam. I'm wondering if you've had any women's clothes recently stolen? Ones specific to the play?"

"Not sure. We'll need to check. The wardrobe rack's backstage."

Anna and Friday followed Sam up the short staircase to the right of the stage, hot on his heels. She bumped the edge of a picture frame in her eagerness and lurched to grab the artifact before it crashed to the floor. It had been set aside rather haphazardly by someone next to the open stage where three men were busy working on the set.

But it was the image painted on the canvas that made her eyebrows rise in disbelief as she held it in her hands. The dark, gloomy work streaked with muddy reddish-brown and rendered in overall muted oils had a menacing edge to it, appearing the product of a depressed artist's mind. There was a headless figure standing mid-center in the twenty by sixteen-inch painting. It was off-putting and sinister, the dark shadows looming uncomfortably in the background, a bed the focus in the foreground. Perhaps she'd go so far as to say it was an unbalanced mind that had seen it in their mind's eye and painted it, letting a dark, hazy presence into the world that it could well do without.

"Ah, Jack the Ripper's Bedroom caught your eye," Sam said, noticing Anna had stopped and was holding the painting gingerly by the edges.

"Walter Sickert?" Anna said, reading the signature. His last name seemed appropriate enough.

"Yes, but only a reproduction lent to us. Alas. No money to be made."

"Somebody pays good money for one of these?"

"Hmm, yes, it has historic importance. And it's the perfect addition to help set the mood for the play even though it wasn't painted until after the murders occurred in Whitechapel. Sickert painted it when his landlord filled his ear with stories of the infamous Jack having lived in her boarding house, residing in the very bedroom Sickert rented."

"How did you get it?" Friday gave a low growl, staring at the painting with intense dissatisfaction. Her companion had good taste in art. Something like this uneasy image would never grace her walls. Epic landscapes were more her thing. Wide open spaces, mountain ranges, realistic images of earth that gave the eye respite. Lightened the soul, not increased its load.

"It was lent to us specifically for use in our production. One of the actors brought it in. Not certain where they got it, but I could ask around?"

"Please."

"The clothing rack's over here." Sam pushed aside a sliding wooden wall perched on wheels that appeared to be part of the set, to reveal a long, overstuffed clothes pole hanging between two long silver chains screwed into the ceiling. "It's makeshift, but it will do. Okay, what specifically are we talking about?"

"A couple of petticoats, a long brownish dress, a black bonnet with black ribbon." Anna wished she could bring up a photo on her phone, but that would have to wait until next of kin had been called and, of course, soon as Josh sent her one. She'd managed a decent look at the clothes JJ was wearing, but being on the wrong side of the yellow tape didn't offer many details.

"The bonnet would be an easier place to start. The few hats we have need of are in boxes on this shelf." Sam strode over to a series of temporary metal shelves leaning against the side wall, pointing out the array of fanciful containers festooned with flower images or pastel watercolors.

"Great. Only six boxes to check." Anna carefully opened the first hat box, admiring the pastoral image of a long-ago garden party with women in flowing gowns and holding frilly umbrellas printed on the lid. A beige straw bonnet with a blue ribbon for tying under a person's chin lay nestled inside.

The second box held a man's dark-brown felt deer-stalker hat. "Did you borrow these from the museum?"

"All except one. Most of the clothes are from there as well."

She opened a third box, sneezing from the dust mites that inhabit old feathers and fabrics. The peacock feather was pretty, but nothing like the one she'd seen.

Her eyes filled with sympathetic tears, and she pulled out a tissue from her pocket. After blowing her nose, she resumed her search. Gingerly pulling the lid off the fourth box that appeared more fragile than the others with a crack running through the image of a soft pink peony flower, she peered inside. Empty. "Bingo. Did this one come from the museum?" Anna pulled out her phone and took a photo of the empty box and then put the lid back on and took another one.

"Can't say for certain."

She took photos of the other five boxes as well and also the hat inside each one. She'd check in at the museum later, see if the hat that was supposed to be inside the peony box was the same hat found near the victim. She sent a quick text to Josh asking for a photo of the crime scene, giving the details she'd learned. If the items were stolen, maybe their suspect was local? A knot formed in Anna's stomach.

"How long could this hat have been missing?"

"I'll have to ask around. The cast doesn't arrive for rehearsal until later today. Most people have day jobs, so we have to do all our preparations in the evening." Sam shrugged. Right, small-town productions never paid the rent or put food on the table. Mostly, a volunteer effort done by a few people who'd dreamed of being actors at some point in their lives and now enjoyed entertaining their neighbors. Any money made usually went to charity.

"I'll come back later."

"I think you're going to need a photo of the dress and undergarments to check the dresses. As you can see, we have a lot of them. The actors are still making their final choices. Hard to tell if one is missing otherwise. Someone should have a list. I'll need to check on that too."

"How about the petticoats?"

"They're hanging with the dresses, corsets, and skirts, pinned to the hanger." Sam shrugged.

Anna took a quick look down the rack, but Sam was right, the drab fabrics all looked rather the same, and without documentation like a list, it was impossible to tell if a specific garment was missing.

"Thanks, Sam. This was very helpful. I'll check back with you later." She turned to leave.

"Thank you for helping my daughter. Raylene's come around since you eliminated those nasty photos online. She's going to take computer programming at the Northern College come graduation next year." Sam beamed with pride. "Wants to follow in your footsteps."

"She wants to become a private investigator?"

"No. But she does want the skills to help people online. I think she's thinking more law enforcement. A desk job behind the scenes, going after perverts and scammers alike. You made quite the impression on her."

"Good to hear, Sam." Anna could use some positive news. She'd need to dig deep, maybe deeper than she ever had, to brace herself for what was coming. A firestorm loomed on the horizon, waiting to consume any unwary soul in its path. It was becoming clear to her.

This was no ordinary suspect. Organized, clever, prepared, so devious he'd stuck around, even after taunting them he would. Everyone had been caught with their pants down, her included, and now they were playing catch up. And it was only a matter of days until he would strike again. The thought sickened her beyond measure. Each of the original crimes had escalated, ending in the worst imaginable incomprehensible slaying of all: Mary Ann Kelly's backstreet butchery.

EIGHT

The heartbreaking cries of an upset baby, a barking dog sounding too much like a pit bull or other large species for comfort, and a blaring television greeted Detectives Pace and Browne as they walked up to the screen door. Josh scanned what he could see of the living room before rapping on the doorframe. Other than the pit bull he expected showing up and adding a few menacing growls to his limited repertoire, a host of assorted household and baby items strewn around behind him, no one could be seen. He knew the dog's gender soon as he jumped at the screen, his paws hitting the mesh and threatening to tear a hole straight through it.

"Anchor Police," he said, trying to be heard over the racket. He knocked louder this time, the screen door flexing and threatening to give up the ghost.

"For fuck's sake, Fred, shut the fuck up!"

"Fred?" Browne said, glancing over at Josh, his eyes wide and his face pale as Josh had ever seen it. Browne had a thing about dogs having been bitten as a kid. Bad one too, the dog had rabies and he'd had to undergo painful stomach shots.

"You can wait in the cruiser. I got this."

"Nah, I'm okay."

Josh shouted again when no one came to the door, "Anchor Police Department, we need to speak with Bella Johnson."

"I'm coming for Christ's sake!"

Finally, a frazzled, anorexic, stringy-haired girl looking about sixteen or seventeen going on forty came to the door. She pushed the dog to the side, admonishing the annoyed creature. "Go to your room. Now!" She pointed the way with a wave of her arm and a stern look that could flatten an entire battalion.

Surprisingly, the dog slunk off. Though not happy about it as he demonstrated when the mutt turned in the doorway and barred his teeth at them before vanishing from view.

"What do you want? It's not even seven in the morning."

"We need to speak with Bella Johnson."

"I'm Bella. What's this all about?" She crossed her arms over her thin chest, glaring at them as if they were the ones who'd caused her shitty living situation and pleasant attitude. "I ain't using, if that's what you're here about. Been clean since Jodie was born. That's my son."

Ah, the one still crying his poor little lungs out in the distance. "Your mother—"

"What? She was supposed to be here by now. She promised to bring me a cinnamon latte from Joe's. She was turning tricks last night—" Bella stopped and pursed her thin lips as she appeared to realize how incriminating her words sounded.

"I'm afraid I have bad news. Can we come in?" Josh asked, sensing Browne tense up at his side.

"Yeah, guess you'd better." She narrowed her eyes.

"We can wait while you tend your son," Josh offered, stepping over a toy dump truck and a pile of baby clothes housed in a plastic hamper that had seen better days.

She waved her arm. "He's fine. Just like his daddy. Never shuts up, always wanting the tit. I ain't got any more for him at the moment. Little monster kept at it all night. Spits up the formula. Mom went to the trouble of buying it too. What have you got to tell me? What happened to Mom? It's my mom you came to see me about, right?"

"Perhaps we could sit down?"

"I'm fine." Her face pinched up. "Say what you have to and leave."

"I'm sorry to inform you that your mother was found this morning. Over on Deerhorn. She's deceased as of a short while ago."

A moment of silence, even from the baby, as if the whole world were holding its collective breath.

Then the maelstrom started up again. The baby broke into a fresh fit of temper, the dog began barking, and Bella broke into tears.

"I'm sorry. Is there anyone we can call?" Josh asked, uncertain of what to do. She might attack him if he touched her or sic the dog on them. He couldn't chance it with Browne shuffling uncomfortably at his side.

Bella wiped her nose on her sweatshirt sleeve, her eyes bloodshot. "What happened? Did Ray hurt her? That asshole. You'd better catch him and fry his ass. It was Ray, right?"

"We have no suspects as yet. Who's Ray?"

"Ray Bendrick. He's a fucking fucktard! Always after Mom to give him money. Threatening to beat her up if she doesn't. He preys on women. My mom was too good for the likes of him."

"Where can I find this Ray Bendrick?" Josh asked, his stomach souring.

"He hangs out around the pool hall, Joey's Bar & Grill. Not sure if he has a crib, probably just sofa surfs. Piece of shit. If he's harmed my mom, he'll pay for it." Bella's eyes narrowed to a squint, the tears drying up in her newfound anger. "You'll get him, right? Send his sorry ass straight to jail and throw away the key?"

"We'll question him. Find out if he was involved," Josh assured her.

"You'd better do it or I'll sue the ass off the police and this lame-ass town."

"What was your mom like?" Josh asked to get her mind off the suspect and into calmer waters.

Bella looked younger as she spoke of her mother, her eyes lit up with better memories. "Best mom ever. She did everything she could for me. It was me that screwed things up. Taking drugs and getting into trouble, getting pregnant. She's helping us out. I don't know what I'll do without her help. Jodie's a difficult baby."

"You might want to check in with social services. They can help you," Browne volunteered.

Bella's mouth twisted. "Yeah, right, so they can tell me how to live my life. Question my ability to be a mom. No way. Jodie and me will figure it out, thank you very much."

"If you think of anything else, please give us a call." Josh handed Bella a card printed with his name and number.

Bella sniffed. "Just take down that Ray bastard before he jumps town. That's all I want."

The clicking of nails on linoleum suggested it was time to go. Especially when Fred poked his head around the corner, his teeth exposed, his nose twitching. When he smelled the fear wafting off Browne, more obvious now that the air had warmed from the body heat of the crowded room with the pair of them wearing long sleeves and jackets, the decision was made in red-rimmed eyes. He charged right at them.

Josh scrambled to push his partner out the front door, but the action delayed his own retreat. He was halfway through the doorway, attempting to close it when the dog attacked. Bella tried to make a grab for him, but his teeth clamped painfully into Josh's calf, tearing through his pants.

"Shit, that hurts!" Josh shouted, trying in vain to shove the maddened animal off his leg. He was about to draw his taser when Browne got to his device first. The dog let go of Josh after a few seconds later when the electrodes sent enough voltage through Fred to make him uncomfortable enough to remove his massive jaws from his flesh.

"What did you do to Fred?" Bella screamed. Fred lay on the floor, panting, Josh's blood staining his muzzle.

"He'll be okay in a couple of minutes. It was set to low voltage, far less than for a human suspect," Josh found himself reassuring the young girl. He stumbled outside and sat down on the cement step, assessing his chewed-up calf muscle through his torn pant leg, worried the sharp teeth had grazed the bone making infection more likely.

Browne was already calling for assistance, speaking

into his shoulder radio in a rapid staccato, receiving statements and questions in return.

"They'll be here shortly, buddy. Do you want some water in the meantime?"

"Yeah, thanks."

Browne hurried off to the cruiser to fetch a bottle. Josh got why Browne had suffered all these years ago even more than he had before. Not a good feeling being accosted by a maddened dog. Hopefully he wouldn't need rabies shots. The dog didn't look rabid, just plain mean.

"Fred fucking peed on my floor!" Bella poked her head out of the house like she expected one of them to clean up the mess. Browne ignored her and handed Josh the water. He took a long swig of it, wiping his mouth with his sleeve. The dog had begun to bark again, though not as loudly. And least he'd be fine. Well, for the moment. All of this had to be reported. A child couldn't be living in a household with a dangerous animal.

Surprising Browne hadn't pulled his gun. Not that Josh condoned any mistreatment of an animal. But sometimes one has to do what is necessary to stop things from escalating to save your ass. But he hadn't seen it coming and that angered him more than anything. Only consolation, he hadn't been bitten on the butt.

"That went well," Josh deadpanned, causing Browne to snort and shake his head, keeping an eye out that the screen door remained closed.

"Yeah, just great." Browne looked worse for the wear, his skin pale and clammy.

"Thanks, bud." Maybe his new partner would get over his fear of dogs now that he had stopped one in its tracks.

Browne nodded. "Doing my job."

The whine of sirens pierced the morning air. Josh got up, shrugging off Browne's assistance, and limped to the street. He needed to get the wound flushed out, stitched, and bandaged, then track down Ray the pimp. Ray Bendrick was top of his suspect list at the moment. Add to that growing list of persons of interest, the unknown truck driver that Anna had texted him about, the one she'd discovered on camera leaving Fast Eddie's and the suspect who had stolen the hat from the Elks Hall. The case was already shaping up far too much like the one back in 1888 when the suspect list became endless for comfort. And it wasn't even noon yet.

NINE

Anna strode into Cross's office after instructing Friday to remain in the truck. Animals weren't allowed inside the M.E.'s stomping grounds, a small building tucked in behind the local Anchor hospital. With the now known connection of the man dating her sister, she felt certain that he wouldn't want to piss her off by sending her away without answering at least some of her questions. Being a PI and not a cop had its drawbacks, more so with those having official titles than the general public who gave her far less grief. Some police turned a deaf ear and a blind eye to her exploits, others were offended, especially if she solved cases first. Not her fault. But Josh had texted her that he was indisposed for the moment from a small incident and would catch up with her later, so she was on her lonesome.

"Anna," Cross said, looking up from his computer screen, his fingers still flying over the keyboard. She remained silent and let him finish. Cross looked even more driven than usual, his eyes shadowed and his skin taunt. The gleam in his eyes spoke of high intelligence, something he was known to demonstrate on cases, helping the police to solve cold cases with his excellent forensic skills. "What can I do for you?"

"Julie Ann Johnson. What can you tell me? I'm working the case with Josh, but he's been detained at the hospital."

Cross grimaced but didn't question her involvement further. "Terrible thing."

"Have you started the autopsy? Any information you can give me would go a long way to helping me find her killer."

He appeared to be evaluating whether or not to share anything, then nodded once.

"I'm about to begin. I was working on my preliminary report. Care to join me?"

Stunned by the invitation, Anna answered quickly without even considering the consequences. "Yes."

"You'll need to keep this to yourself."

"Of course." Maybe his dating her sister had opened a door for her? She never in her wildest dreams ever expected this to happen. Was it even legal? Could Cross get into trouble if it was exposed? It would never come from her, that was for certain. Normally Josh would be here, but she was standing in his place today. Something she took very seriously.

Anna steeled herself, her stomach folding in on itself, as she realized what she was about to bear witness to. But this was an unexpected opportunity and she couldn't wuss out of when a woman's life was on the line. The clock was ticking so loudly for the next victim she swore a horde of blood-hungry insects had taken up residence in her head. She focused on her breathing in efforts to dim the noise. Quell her discomfort.

"You'll need to suit up."

She followed Cross's example and followed him into the back room. The body was laid out, already undressed and ready for the procedure.

A few queasy moments later and Cross was speaking directly under the overhead microphone that would record his words as he worked. He first summed up the injuries.

"The victim's throat has been cut from left to right, two distinctive cuts starting on the left side one inch apart, the windpipe, gullet, and spinal cord being cut through. The top cut just below the jawline is about four inches long, the lower one eight inches long. A bruise of a thumbprint on the right lower jaw and one on the left cheek as if the face was held while the throat was slashed. The suspect most likely stood behind the victim, strangled her to stop her from struggling which is why the petechia in the eyes and explains the lack of blood on the ground where the victim was found, using his right hand to draw the knife across her throat twice. The abdomen has been cut open from center of the bottom of the ribs along the right side, under pelvis to the left of the stomach, where the wound is jagged. The omentum was also cut in several places. Two small stabs on the pubis. The victim has been effectively disemboweled. It also suggests some rudimentary knowledge of anatomy or at the very least someone schooled in what injuries were inflicted during the original crime. The knife edges are sharp and the wounds appear 'ripped' rather than stabbed."

Cross looked at Anna over his mask, his eyes dead serious, glittering with intelligence. "I have read the autopsies of the cannon five victims of the so-called Jack the Ripper as have most medical examiners I would imagine, and these injuries align exactly with the first victim back in 1888. It's uncanny."

The information was brutal. It also sounded familiar. She must have read it online about the original victim. Mary Ann Nichols.

"The skin of the forehead below the hairline and above the eyebrows has been cut into and distinctive marks left behind by the sharp point of a knife blade. The edges of the wounds are very defined. The wounds spell out the word M A N, with an inch between letters. It covers the entire forehead and was done after death, same as the stomach wounds."

"What's that?" Anna pointed at an imprint on the victim's jaw line, stepping closer to have a better view. "Looks like some kind of pattern or design? A ring?"

Cross moved the overhead magnifier closer to inspect the area. "Hmm. Maybe."

It looked rather distinctive to her. Sort of a graphic series of chain shapes about three-eighths of an inch in diameter, interlocking. A decorative ring that was pressed into the skin when he grabbed her face? She counted three chains before it faded off into a partial one. It could be a good lead. Who wore such distinctive jewelry in town? Or better yet, maybe this would prove it was a stranger?

"Can I get a photo of that image?"

Cross shrugged. "You'll have to go through normal channels for those, I'm afraid."

Anna's fingers twitched to grab her phone and snap a photo anyway, but Cross was already breaking protocol allowing her to observe the autopsy. Without a photo, she would have to rely on memory. "How soon until you have test results?"

"I'll put a top priority on them for the lab. No

evidence of any semen emissions, but I will send in all the swabs in the hopes of finding something. Maybe we'll get lucky and find a hair or other fibers. Her clothing will also be methodically gone over. We'll find this bastard, no fear. He can't hide in the shadows forever. Not with all the forensic science that exists now that didn't in Victorian England. Back then they even believed the image of the murderer could be seen in the eyes of the victim, the retina specifically. They took photos of the eyeballs, calling it an optogram, hoping to find a clue. Some murderers even went to the trouble of taking the eyeballs to avoid detection. Of course, they also believed foul odors or miasma caused infections, that most ailments could be cured by electric shock, that the shape of a person's skull determined their personality, and thought transference or telekinesis, the ability to help an unhealthy brain become normal by transmitting healthy thoughts to the afflicted, could ease the suffering of the mentally ill."

Anna glanced at a slight movement on the monitor on the wall, distracting her attention away from the autopsy table and Cross's oddly liturgic recital of disturbing facts. She caught a glimpse of a police officer just getting out of his vehicle. Good timing, she didn't want to see the poor woman cut into any further, something Cross had no choice but to do if they wanted answers.

"I'll scram. I don't want you getting into trouble. You're too valuable for this community to lose. Thanks for this. I owe you one."

She made it out the door and met Browne halfway down the hallway.

He seemed surprised to see her. "Anna. I was at the hospital. Are you on your way now?"

"Should I be? I thought it was only a small wound?"

"Crazy dog tore out a heck of a chunk of his calf." Browne shook his head in anger.

Damn it, Josh had underplayed things. Not the first time.

"I'm on my way." Anna rushed out the door, leaving Browne to stare after her.

TEN

Detective Josh Pace shoved his hand through his short hair in frustration, upset over losing precious time sitting on the hospital gurney waiting for the nurse to come back. She had yet to give him a prescription for antibiotics and to finish bandaging his wound that had required twenty-seven stitches. A fellow officer had come and gone in the meantime. Detective Spencer Harrison, a new hire, caught him up to speed on the investigation. While he and Browne had been informing the victim's daughter, which had gone so well, Harrison had been going door-to-door in Whitechapel. He filled in Harrison about the prick, Ray Bendrick, the victim's pimp and part-time boyfriend. The asshole needed to be found and squeezed next. Something Josh was itching to do.

But damn it. No one had heard or seen anything on Harrison's scouting tour. Or at least anything they would admit to, though the detective had asked questions and strived his best to have those interviewed see it was in their own best interests to help solve the case.

The uneasy sense of this escalating like back in 1888 with no obvious suspects and not enough hard evidence ate at him. He reminded himself that they had the meticulous Cross on their side. Forensic science and profiling unavailable a century ago could break this case wide open before another victim was murdered. But his job wasn't made any easier by the residents of the area being close-mouthed and uneasy around cops who arrested those dealing drugs or plying illegal trades as a matter of course.

Anna burst into the room. "What the hell happened, Josh? You said it was nothing."

She rushed over, looking like she wanted to throttle him. She gave him a quick hug before stepping back and taking a closer look at him. He looked less than detective-like with his pant leg cut off at the knee to allow for the tedious stitching together of his wounds.

"I'm fine. Just tore me up a bit. Might look a bit less appealing in shorts, but I can always get a tattoo over it. Waiting for the nurse to finish it up."

Anna bent down and inspected the wound, turning his leg enough for her to view the entire wound. "Holy shit, that looks bad. No tattoo's going to fix that, sorry, buddy."

Josh shrugged. "I can't see it from the front, so not my problem." The wound was untimely though, going to make it a bit harder to move around. He'd have to suck it up and take painkillers to blunt the worst of it.

"Why did the dog attack?"

"I'm not a mind reader. But he had no provocation. Most likely he'll need to be put down."

Anna turned white as a ghost, her lower lip trembling.

Josh didn't like it any better than Anna. "Sorry, but

he'd in a home with a baby and once a dog bites and gets a taste of human flesh—"

"It's okay. But you gave me a hell of a scare."

"What have you found out?" Josh asked. He hoped the nurse would get a move on. He needed to get out of here and straight back on the case. Antibiotics would take care of things until the wound healed. He was warned to use a crutch to avoid putting any stress on the leg for the next few days, to avoid tearing open the stitches.

"I texted you. I talked with Fields and then with Cross." He checked his phone and read the unopened text from Anna.

He pulled up his camera roll and showed her a photo of the victim fully dressed.

"They need to see that photo over at the Elks Hall. A similar bonnet is missing from wardrobe, but the dress needs to be identified as being there or not."

"I'm on it," Josh said.

"What did Cross share?" Anna had a certain look in her eyes. Like she had a secret. No one else would notice, but Josh knew her too well for them to keep anything from each other.

"Spill it."

"He was in a generous mood. Apparently, our sister and him dating has given me a royal in."

"Zoe and Cross are dating?" Josh stopped fiddling with his phone. He was uncertain if he liked this new development. Sure, he was okay as guys go, a workaholic which was good for the town, but dating his sister, yeah, that's a whole other thing.

"Yeah, for a couple of months now. They've being seeing each other on the QT. Zoe told me about it me before the shit hit the fan and we got pulled into this new case. I was going to have everyone over for a barbeque." Anna shrugged. "Probably not going to happen now. Everyone will be too busy."

"We should still make the attempt. For Zoe's sake," Josh suggested. He needed to see what was going on for himself. Sure, Cross was a standup guy in his field, but this was totally different.

"Yeah, you're right. Life can't come to a halt every time we have a case or we'd never live at all. And case or not, everyone still has to eat."

"So, what did Cross share?"

"I got to observe the body and inspect the wounds."

Josh felt his eyes widen. "Really?"

Anna shuddered. "It was horrible, but I think I discovered a clue. An imprint of a ring on her jaw. Looked like it was made of chains. Fairly certain I saw three links. A fair-sized ring to have made the imprint. It was where her head was held for him to—well, you know."

"Good sleuthing. I'll need a photo of it for comparison." He filled Anna in about Ray Bendrick to a string of expletives from his adopted sister. "Best-case scenario. Cross finds the evidence to prove a conviction and we can identify someone already in the database." Anna didn't have to tell him the clock was ticking. What poor woman would be next if the murderer couldn't be identified in time?

The nurse bustled into the room and got right down to bandaging his wound.

"No stress on the leg, I'm warning you. That was a major bite and the stitches will break open if you're not careful. Leave an even bigger scar." She finished up and handed him a bottle of pills. "Four times a day with food."

"No problem." Scars on the outside didn't faze Josh,

not nearly as devastating as scars on the inside. His pal Tom came to mind. He'd been gone for a few days now. His sister Laura's death was still pressing on him, then his mother had developed dementia soon after her daughter had been murdered. Now he'd gone back to Nome to deal with arrangements for permanent care since home visits weren't enough anymore. He worried his old friend since their soldering days in the sandbox was on a bender. Last time they'd talked, he'd been slurring his words. He needed to come back to Anchor and join the AA program. It had worked for his friend once before, after the horrors of war had eaten away at him, a second round maybe in order.

Like Anna could read his mind, she brought him up the man preying on his mind next. "I should call Tom. Maybe he's finished up in Nome and can come home?"

"I'll do it," Josh said. "He's had a lot on his plate what with his mom getting sicker." He turned to the nurse. "Where do I get a pair of crutches? I gotta get a move on."

"I'll fetch them," Anna volunteered. Good, she'd be quicker about it. He'd feel bad about thinking the nurse could move a bit quicker, but a woman was lying dead in the morgue and that tempered any guilt.

Anna hurried from the room. The nurse gave him a look of admonishment. "Don't forget what I said. And you'll need to come in for three rabies shots, scheduled over the next three weeks until we know if the dog was infected."

"Right." He kept his tone neutral with some effort. Could this whole thing be more inconvenient? Stitches and shots and taking antibiotics. Not what he had in mind heading into a criminal investigation, shaping up to be the worst Anchor had ever witnessed.

Anna came racing back into the room carrying the already hated crutches. "Here we go."

Josh sighed and got to his feet, placing his underarms over the padded tops. He stepped onto his good leg, wishing he'd been a whole lot quicker this morning. He navigated through the open doorway and started down the hallway.

"This is not annoying at all." He grimaced, giving Anna a crooked smile as she followed at his side.

"Yeah, right." Anna rolled her eyes. "But it's got to be done. Don't be a martyr and hurt that leg further. You hear me?"

"Yes, *Mom*."

She swatted his arm. "You're older than me."

"Damn right, and deserving of all the honors and privileges it warrants. Remember that, baby girl."

This time the squint in her eyes bore ill will. Josh hastened his pace. Anna, when she wasn't riled, was a woman to be reckoned with riled, well there was no stopping her.

Outside the hospital, he stood there and realized he shouldn't be driving, at least for a couple of days. He pointed at his cruiser parked a distance away on the hospital lot, pointing it out with the bottom of his crutch. "Would you mind driving me back to the station?"

"No problem-o, baby boy."

"Touché."

While he waited for Anna, a van suddenly pulled up alongside the curb. Out popped Sasha Perkins, the news woman for Anchor's only home grown TV station. He groaned. Last thing he needed in the world right now was a nosy reporter.

"Detective Josh Pace. Could I have a word?" Sasha

asked, striding up to him with a determined look on her well made-up face. Camera ready as always, she was the darling of ANBC or Anchor News Broadcasting Corporation. Her camera man followed her at a trot.

"Good morning, Sasha, or maybe I should say afternoon." He'd lost track of time in events of the morning. They'd flown by in a whirlwind of activity. And yet he felt like he was standing in quicksand for all the good it had done the investigation to date. He wanted to be in numerous places all at once. Too bad cloning wasn't a possibility. Yet.

"There was a woman's body found early this morning. And I have it on good authority that when you went to notify next of kin, you were bitten by a rabid dog. Can you release the victim's name now?"

"If you know that much, surely you must know who the woman is by now? And it's not been proven to be rabid as yet. The dog, that is." Sasha always rubbed him the wrong way. Well, maybe newspeople in general, if he was being truthful. Always prodding at people, opening wounds and speculating to sell news. Sure, it was their job, but he'd found it grating, nevertheless. And their weird ability to hand out terrible news, then jump to something entirely different that made them smile at the viewer baffled him.

"I just need you to confirm the name."

"No comment."

"Did you know another letter has been sent?"

That took him off guard and Sasha immediately capitalized on it. "He's saying he'll never be caught, thumbing his nose at the police department. That in eight days another victim is going down. Did he carve the initials of the woman from Whitechapel into her forehead? Can you confirm that at least?"

"No comment." Josh gritted his teeth, willing Anna to hurry up.

Sasha dropped the microphone to her side and gave him a beseeching look. "Okay, I can tell you're not happy about my being here, but women in Anchor need to know this, to be prepared in case the monster comes after them. I'm trying to do a job that needs doing, Detective. Not speculate or cause the department any embarrassment. Okay?"

She had a valid point. Women did need to protect themselves more now than ever. "You're right. Women do need to be warned, prepared, keep an eye out for each other until he's caught."

"Or she."

"What?"

"There's been speculation in recent years of the original Ripper being a female. Jill the Ripper. Mary Pearcey in particular. She was executed in 1890 for murdering her lover's wife and child with a carving knife. A witness back in 1888 said she saw the fifth Ripper victim, Mary Kelly, hours after she was murdered, the chief inspector in the case suggested it might have been the female killer escaping in Kelly's clothing. There is further speculation that the murderer was an abortionist with anatomical knowledge providing an easy way to get close to an unsuspecting victim."

Josh shuddered at the gruesome revelations that the cameraman was dutifully recording. "I wasn't aware of any of that. Far-fetched to think a woman would do such a monstrous thing. But then to think any human was capable of such harm." He shook his head letting his words die away.

But Sasha wasn't to be deterred, continuing with her avalanche of brutal facts. "An Australian scientist, in one of the more recent efforts to crack the long-cold case, used swabs from the licked seals and stamps of some of the letters from the original Jack the Ripper case. The very ones believed to have been sent to police by the suspected murderer. He was able to construct a partial DNA profile of the sender. Though the results were inconclusive, they indicated that the samples had more than likely come from *a woman*."

He caught a glimpse of movement from the corner of his eye. Anna, *finally*. "If you'll excuse me, my ride's here."

He scrambled over to the passenger side of the vehicle, nearly toppling himself getting used to the new crutches. He felt Sasha's eyes boring into his back. Great. He stopped and turned back to stare at her over the roof of the SUV.

"You have my word, Sasha, that I will do everything possible to find this criminal and bring him to justice. We won't rest until this monster is put away where he belongs. You can quote me on that." He stared her down as he made the promise.

She nodded, the look in her eyes one of great zeal. He had to remind himself she only wanted what most people would desperately want going forward. To bring the perpetrator to justice and end this disgusting copycat killing in its tracks. And take the power of good back from the evildoers of history.

ELEVEN

"What did Sasha Perkins want?" Anna asked.

She let Josh navigate by his lonesome getting into the passenger side of the Anchor Police Department's SUV with the new crutches. He would have to get used to the inconvenience. And if she offered to help, she was one hundred percent certain he'd wave her actions away with extreme prejudice. It didn't faze her. She was just as independent.

"The usual. To catch a detective unawares and get a quote that would make us look bad. Inept. Sells more papers than telling the public we are on top of things."

"Yeah, but it looked like you handled it fine."

"She spouted some theory about a woman being a suspect in the original case. I need to read up on it. Not something they teach at the academy."

"Our sister's an avid Jack the Ripper fount of knowledge."

"Really? I didn't know that about Zoe. And there's been another letter sent to the press."

"Damn it!" Anna tossed her phone at Joss. "Here, look it up."

Josh read the letter out loud, his voice contorted by anger.

"Dear Boss, Saucy Jack is back! He promised to make his first appearance on August 31st and so he has, his reanimated spirit living in yours truly. Take note of how very sharp my knife was when I applied it so diligently to her diseased flesh. I precisely ripped into that creature who prowled the dark streets of Whitechapel, spreading her vile exploits on an unsuspecting public. You should be thanking me for protecting all of you from her disgusting exploits. Jack the Ripper. PS. Expect this to continue until I clean up Whitechapel. We have a date on September 8th if memory serves me correctly."

Anna pounded the steering wheel with her hand so hard she winced. "I feel sick to my stomach hearing such vile shit. We have to catch this bastard. He's mocking everything we stand for."

"I'm calling Tom right now."

Anna kept her wits about her with some difficulty, the anger surging through her making it hard to concentrate on driving.

"Hey, bud, how's it hanging?"

Josh had put the phone on the speaker setting so she could hear Tom's response. "It's hanging lower than yours."

Anna rolled her eyes. At least, nothing changed in the men's universe. Not a bad thing. At least it was something to lighten the load.

"Say, are you about done in Nome? We could use your help."

"Yeah, I heard. Jack's back."

"Anna's here with me right now. Driving me home from the hospital. Stepped right into it with a pissed-off dog."

"Sorry to hear that. Is the dog okay?"

Anna choked back a snort of laughter.

"He's getting shots for rabies, but he'll pull through. But we could use your help on this one. Clock's ticking."

"I'll catch the next flight. Pretty much set here. Least all that I can do for Mom."

"Great. Text me when you get in."

Josh hung up on the call. "When he gets to town, I think we should try to talk him into going back to AA."

"He can stay with me. I got the room now." Anna immediately warmed to the idea. Tom was good company and he got along famously with Friday.

"Not sure if that's a good idea," Josh said, giving her a strange, penetrating look.

She shrugged. "It will save money and offer him family support. I think it's a good idea. Why don't you?"

"Now don't get all touchy about this, but the facts are you had a problem with drinking for a while there if I remember correctly after Tia was murdered." Josh studiously avoided her probing glance she shot at him.

She felt her spine stiffen, then backed herself away from the outrage by taking a couple of steadying breaths. He was right. "Even so, I have plenty of room and I have too much to do and live for now to fall back into that quagmire. If I do, I'll join AA right alongside Tom. Promise."

Josh groaned. "Last thing I need is both of you drinking like fish."

"I don't intend to head into that territory again, so stop your fussing, *Dad*." What was his problem? Tom needed a place to stay. She had a place. End of discussion.

"Guess I deserved that one."

"Yeah, you did!"

"I was worried about Tom and you, you know, sharing the same living space." Josh threw the words out there and they landed uneasily in a pile between them when he didn't meet her eyes. Again.

"Tom and I are colleagues. Nothing more, not that it's any of your business." Josh squirmed in his hot seat and she relented. The poor guy was in pain after all. "Sorry, I'm a bit testy today. This new case—someone wanting to be the new Jack the Ripper—it's got me in knots."

"Yeah, me too."

Anna pulled into the detachment's parking lot, parking alongside the row of five police vehicles. It was then she noticed a large white news van trolling the lot. Not the local news either, but a national station. Had this case reached so far afield already? The thought was alarming and she nudged Josh to take a look. "We're already making headlines."

"How did they get onto this so soon?" Josh blew out a rush of air, his brows drawn together. "Just what we need. Being under the microscope."

"Maybe they can help with surveillance in Whitechapel?" Anna tried for a lighter, more positive spin.

Josh scoffed. "Trust me. They'll be safe in their beds long before *he* strikes again."

Anna turned serious, her mouth drying up with worry. "We can't let him strike again. Maybe we need to get the whole town out on patrols?"

"You can't stop normal life, work, and school, and getting on with living, Anna. I'm sorry. That's what the police are for. Doing what we do allows the average Joe citizen to live his life unencumbered by such things. And I wouldn't have it any other way. It's our job to serve and protect the public."

An idea struck her. "Can we trade phones for the next hour?"

"Why?"

"You got a photo of the victim's clothing and I don't. I want to run it by Sam. Confirm if it was stolen or not?"

"Okay. But hurry and get it back to me. I don't need the fallout if anyone finds out." He didn't need to say the importance of him not being put on probation or suspended right now. Not when they had a killer to track down.

"Cross my heart." Anna made the sign of a cross on her chest.

They both watched the white van turn onto the street and park at the curb. Then Josh opened the passenger door, preparing to head into the station.

"Want me to run interference?" Anna asked with a nod toward the vehicle, watching him pick up the crutches and place them under his arms.

"Naw. I can handle them."

Anna jumped out anyway, deciding at the last second to head over to the detachment to make it easier for Josh. There was no electronic eye to open the door at the back of the police station. "At least I can hold the door open for you."

Josh gave a curt nod and she hurried to follow him down the sidewalk. He was already fleet of foot on the crutches, determined to get on with things. She could only imagine how his leg was going to throb once the freezing came out.

She pulled the steel door open after Josh used his

electronic key to disengage the lock. "I'll be back shortly with answers." She also hadn't heard back from the trucking company since the second phone call and the office manager promising to get her the information she'd asked for. What was taking so long?

She caught movement in her peripheral vision as the heavy metal door slammed shut behind Josh. The news-people were on the move, striding across the parking lot, headed in her direction. She made a dash for the cruiser and got inside just in time. She'd also need to return the police vehicle when she brought back the phone. Anchor Police Department would most likely not appreciate they were getting two detectives for the cost of one. But at this rate, she was a consultant at the very least.

She drove past the sullen-looking news crew, having stymied their attempt at getting a quote, barely managing not to make a rude gesture. Memories of another case, her own stepfather's death row sentence carried out earlier in the year, made the bile rise in her throat. The media frenzy back in Lexington, Kentucky, where she grew up and her mom was murdered, still stark in her mind nearly two decades later. It had become so bad, the Pace family, after adopting Anna, had moved the whole family to Anchor, Alaska. Sure, the press had a job to do, but more than likely they'd be in the way here, stirring up trouble with endless specula-tions about the murderer. Last thing Anchor needed. More determined than ever to find the killer and end the possibility of the death of another innocent woman, Anna sped off back to the Elks Hall. She didn't like the sensation the Ripper had her running in circles today. It didn't bode well. Felt even worse. Like something bad was chewing away at her insides.

This all had come out of left field, even with the

warning. She'd been so certain a serial killer could never strike in her adopted town ever again. Hadn't this town already been afflicted with more than their fair share? At that moment, a premonition hit her. Struck her hard, making her gasp aloud. This case would be the worst of her life. Something more than evil lurked beyond the shadows. Something so vile her mind could never accept it. And someone she cared about was in terrible trouble. Who? When the universe provided no answers, just the sensation of knowing it to the depths of her being, Anna struck the steering wheel so hard her hands throbbed in pain. *Get a grip. This too shall pass.*

But when? She silently screamed.

The lonely howl of a wolf echoed in her mind, trying its best to push away the bearer of bad omens. But still the unease lingered. Before this case was done, her world would be changed. Forever.

TWELVE

Tom Jackson strode in the front door of the Anchor Police Department, keeping a lookout for his friend Detective Josh Pace.

He hurried down the wide hallway past reception, waving away any assistance, and headed for Josh's new office. He rapped on the doorframe. Josh looked up from frowning over his computer keyboard, the strain on his face obvious. Shit, he was in a lot of pain.

When his friend struggled to get to his feet, his glance took in the crutches leaning against the desk.

"Stay seated. I heard already how a dog got the better of you. Hope he's had his shots."

Josh's face creased into a grin. "I can only hope. Good to see you, buddy."

"Yeah, me too. Wish it could have been under better circumstances. What's the verdict?"

"A flesh wound. It's going to be worse for that poor mutt."

"Yeah, bad owners make me pissed off."

"In her defense, I was there telling her of the death of

her mom. She was distracted." Josh shrugged, his face showing the strain of the case again. Or maybe that was the effect of the wounds left by the dog attacking? No, more than likely, knowing his friend so well and what he cared about, family and community, it was his worry over his fellow citizens that had him tied in knots.

"Well, I'm here now, what do you want me to do first?" Tom pushed back at the headache that lingered from last night's drinking binge. Now that he was on the case, he'd have to ease up, maybe even dry out until the murderer was caught or killed. He leaned more heavily toward the second option, figuring that anything else was a waste of time. Sooner this monster was yanked from the streets with all due prejudices, the better.

"Where are you going to stay? Anna's thinking to invite you to her new place." Josh avoided his eyes, looking somewhat uncomfortable. He was beginning to suspect his friend might be holding a torch for his adopted sister, but still, if he wasn't going to act on it himself, seemed wrong to stand in her way. Tom had to admit, Anna brought out the best in him. They'd made a good team during their first case working together, dispatching the killers of Laura straight to hell. The death of his beloved sister still burned him to the bone. Probably always would. But at least her murderers were in the ground, never to harm another woman. And to think another such evil entity had raised its vile head in Anchor. Seemed beyond belief.

"I'll probably check in with Anna then. Do you need me to do anything first?"

Josh scrubbed his hands through his short hair, making Tom aware he had something on his mind.

"Spill, what is it?"

"Have you thought about attending AA meetings again?"

Anger instantly filled Tom, his stomach clenching. He tamped down as much of it as he could. After all, Josh was only looking out for him. Still, it stung.

"Shit, Josh, who has time for that?"

"Always time to look after yourself. No good to the team if you're drinking like a fish. Not that you don't have the right—all you've been through with Laura, and now your mom—but Anna's newly recovered from a similar affliction by only a few months. I don't want you drawing her back into the dark times. We clear?"

"You're her brother, and I appreciate your sticking up for her, so I accept that. But Anna brings out something good in me. Something that makes me want to be a better man. You have my word. I have no intention of causing her any more grief. I'll find a meeting if that makes you happy. Today. Soon enough for you?"

Josh nodded. "Fine. Then we have an understanding. In the meantime, check in with Anna. She's over at the Elks Hall going through costumes trying to see if the one used in the killing is the same."

"What kind of sick fuck dresses them in period pieces?" Tom shook his head with disbelief.

"Beyond me. But believe me, when I get my hands on him…well, suffice to say he's going down, with or without benefit of law."

———

The Elks Hall was dimly lit when Tom strode through the front doors. All the lighting was focused on the stage centered to the back of the building. A couple of workmen were milling about, moving furniture around while the director sat in the front row and barked directions. No one looked to be having a good time.

On each side of the raised platform, a staircase provided easy access. Tom decided not to interrupt the harried director, instead choosing to descend a set of stairs to gain access to the back area which no doubt would house the wardrobe. He'd bet dollars to donuts that Anna was hard at work sorting through the clothing checking for missing garments. He hoped she'd found someone that would recognize the clothing of the victim, and verify those had been stolen from the production.

The busy stage crew didn't stop him and he slipped quietly into the back room. Yes. There was Anna, talking with a young man who looked rather uncomfortable under her scrutiny.

"I *need* the list of items that were donated. Surely someone has it? Otherwise, how would you know who to return said items to?" Anna's voice was raised in frustration. But she looked good. So good his heart gave an uncomfortable lurch.

"Yeah, someone should." The young man scratched his head. "I guess I'd better call around?" He said it like he wanted an excuse, any excuse, not to.

"Guess you'd better. Since it's a matter of life or death."

The young man blanched and his fingers began working his phone in a furious manner.

When Tom took another step forward, Anna realized someone was there and glanced his way. A smile instantly brightened her face.

"Tom," she exclaimed, rushing to embrace him. "Good to see you." She stepped back from him when he'd have liked the hug to continue. Indefinitely, if it were possible.

"You as well. You're looking good, Anna. Sorry I've been MIA with all this going on."

"How were you to know? And you had important things to take care of. How's your mom doing?"

He shrugged. "*It is what it is.* Good days and bad days, heading to more of the latter."

"Sorry, that sucks."

"Well, I'm here now. What do you need me to do?"

"Did you see Josh yet?"

Tom cleared his throat. "Yeah, and he mentioned something about my staying at your new place?" It was such a bad idea, being around Anna for more than working the case, but nothing could stop him from accepting it. Nothing on God's green earth. Not when it meant he could be party to that smile once in a while.

"I thought we could bivouac together. Though my new place does have all the amenities of a good four-star hotel. Five, if I got a decent chef onboard."

"That's what you got me for. I've been known to hold my own in that department." Tom was happy to offer something in return for her generous hospitality.

"Great. We're all set then." She turned back toward the flustered kid. "Anything yet, David?"

"Ah, working on it. I think Eileen might know something. She's the old lady in charge of donations."

Anna glared at the boy. "You might want to rephrase that."

"Ah, she's the nice woman in charge of donations."

Anna nodded. "Okay. Where can we find this Eileen?"

"She works at Goodwill in the mornings. But she'll be here soon. Tonight's a big rehearsal and she's helping with that. She always comes in early." The kid looked like he wished Eileen would pop in right now and take the focus as far away from him as possible. Even now he was edging toward the stairs.

"Okay, we'll wait. Want a coffee? We can catch up more while we wait for Eileen. Bring you up to date with the case."

"Sounds good. Where's Friday?" Tom suddenly realized his favorite mutt was missing.

"With Charlie. She was upset by events of the morning. Well, you know." Anna didn't need to fill in the blanks as they headed side by side down into the main hall, headed for the canteen. He knew the entire tale of her twin sister Zoe being kidnapped by the disgraced mayor of Anchor, an asshole who called himself The Buck, who tried to use her to cover his killing of his wife and her lover. Anna had sorted the whole mess, even though she'd been under suspicion by a couple of police detectives. One who proved corrupt. You couldn't write this stuff as nobody would believe it, yet in the land of the midnight sun, stranger tales had been told by inhabitants right from early days onward. Strange tales that made the blood run cold, like that Robert Service guy wrote in one of his poems. Tom shook his head. And now this. A Jack wannabe. Why? He read as much true crime as anything, and still, he couldn't get a handle on why some people did what they did. Maybe it really did come down to evil. Because take away shitty home lives, lame excuses like alcohol or drugs, nothing that lots of people have endured and not turned into monsters that murdered the innocent, and what are you left with?

"Two coffees, black, Mrs. Jones," Anna instructed the elderly woman running the canteen. "Want anything to eat? Might be a while before we can get around to it again."

Tom checked the few items available on the chalk-board. "Yeah, I'll have a hot dog. Mustard and ketchup, hold the onions."

"Make that two, thanks," Anna added to the food to the order and placed the money on the counter. "Keep the change."

"Nice tip."

Anna had paid twice what the food was worth.

"The money goes to charity."

The woman with the soft white curls and beaming countenance quickly obliged, handing the food over, wrapped in thin aluminum and set in a cardboard tray. A few round tables were placed nearby and they nabbed one, the only customers at the moment.

They quickly consumed their fare, then Anna filled him in on the facts she'd gleaned so far, from checking out the surveillance tapes at Fast Eddie's to the straw bonnet being missing. The unusual ring sounded like a good lead, and he tucked the information away.

Her phone rang and she looked pleased at the caller.

"Gotta take this one."

She got up and began to walk and talk, an action she was famous for.

"Yes. Uh-uh." She nodded as she spoke with the unknown caller, her eyes gleaming with intelligence showing how focused she was on the case. If anyone could solve it, save future victims the ordeal, Anna was their best bet. She'd move heaven and earth to find justice. Then take it into her own hands, if necessary. An unusual woman. One he was proud to call his friend.

She frowned then, not liking the answers she was getting. When the call ended, she slipped back into her spot at the table, her mouth twisted with disgust. "Seems Northern Star Trucking has shitty record keeping or one of their drivers is hiding his actions by faking his log. No truck was scheduled to be in this area last night. So, it's going to be a hard slog to find out who was driving the one observed on camera last night. But each truck has a tracker, right? Damn it, someone's hiding something."

"How about I mosey over there and ask some questions? Their main office is in Fairbanks, right? Just a few hours' drive. The drivers are more likely to spill something in person than not. Or one of the shop diesel mechanics might know something?" Fairbanks was southeast of Anchor, a small city. "I'll stay over if necessary. Buying drinks for the guys is often the charm if I can't get the information from the security department. That will be my first stop."

"Good idea. You got a rental lined up? If not, take my truck. I've bought a second one." Anna shared the photo she had of the trucking guy with him. He took a good look and nodded.

"You adding to your fleet already?" Tom finished the dregs of his coffee.

"Figured it would make sense. I also leased a van."

"I'll take you up on the offer. Saves time."

Anna tossed him the keys. "I'll catch a ride with Charlie and pick up my other one. The way she's feeling, I might need to invite her to stay over as well. This whole Ripper situation has got her upset. She took me in when my house was exploded to smithereens. Least I can do."

Much as he wanted Anna all to himself, he found himself nodding. "Good idea. We gotta keep everyone safe, and perception of safety is as important as reality. Most women will be just fine, but that doesn't change the fact none are going to feel safe until the monster is taken out of circulation. That kind of stress is bound to have a negative impact."

"You always manage to surprise me with the range of your understanding of human nature, Tom Jackson."

"We aim to please. I'll keep in touch." He got to his feet and Anna followed suit.

"I think I'll check in with David again. He's the guy who helped me this morning discover the bonnet was missing. I wonder what the holdup is with Eileen? Oh good, there she is now."

Anna kissed his cheek, a nice surprise. "Stay safe."

"Always." Tom walked away, a spring in his step. Brutal as this case was, being with Anna again and having a new job to focus on, even as horrendous as the facts were, was the best ticket to staying off the bottle. *One day at a time* was more than a cliché for him, it was a reality.

THIRTEEN

"Eileen! If I could have a word?" Anna raced toward the woman, zeroing in on her, wanting to garner her attention before she got accosted by anyone else.

"Oh, Anna, surprised to see you here." Eileen gave her a distracted look. "What can I do for you, dear?" The woman was seventy-five if she was day, but she was robust and still in the game. Anna wished for as much wherewithal when the time came. Work with a purpose, the answer to staying vital.

"I need to know if some clothes have gone missing from wardrobe. I was hoping you had the list of donated items so that you can return them when the play's finished?"

"As it happens, I do."

Anna let out a sigh of relief. "Finally, someone who knows something." She complimented the woman before following her up the stairs to the back area. Three times today. She sneezed, her nose twitching as she drew closer to the stuffed rack of dresses and suits.

"What specifically were you looking for?"

Anna pulled out her phone, sharing the photograph.

"Oh my. Is that blood?" Eileen peered closer at the image; her eyes wide behind her wire-rimmed glasses.

The photo didn't show the face of the victim, but it was impossible to hide the dark areas where blood had seeped into the neckline of the dress.

"Yes, I'm sorry to say. Can you tell me anything about who donated it? If it's one of yours? I discovered a bonnet missing from one of the hat boxes piled over there as well. It was found next to the woman in this photo."

"Is that the dead woman? The one who was murdered last night?" Eileen lay a trembling hand on her chest and moved back a faltering step. Anna went into high gear, helping her to sit down.

"Are you okay? Should I call 9-1-1?"

The woman shook her head. "I need a moment. Perhaps something to drink?"

"I'll get you some water. I'll be right back." Terrible guilt for upsetting the older woman added a burst of speed to her charge down the stairs two at a time and over to the canteen where she requested the water. Racing back to wardrobe, she helped Eileen take a few sips.

"Brandy would be better," Eileen gamely said, making an attempt at a weak smile.

"I'll buy one for you. Finest top-shelf brand Anchor has to offer too. I'm sorry, Eileen, it wasn't my intention to upset you. Are you okay? Maybe I should call 9-1-1? Get you checked out to be on the safe side."

"No, I'm better now, dear. Bless your heart."

Eileen did look like she was coming round. Anna pulled up a stool and sat down beside her. She'd keep an eye on her for the next while, make sure she was all right.

"How are things going with the play?" she asked. "Have you watched it in its entirety yet?"

"Seen lots of bits and pieces, but not a complete run through like tonight. Looking forward to it. Dr. Druitt is beyond excellent in the lead part. You really believe he's both Doctor Jekyll and Mr. Hyde. He can change on a dime that young man. Fine actor. Not sure why he went into the medical field with a talent like that." Eileen shook her head. "It's a waste."

Anna was stunned. Dr. Druitt was acting in the play? And he was good? Her GP since she was a teenager could hardly be classified a young man. Not to mention she'd never heard a whisper of his ever wanting to act. Unlike Sunday Rose who'd dreamed of Hollywood all her young life. Why had she not known about this? Of course, he had every right to do something less serious than medicine in his spare time. She guessed she hadn't realized he had any. Like many towns, Anchor was short of medical personnel.

"Does he have an understudy?"

Eileen laughed, making a scoffing sound. "What? In our small town? And he was nice enough to lend us that reproduction of a painting that is perfect for our set. Painted it himself, he did. The man is multi-talented. Looks exactly like what one would expect in that time period. So perfectly ghoulish, it sends shivers down this old spine."

Druitt painted the Ripper painting? The guy was multi-talented. She'd give him that.

"Anna Hale. Why am I not surprised to find you here? I should hire you on as a detective. Save the middleman. Is Sam around, Eileen?"

Anna whirled around to find Police Chief Davis staring at her with flint in his eyes. She slipped Josh's phone into her pocket, not wanting the man to get wind of it being in her possession.

"Chief Davis." She was about to say more when Eileen interrupted her.

"I think I will take you up on your kind offer to drive me home, Anna. I am feeling a bit off. You can find Sam downstairs, Chief Davis." Eileen pointed in the direction of the man; her expression vague.

Grateful for something to take the focus off her, Anna helped Eileen to her feet who fussed about grabbing her purse before allowing her to escort her away from the situation, all under the chief's watchful eye. Davis was a decent lawman, but he was less than enthusiastic about her always interjecting herself into crime investigations. Someone always ended up dead.

"Thank you." Anna spoke quietly, helping Eileen into the front set of her vehicle.

"Buy me that bottle of brandy and we'll call it even. Davis doesn't always appreciate what's right under his nose. You're the finest detective in Alaska is what I think." The woman patted her hand, then buckled her seat belt.

Anna had to laugh, though her face heated at the unexpected compliment. "You're a clever woman, Miss Eileen."

"I also brought that list with me you wanted to check."

With that Anna bestowed a huge smile on the woman. "Did I mention how clever you are?"

"Yes, dear, that's been established. Now let's check the list. Pull over at the closest liquor store and we can kill two birds with one stone."

FOURTEEN

Anna slipped into the liquor mart, hoping not to run into anyone she knew other than the cashier. Her reputation for drinking in the past made her susceptible to feeling guilty for shopping for alcohol more than once a week. She'd already bought a few bottles two days before in preparation of celebrating her new home with friends and family when they happened by, but not any top-shelf brandy.

She refocused and hurried her step to the back of the store, hoping to get in and out like a ninja. A disquieting thought for a split-second was how Jack the Ripper could be thought of in that way. Five times in 1888 he'd managed the feat. She shook her head. Impossible in this century, too many checks and balances in place, far too many tools available. She was recognisant too of Eileen waiting outside, her intel on the clothing and her interference with the chief priceless, so she needed to hurry this transaction.

"Anna Hale. Nice to see you."

She whirled around at the pleasantly spoken words, catching sight of Dr. Druitt.

"Dr. Druitt. The man of the hour."

The middle-aged man gave her a quizzical look, his eyebrows dark slashes against his pale skin. He looked like a man who hadn't seen the sun in quite some time. Probably due to his responsibilities at the hospital, which begged the question how had he found time now to act out the role of the main character in a play? Though his dark eyes were shadowed, his features combined to make him a stereotypical average-looking Joe. Someone you'd pass on the street and not take much notice of. Middle height, though perhaps a bit thinner than the norm in his age bracket. He certainly didn't give the aura of being a man who could command an audience let alone leave them spellbound. Maybe Eileen was exaggerating his ability to sell tickets? But then she didn't appear to suffer fools gladly. A conundrum. Maybe she needed to take in a performance of the play, check it out for herself.

"The man of the hour?" He gave her a quizzical look.

"Eileen Merrit was filling me in on how impressed she was with your acting ability."

"Bit of an exaggeration," he said, but the telling gleam in his eyes suggested he relished the compliment.

"I'm more impressed that you managed to find the time."

He liked this comment far less than the previous one, the corners of his mouth turning down. "Well, it was kind of a now or never situation. My wife insisted. Grace has a soft spot for the theater and knew of my theatrical experience from college. I took a few courses in the field before homing in on medicine. To say my parents were relieved is an understatement."

"I had no idea." Anna shook her head.

"You can't be expected to know everything about everyone in town, Anna. How are you doing? Are you finding it easier to get through each day now? Less grief struck about the past?"

He didn't need to mention they both stood in the liquor store, his words grating on her. Was he suggesting her buying liquor was suspect? Well, look to yourself, buddy, so are you.

Like he could read her mind he continued, "I should talk. I'm buying a bottle as well. An anniversary gift. Eighteen years. Grace must be a saint to put up with the likes of me for so long." He held up an expensive bottle of wine as proof.

"I'm buying for a friend to say thanks." *Thanks for the intel about Dr. Druitt, Eileen.* For the first time she saw the man in a different light. Not quite so favorable. Or maybe it was her own guilt? She had more than enough guilt to last ten lifetimes.

"Well, I'm off. Rehearsal starts soon."

"Break a leg," Anna said.

His expression turned quizzical. Then cleared as he caught the reference. "Right, thanks."

Should she be adding the good doctor to her suspect list along with the truck driver, Ray Bendrick, and the thief of the clothing and bonnet? A bad feeling came over her. Like back in 1888, she suspected the investigation would grow tentacles, pointing at numerous suspects as more facts revealed themselves. Worst-case scenario, all proved circumstantial. No, they had forensics in their corner this time round. That had to be their salvation. She sent a mental *hurry up* to Cross. If anyone could nail down this bastard, he could.

She strode over to the small brandy section of the

store, losing focus on securing a bottle, but instead her mind playing over the named suspects listed in the original case. Though the list never seemed to quit growing in the twenty-first century, the actual group had been small back in the day according to police reports. And strangely, one was named Montague John Druitt, a man who drowned himself in the Thames after the final murder attributed to the Ripper. A shiver made its way snake-like down her spine. Surely it couldn't be. She shook her head, no, it had to be a coincidence. Like the convergence of so many odd things that had drawn a mad killer out from the shadows: the book, *I Know Jack*, the renaming of an area to Whitechapel, the Doctor Jekyll and Mr. Hyde play produced in town, all too similar to the time period to be believed in a work of fiction. Together they had created a perfect storm. An evil opportunity in the mind of someone so nefarious the idea alone would go down in the annuals of history. Only difference, this time Anna would make certain the case was solved. No matter what it took. The bastard was going down.

She realized she'd better get a move on as she needed to trade phones with Josh. She grabbed the most expensive bottle of brandy off the shelf and headed to the checkout counter. Not worrying about money was a blessing. Maybe if she could even see her way to buying the equipment to set up her own DNA testing lab right here in Anchor? While providing jobs, it would speed up processing of evidence in current investigations and cold case files. Tom would be onboard. It would help with his new focus on missing persons. Some crime labs had even gotten rapid testing down to two hours, she'd read recently. The idea grew on her, adding a new buoyancy to her step as she hurried outside to her vehicle.

FIFTEEN

Tom strode in the front doors of Northern Star Trucking, intent on speaking to someone in the security department. Someone obviously knew something. Trucks are tracked for safety measures. He just had to have a good reason for someone to give up the information he needed. And he had an idea of how to go about it.

"Good afternoon. I wanted to speak to someone in your security department. Could you let them know? I'm Tom Jackson by the way. It won't take but a few minutes of their time. I wanted to thank them for yesterday."

The receptionist's eyes grew larger. A young girl who looked fresh out of high school, trying to look grown up in her white shirt and black pencil skirt, her face overly made-up. "Right. That would be Gerald Rainy. I'll let him know you're here. If you'll have a seat."

Tom remained standing, staring out the window at the lot, sizing up the operation. It looked prosperous; a lot of newer trucks lined the lot. Not thirty seconds later a short, heavy-set man clomped down the hallway, the sound drawing his attention. The man stopped to talk with the receptionist, doing his best to chat her up for a least five minutes before bothering to look over at his visitor. He renewed his noisy walk across the floor, seeming incapable of lifting his feet, stopping in front of Tom.

"You wanted to see me?" At least the tone was neutral.

"Yes, I only need a few minutes of your time."

When it looked like the man wanted to speak right where they stood, Tom commented, "If we could speak in private?"

"Okay, sure." The man sighed and led him back down the hall and into one of the small offices.

Tom took a seat in one of the two available, taking in the messy workspace, the steaming cup of coffee and half-eaten danish on the desktop. Tom had interrupted his late-afternoon snacking, though it hadn't taken long for Gerald to answer the pretty receptionist's call. Tom required sustenance himself, promising to stop for a cheeseburger before leaving town. Sweets weren't his thing.

"What can I do for you?"

"As I told your receptionist, I wanted to thank one of your truck drivers. They were in Anchor last night. The guy let me cut into line when I was racing to the hospital. He probably doesn't even know his courtesy went a long way to easing my mind. My brother's wife had twins not long after. We barely made it to the hospital. A boy and a girl. I was filling in for my brother while he's away working."

Gerald's eyes popped open at that bit of intel. "Congratulations, you're an uncle. First time?"

"Yeah. I get to practice on them. Gonna need it, got my own coming in a few months."

"Last night in Anchor. Let me check."

Tom glanced at the man's hands while he worked the keyboard of his desktop computer, a plain gold wedding band clearly visible on his left hand. And the guy was trying to make time with the receptionist. Dream on, buddy.

"Hey Gerald, have you got that report for Tomlinson ready?" A man popped his head around the door of the office, his expression harried. Then the man caught sight of Tom. "Sorry, didn't realize you had company."

"Yeah, it's finished. I just need to help this fellow on an inquiry about one of our driver's and I'm on it. Apparently, one of the truckers did something nice last night in Anchor."

"Anchor?" The new guy's eyes narrowed. He opened the door further. "That's twice today that name's come up. What's the deal?"

"I was wanting to thank one of your drivers for a curtsy yesterday. Our world's gotten so rude—I thought it important to mention a good action."

"The guy's brother had twins last night," Gerald filled in the blanks. "Glad it's not me. One at a time's enough. Imagine two crying babies." He shook his head in sympathy. "One's enough to drive a person crazy. And if they get colic, look out."

"And you drove all the way up here just to say thanks, from Anchor?"

Tom shrugged, wishing the guy would shut the hell up and get out of his way for another thirty seconds. "I was headed this way anyway. Picking up some parts for my John Deere tractor. We don't have a dealer in Anchor. Thought I'd take a few minutes and drop by. Doesn't cost anything to say thanks, right? Make someone's day."

"Did he help deliver the babies?" Idiot wouldn't just let it go.

"No, nothing that dramatic. But his courtesy meant we got to the hospital in the nick of time." He laid it on thick, then turned back toward Gerald as if to block out the interloper. "You got that name for me? I gotta get back on the road soon."

"Yeah, here it is."

"Hold on a sec, Gerald. We can't give out that kind of information to a complete stranger. Did you check this guy out? Look at his ID?"

Gerald glanced up from his computer screen, a slight confusion glossing his eyes. Tom wanted to jump the desk and read the name for himself. He didn't want to have to spill the real reason he was here if he could help it. They'd know soon enough.

Gerald's eyes cleared, seeing a path ahead. "Right. It would be best if you tell me what you want to say to the guy and I'll pass it on personally. A win-win."

Tom inwardly groaned. *So close.* "I didn't realize you were running such a cloak and dagger operation. I was trying to thank someone personally and you make me out to be some kind of criminal."

"Hold on. No need for that." Gerald waved his arms about, his face turning beet red. "No one's accusing you of anything."

"I think your time here is done." The asshole in the doorway put in his worthless two cents.

Damn it. "Okay, I'll come clean. A woman was murdered in Anchor last night. A brutal slaying. And one of your drivers was seen on a surveillance camera heading into the area where she was killed just before it happened. I need to talk with the guy. Find out what he knows. Clear him of the crime before the cops get onto him."

"Who are you? Who do you work for?" Doorway guy demanded. Tom checked. His hands were free of any jewelry.

"I'm a private investigator, working for Lone Wolf Investigations." He pulled out his wallet, flashing his ID.

"So you came here under false pretenses. I think it is time for you to leave."

Gerald said nothing, looking conflicted. Maybe he could appeal to him?

"A woman is dead, with the promise of another body in eight days. The clock is ticking on this. Do you really want to be responsible for holding up an investigation and letting the killer slaughter another innocent woman?" It was impossible to hide his sense of outrage. And why bother? Maybe these two needed to have the lead shook out of them.

"Does this have something to do with that letter that Anchor printed a few months back? From the copycat Ripper guy?" Gerald asked, his eyes now rounded as an owl's. The infamous letter had made it to the far reaches of Alaska like an AI-generated wildfire. This current crime would do the same, probably be circulating throughout North America by tomorrow's sunrise. Nothing travels faster than bad news.

Tom nodded. "It does. My partner tried to get this intel through proper channels this morning, but it led to a dead end. Someone's hiding something here. And if the press get wind of it, you can bet your bottom dollar that Northern Star Trucking is going to take a huge publicity hit. And it won't be a good one. Definitely not good for sales."

"I think maybe we should cooperate," Gerald said, looking to his boss.

Dead silence for a few seconds, while the doorway guy weighed the two less than optimal options as to which was the worst for the company. Snitch or bad publicity. He might feel sorry for them if he had the time.

"Fine. Give him the name. Send that report. *Now.*" The guy vanished from view, taking the scowl with him.

"Who was that guy?"

"Will. He's the general manager. The guy you're looking for is Brad Sorenson. Lives in town." He recited off the phone number and Tom keyed it into his phone.

"Thank you." Tom stood and offered his hand. They shook and Gerald eyed him curiously.

"How do you like the PI business?"

"Only got dropped into the tradecraft a few months ago. So far, so good."

"What do you mainly do?"

"Hoping to work on some cold cases, missing persons. Right now, trying to stop a killer. I'll leave you to send that file."

"Yeah. Don't want to keep the GM waiting. Must be nice to be your own boss."

"It has its moments."

SIXTEEN

"I know where my daughter Kelly is! You have to go get her for me. That's what you do, right? Find missing people," the woman half-screamed into Anna's phone. It took a second for her to recognize the woman's shrill voice. Sonja Smith, a woman she'd run into often at the pharmacy, one of the clerks.

"Please, slow down, Sonja. What about Kelly?" Anna hadn't heard anything about her daughter being missing. It must have been very recent. She didn't know much about the girl other than she'd dropped out of high school last year and didn't graduate with her classmates, disappointing her mother to no end. She did remember that Sonya had mentioned celebrating her eighteenth birthday in June.

"My friend Meghan spotted her a few minutes ago at the Yellowbird Motel. You have to talk to her, Anna. Get her to come home. She won't listen to me. She needs help."

Sonja couldn't call the cops. Kelly was eighteen. Legal

age. But she was in danger. Especially with a murderer on the loose in Anchor.

"When did she leave home?" Anna needed a few facts. Running in blind was a bad idea.

"Three days ago. We had a terrible fight. I found drugs in her room. Then when Bear came home, she took off. They don't get along. Never had. He's strict with her. But this time she wouldn't listen. She said some awful things. Called him every name in the book. He got so mad I thought he'd have a heart attack."

"What did she accuse him of?" Anna asked the question in as neutral tone as she could muster. A clearer picture was emerging and it made Anna's stomach fold in on itself.

"I can't say it over the phone. It's too vile." Sonja's voice broke and Anna knew then what the real deal was. White-hot anger pumped through her body, firing up very nerve and muscle, giving her the juice to run into any situation that would save a young girl from a bad man.

"I'm on my way. I can't promise anything, but I will talk to her. Try to persuade her to come home." This was the first time Sonja had asked for Anna's help. No matter if the timing could be better, this took priority with Tom still in Fairbanks and Josh on duty round the clock. She glanced at the time. Midnight. Well at least her regular late-night caller had deceased their harassment a few months back right after the Sacred Ground Case came to its brutal but satisfying conclusion and Dr. Molly, the town's psychiatrist left town for parts unknown.

"Thank you. Please tell her I'm sorry. That things will be different now. Tell her that I love her."

"I take it you've thrown Bear out?" Anna asked. The

chances of persuading Kelly to go home became near zero if he was still in residence.

Silence for a few seconds.

"Tell her he's gone if she'll come home. I give my word."

"You should throw him out for your sake, Sonja. Not only your daughter's." She threw the advice out there, hoping it would land. Be taken the right way in the spirit it had been offered.

"You don't know what it's like!" The sharp tone was back. Defensive and grating.

"No, I don't. But if I get her to come back, you'd better throw him out right now or you have no hope of keeping her off the streets, Sonja. You know I'm right. You'll lose your daughter—probably permanent this time. There is a short window of opportunity to get this right and it closes far too quickly for you to even consider hesitating on doing what's right."

"I'm sorry. You're right. Please, get her to come home. I'll make sure he's gone for good."

Anna wasn't sure she believed her, but the woman sounded determined. "If Bear is still there when I come over there with her, she's not staying. You know that. And I can't leave her there with him in residence." If nothing else, she'd take Kelly in herself for a few days. Help her get settled.

"Bring her home. I promise to throw him out tonight. If I have to sic the cops on him."

Anna considered exactly what she could do to lessen any chance of someone being harmed over the situation. One of the most dangerous times in a woman's life is when she's leaving a significant other, especially if they are known to be abusive. They never ever take it well. "Someone needs to be with you when you do that. He might turn violent." Bear had a bad reputation in town. "I'll take her to a safe place if I can get her to come with me, then help you with Bear."

"You'd do that for me?" The relief in Sonja's voice was palpable.

"Yes, of course. I'll be in touch." Anna hung up on the call. She'd take Friday with her. She thrust her Glock into her shoulder holster and pulled a light jacket on over her jeans and sweater. Hard a situation as it was, at least it was something she could do tonight that might bear fruit. Talk a young girl away from the abyss. Make sure the right things were done. Her extra guest rooms were going to come in handy, handier than she'd even realized when she'd requested the builder to add extra suites to the house plans.

"Want to go for a ride?" she asked Friday, lounging on the sofa though his eyes were on alert as if waiting for something. He jumped off immediately, ready to go to work. Her wolfdog matched her determined stride out to the attached garage with the extra stalls and work-shop she'd had built to replace the old one. At least she'd been able to make some definite improvements when her home had been blown to smithereens.

They climbed into her GMC half-ton with four-wheel-drive ideal for Anchor's long winters and the perfect color to her mind, a stealth-like gray that blended in well to most landscapes. Anna maneuvered the vehicle down the driveway to the road. She headed for the Yellowbird, her mind busy on considering ways to approach Kelly in efforts to talk her into going home and giving it a try again. She landed on the truth as the best persuader.

It was a short drive to the motel. A rundown array of old log cabins, refurbished and brought in from around the countryside, hidden behind a stand of fir trees. Lots of small buildings littered the area around Anchor, left over from gold rush days, the town's main claim to fame. They were meant to add a nostalgic flavor to the motel, but instead looked forlorn to Anna as she pulled up in front of the motel's office. However, the business had done a fair trade in people wanting a bit of privacy for their chosen activities over the years, back when George was the owner.

She missed seeing George Stubbs perched on his usual stool as she checked into the office, leaving Friday to guard the truck. A man slicker than used motor oil, good old George. After his nephew Jason had been murdered by the Black Rose Killer, he'd boarded it up and retired. It had only been recently reopened for business when some enterprising person had purchased the seedy place. She hadn't met them yet. She hoped they planned renovations, but from the look of the place it was it worse shape than her last visit.

The office was deserted. George's favorite stool still stood near a window, worn down smooth from the years of his sitting on it watching the world pass by. She rang the night bell.

A woolly mammoth of a man came lumbering in from the back area, his black beard and hair about taking over his face and upper chest. A cross between Jack Sparrow and Jason Momoa, his size was what stood out the most. Well over six feet, his shoulders looking padded with enough muscle to flatten the best field of football players one could assemble. Or plow a field for that matter.

"You wanna room?" he asked, looking her up and down.

"No. Looking for intel." She slid two fifties onto the

rough surface of the counter pitted with the abusive of decades past. Kept her hand over the money, waiting for his reaction.

He shrugged. "Sure. What do you need?"

"No, who are you? What are you doing here?"

"Okay, I'll bite. Who are you and what are you doing here?" He appeared indifferent, though his eyes had a certain sharpness suggesting his nonchalance was an adopted attitude.

"Anna Hale, private investigator. I'm here looking for a lost daughter. Kelly Smith." Anna pulled out her phone and showed him a photo.

He grunted. "Came in last night with a couple of big guys. Cabin six."

"Bigger than you?" She took her hand off the cash and he pocketed it.

"Nah, but not as nice."

Anna snorted. "How's George Stubbs doing?"

The big guy scratched his full beard that looked enough like a Brillo pad that it might just leave deep cuts on his fingers. "Not so good. Lives in a personal care home in Fairbanks. Cancer has turned him into a skeleton."

Anna couldn't imagine the obese George skin and bone. A wave of sadness washed over her. Much as George has his proclivities, he'd helped her out in a time of need. Lent her a gun that saved her life. A quid pro quo situation that had turned out better for Anna than his teenage nephew, murdered by the Black Rose Killer. Had that brought about his decline? He'd never gotten over it, wore his grief like a black shroud. She understood. Grief became part of a person, burrowing into their DNA.

"Sorry to hear that. He was an okay guy. Helped me out once."

"Fascinating as this all is, I got an early call. I'm intending to fix this place up. Can't afford a carpenter, so going to do it myself." He patted his pocket he'd tucked the money into. "If you need any more information, don't hesitate to ask. I'll add it to my building supply funds."

Good, an ally she could count on. She appreciated that he hadn't hit on her. Not even mentioned her likeness to a certain actress that had been often mentioned in comparison to her looks. Or maybe that was fading now with her inattention to caring much about her appearance other than staying clean. Only exception, making a honeypot play to land some intel about a case. Most men make that exercise too easy. And the more obvious the goods, the quicker the results in her experience. "Good. I'll be taking you up on it from time to time. You armed?"

He snorted. "Running this joint, crazy not to be. I see you are too."

She nodded. "I didn't catch your name?"

"Zeke Law." This time he held out his hand, swallowing hers in a strong grip that lasted the exact right amount of time.

"Good to meet you, Zeke Law." She recognized the tattoo on his forearm. He'd been in the military. War ink. Something else they had in common.

"Nice doing business with you, Anna Hale."

"Likewise."

She strode from the office, intent on finding Kelly. She headed for her truck first, wanting Friday to have her back in case everything went sideways. He shadowed her up to the cabin door marked with a faded six, and stood alert at her side as she knocked three times briskly.

It took two more tries before the door was eased open and two eyes peered around the doorframe, dark rimmed with thick kohl.

"What are you doing here?" Kelly sneered, obviously recognizing Anna. Teenagers made it an art form, the put-upon attitude that so endeared them to adults. Anna ignored the rudeness. Oil off a duck's back as her southern receptionist, Charlie, would say in her lovely drawl.

"Can I come in?"

Kelly shrugged and opened the door wider. She was dressed in a short electric blue stretchy number that barely covered the essentials, her face looking far more worldly than her eighteen years would suggest. Kelly was a pretty girl, slim and athletic in school, but none of that solid background was visible in her current appearance. The dress screamed street-walker.

"Are you alone?"

"Yeah, Gus and Leon are out buying—beer. They'll be back soon," Kelly corrected her statement mid-sentence. "Why are you here?"

"Meghan called your mom tonight. Your mom wants you to come home. She's upset. Blames herself for what happened."

"*Phttt.*" Kelly sat down on the unmade bed and studied her fingernails.

Not much to work with there. "She's throwing out Bear tonight so you can come home and be safe."

"Heard that one before. The guy's nothing but an asshole. Treats my mom like shit but she *always* takes him back. He matters more to her than me." The glint of anger in her eyes told the tale.

She launched into her speech, hoping Sonja's promise was the real deal. "This time's different, Kelly. She means it. She's going to call the cops on him if he pulls anything. I'm going to help her with that. Tonight. And if you like, you can stay a few days with me. I got lots of room in my new place. After you get your bearings, then you go see your mom. I'll go with you if you want. But I promised her I'd see you safe. You can come with me right now. Walk out of here, go back to school, have a good life. This is the moment of decision for you. I think you should grab hold of it with all your might. You don't want to look back at this one day with regret, knowing you could have made something of yourself. Something more than what Gus and Leon are promising you."

A slight hesitation in her eyes gave me a glimmer of hope of this going easy.

Then she flattened her mouth and her tone. "I'm doing okay. Gus and Leon are fine."

"You know what they want you for, right?"

"It's not like that. Gus cares about me. He even said he'd give Bear a beat down if I wanted him to. He's going to teach me things. Promises to make my life better."

Anna shook her head at the idea. "No, that's not the answer. Please come stay with me for a few days. We'll figure this thing out together. I'll even pay for college. What would you like to be if you could be anything you wanted?" The offer came up in the spur of the moment, but it immediately grew on her. Yes, this was what some of the money was for. Helping those right in front of her.

Kelly's expression changed on a dime. Softened. Dreamlike. A small smile erupted on her face. "I love drawing people. If I could be anything I wanted, it would be a person who designs clothes. Really nice clothes that make them feel good about themselves. And at an afford-able price so that even poorer people can look great."

"That's doable. You have my word on that."

"Okay." Kelly got to her feet. She looked as surprised as anyone at what she had so quickly decided to do. "I'll go with you. Right now."

Anna let out a breath of relief. Then heavy footsteps coming in the door sent her risk assessment skyrock-eting from low to extreme in a single heartbeat. Friday growled at her side.

"What the fuck's going on here? Who are you?" a loud, grating voice boomed in the small space. She whirled around, instantly face to face with two lowlifes. Gus and Leon.

SEVENTEEN

Tom strolled into the Jack 'n Coke, a dive bar on the outskirts of Fairbanks, alert for his prey. Brad Sorenson's wife had been most helpful, pointing out the bar the guy frequented most when he was home and not on the road driving his big rig. Hinted her husband needed reminding he had a wife and child waiting for him. Tom offered his sincere sympathy for her husband's long and frequent absences. Then gave his own excuse for seeing his old friend Brad to return some money he'd borrowed a few years back. The woman's eyes had lit up at with the announcement and she'd offered to pass the cash along. Tom said sure, handed over three hundred dollars, and then said he'd like to buy Brad a drink anyway to thank him. She'd obliged and here he was: hot on the trail of a possible murder suspect. He hadn't felt this determined since the last big case with Anna that had led them from the likes of Hollywood to the wilds of Alaska. He ignored the pain thinking of why he'd been called up to solve the murder of his baby sister, Laura. Instead, focused on knowing that he, Anna and Josh had found proper justice for her.

Tom patted his jacket, checking his taser was secure. He was also armed with a 357SIG, snugly encased in his shoulder holster. If the guy had anything to do with the Ripper killing, he was going to be dispatched with all due prejudice. One thing about the grand state of Alaska, lots of places for a body to vanish. The war at home maybe different than the war overseas, but certain sub-humans should be dispatched no differently than America's worst enemies, in his humble opinion. And if anyone thought the war ever ended for a soldier, they were dead wrong.

Tom spotted the guy sitting at the bar, his gut up tight against the wooden rail as he leaned in on his elbows chatting up the unimpressed female bartender. A half-empty beer glass sat in front of him. His dark curly hair so obvious in the security camera photo glinted with some kind of overly-shiny product in the overhead pot lighting, his beefy arms exposed in the short-sleeved black tee. The pretty young girl serving him looked bored by the conversation, only nodding as she worked behind the bar preparing drinks for the busy bar. He was party to an eye roll.

Tom slid onto a stool, leaving one between him and Brad. Brad turned to check out his competition, noting the look of interest in the bartender's expression as she moved over in front of him.

"What can I get you, mister?" she asked. She couldn't have been more than twenty-one or two while good old Brad was nearer to forty than not. His passing as a four out of ten on his best day and her being a ten every day was never going to work. An uncomfortable thought rolled through his mind. Anna Hale was a ten plus.

"A beer, whatever you got on tap is fine. And a beer for him as well." Tom stuck his thumb in Brad's direction.

The bartender pursed her lips as she poured him a beer, then set it in front of him. "You know him?"

"Nah, but I just spoke to Shirley. She asked me to hand deliver a message. I figured I owed him one to soften the blow."

"What's that you say?" Brad asked, his tone belligerent as he tried to figure out what the deal was. "What about Shirley?" Duly noted he didn't want her being called his wife, though hopes of getting the perky young bartender into bed were slim to none. Easier to bring the woolly mammoth back to the tundra.

"I was returning some money I owed her and she asked me to tell you that she's lonely tonight. Her and the baby. Brad junior, right? Wanted me to send you home to help with said baby."

Brad couldn't look more discomforted if he'd woken up with his head sewn to the carpet like in that classic Chevy Chase movie. His eyes darted around the room, realizing the gig was up. The bartender didn't bother to hide her eye roll this time.

"How much money we talking about here?" Was what he finally came up with. Apparently, thinking was an option for Brad when he was out drinking. Could this guy be the new Ripper? Tom had a moment of extreme doubt.

"Three hundred dollars."

The bartender set a fresh beer in front of Brad without bothering to smile and walked away.

"What for? How do you know my wife?"

"I don't know her. But I wanted to find you."

Brad's eye pinballed around their sockets. "You found me. What do you want?"

"You were seen in Anchor last night." Tom drew out a page of paper from his pocket and unfolded it. Smoothed the creases and laid in on the bar. "I've got you here on video. Your company confirms it was your truck. Care to tell me what you were doing there last night?"

"Why the fuck is that your business?"

Tom leaned in closer to Brad, staring him in the eyes. "I'm making it mine since right after this photo was recorded, a woman was killed in the same area you're seen walking toward here. Care to explain what you were doing there?"

"What!" Brad's horror was palpable. "I didn't hurt nobody!" He raised a shaky hand to his mouth. "Murdered?"

"Yes, monster slit her throat and cut her up real bad, copying fucking Jack the Ripper. So, I ask you one last time. What were you doing?"

"I have a girlfriend in Anchor. Leeann Marko. I spent a few hours with her. She can confirm it. Please, don't tell my wife. She has no idea."

"Me telling your wife is the least of your worries. But I'll leave that up to you. The police get wind of this, and you'll be hauled in for questioning in short order."

"Wait! You're not the cops?"

"No. I'm a private investigator. I'm here to prove your guilt or innocence. You'll thank me one day, I promise, well, if you prove out innocent. Where can I find this Leeann Marko?"

Brad shakily gave him Leeann's home address and phone number, his unease making him look like a blowfish that had landed on the hostile bank of a river, unable to get a full breath.

"Nice talking to you, Brad." Tom ambled to his feet, pleased with the results. Now he could head back to Anchor and help Anna and Josh.

He left a generous tip, then made his way out to the street in a far better mood than he'd gone in. Dealing with Brad had been somewhat entertaining and a lot less trouble than he'd prepared for. Most likely the alibi would check out. But if not, he'd be easy enough to find again. And in the meantime, he wouldn't be hurting any more women in Anchor. But his gut said the man may be an adulterer, an annoying asshole, but he didn't have the look of a killer. At least not one smart enough to plan the Ripper killings. One suspect down, how many to go?

EIGHTEEN

Risk assessment: high.

Two men stood in the small cabin doorway whom Anna assumed had to be Gus and Leon. They filled the room with an obnoxious cloud of funky testosterone. *Soap is cheap, assholes.* She shook her head. Thirty seconds and she and Kelly would have been on their way.

Friday growled again, letting Anna know he was ready to strike at her signal. *A wolf always recognizes a coyote.* But these two low-life curs weren't worthy of the comparison.

"Who the fuck are you?" one asked while the other sniffed and swiped at his nose with the back of his hand. A white residue on one nostril suggested the source of his annoyed sinuses.

"Kelly's friend, Anna Hale. My companion here is Friday. I'd suggest you don't move too quickly. He doesn't like it when he feels threatened. The wolf in him, I'd hazard a guess."

"Gus, Anna's here for me," Kelly said. "My mom sent her to check that I'm okay."

Gus's beady eyes ping ponged between the pair of us. He had the look of a tweaker, though not as far gone as drippy-nosed Leon.

"Well, you can see she's fine. Time to be on your way," Gus said.

"Afraid I can't do that. Kelly's taken me up on my invite. I'm putting her through college. She's going to design my clothes in trade."

"What the fuck ya talkin' about?" Gus shook his head as if trying to shake what little brain he had left into paying attention to her impossible word puzzle. Leon stared at her as if she were an alien being from another planet with an extra head. "No way in hell is she leaving here. She owes me. *Bigtime*."

Kelly gasped. Obviously, the information was news to her.

"Is it money you want? How much is her debt? I'll pay it. Right now." Anna pulled a money clip from her pocket and tugged out a thousand dollars. "This enough?"

Leon's eyes sprung open and his jaw slackened. His greedy hands reached for the bills, but Gus slapped them away.

Gus shook his head. "We want ten times that. Kelly's going to be a real good earner. Look at that bod." His sleazy eyes took in Anna. "You could bring in top dollar to if you'd fix yourself up a bit."

"I didn't sign on for that!" Kelly shouted. "You said we were going to Vegas for fun. That you'd teach me how to gamble and win. No way am I whoring, not for you, not for anybody."

Anna held up a hand to the incensed girl, letting her know she would handle it.

"I'll keep that in mind." Anna held out another thousand, the last series of bills her money clip contained. She suppressed her disgust, needing to get clear of the situation first. Later, she could have the luxury of anger flood her system. But right now, it would only get in the way. "This work as a down payment? Two grand for doing nothing more than the right thing? More than fair, I'd say."

"It's a start. Bring the rest, then we'll talk. Can't let her go right now. No collateral."

"No. I'm not leaving here without Kelly. We'll have to come to some other arrangement."

The sharp crack of a shotgun being jerked back and forth as someone loaded a shell into the chamber drew everyone's rapt attention. No mistaking that ominous sound. Zeke Law stood behind the two druggies, holding a Remington .308 like it was a natural extension of his body.

"You heard the lady. Move it. Away from the doorway if you want to keep all your limbs intact. Hands above your head where I can see them. No one has to die here. And just so you know, my favorite gun here is loaded with .30 caliber hollow points. I shoot you in the head and not even your mamas will recognize you for the wake." His steely grin held an edge that could chill the heart of an African lion.

Gus and Leon's expressions shifted from predator to prey in a nanosecond. Both did as the motel owner asked, backing away from the door to give room for her and Kelly to walk away.

"You're crazy, man," Gus muttered. Leon was visibly shaking, his hands swaying back and forth above his head.

"Good timing, Zeke," Anna said. She cut her eyes to Kelly. "Grab your stuff and let's go."

"You won't get away with this shit," Gus hissed.

"We already did," Anna said, then decided they needed a more comprehensive warning. "And keep in mind that I'm a war vet. One with paranoid issues and PTSD, if the doctors are to be believed. I'll give you a head's up. My land's protected by explosive devices. Step one foot on my property and both your asses will meet their maker. Something else to keep in mind. In Anchor, most of us are armed and prepared, and like the Colonel, we'd rather be judged by twelve than carried by six." Friday punctuated her remarks with a low growl, a stomach-curdling sound about like what you'd expect a demon escaping hell to make on judgment day.

"What Colonel? What the fuck is she talking about?" Leon couldn't seem to help himself.

Gus gave him a side-eye. "Shut up. I'll explain later."

Kelly proceeded her out of the motel room, clutching a large stuffed bag. Her body language was encouraging. She even had a spring to her step as she left the prison-like stench of the motel room. Friday escorted the young girl to Anna's truck and the pair climbed in.

"Thanks, Zeke, for having my back."

"No problem. You want your money?" Zeke kept his gun aimed at the two tweakers. "It's wasted on these assholes."

"No. It was money well spent." Anna couldn't hold back a grin at another idea that suddenly surfaced. "I don't care whose hands it ends up in though I'd hate to see it wasted on drugs, if you get my drift. I like what you're doing with the place. But if I were you, I'd send them packing now. Those two aren't to be trusted."

"I intend to."

"You want my help?" Anna asked.

"I got this. Not my first rodeo."

"Or your last," Anna said, leaving him to finish the matter. Zeke Law was going to be an excellent replacement for the former owner, George Stubbs, bless his quid pro quo heart.

Anna jumped into her GMC and turned to Kelly. She was busy petting Friday as he leaned in between the seats, his rump in the back, his tail thudding noisily. Talk about a quick bonding.

Kelly gave her a wide smile. She looked far younger, like the weight of the world had been lifted. "I love the name Friday. Did you really mean what you said? I can stay with you and go to school?"

"Yes. But I would imagine you'd want to live in residence at the school, right? But you can stay with me until then."

"Why are you being so nice to me? Are you into women?" She eyed her sideways.

Anna laughed. "No."

"Good. I'm not either. I mean, I like females. Just not in that way." Kelly shuddered. "A hell of a lot more than guys at the moment. They were going to pimp me. How come I didn't see that coming?"

"They didn't want you to, that's why." Anna pressed her lips together, but she had to ask. "How much have they given you?"

"I'm going straight."

Anna nodded. "We can get you help for that if need be. My sister Zoe has connections in the community."

"I'll be fine."

"No weakness in asking for help, Kelly. Everyone needs a hand up at times. Okay, here's the plan. I'm going to drop you off, then head over to your mom's."

Kelly began to chew at a thumbnail as Anna headed back down the road toward her new house. "Don't worry about me, okay. I haven't been using long. I can handle a little discomfort."

Anna prayed she was telling the truth. That she wouldn't slip away again when the cravings began. She'd ask Zoe for her help in the morning, explain the situation.

"You'll make sure my mom's safe from Bear?"

"Yes, I'll do my level best. You have my word."

A strange swaying motion of her truck began, refocusing her attention. It wasn't mechanical failure, but something else. Anna quickly studied the landscape, observing the rocking of the trees back and forth, even though there was no wind to speak of.

"What's going on?" Kelly asked, her eyes wide with concern.

"Earthquake."

Anna prayed it wasn't the big one again as she pulled onto the shoulder of the road, turning on her hazard lights. Back in 1964, a 9.2 quake hit Alaska, killing one hundred and thirty-one people and damaging property with the ensuing tsunamis that flooded fishing villages and waterways, felt as far away as Louisiana. It was a natural catastrophe and a tragedy never to be forgotten, the second worst one ever recorded in the world.

NINETEEN

"DNA results are in. Nothing we can use to identify the killer. Apparently, he got away clean as a whistle. No trace evidence on the victim. I wouldn't have believed it. I thought every criminal left something of themselves behind, a hair, skin, blood. With those deep stab wounds, the knife should have been slippery as hell. I would have expected some blood from some a shallow cut or two from the murderer's hands to contaminate the scene at the least. Fiber isn't much to go on unless it's distinctive, though better than teeth," Browne said with a deep sigh, slipping his phone back in his pocket.

"Fuck." Josh scrubbed at his face. He needed a shave and a shower. And a couple hours of sleep wouldn't go amiss. His eyes were gritty, making his vision blurry. He wondered how Anna and Tom were making out. He imagined the pair of them snugly cocooned in Anna's new place and it make his gut roil. Then he remembered that Tom had headed to Fairbanks. Maybe he wasn't back yet?

"I gotta hit the bathroom," he said, rising carefully

from his chair while doing his best not to wince at the influx of pain. *Damn dog owners unable to control their mutts.* Inside the men's room, he pulled out his phone and called Anna's number. She'd need the bad news ASAP. Her digging around in the facts of the case were of even more vital importance now without any science to back them up, to point out a suspect. Cross had never failed them before. Of course, not his fault, if there was no DNA or traces of a human left at a crime scene, he couldn't manufacture it. But this was only going to cause more speculation that the Ripper was a myth, a phantom of the night. Josh shivered, not liking the images that came to mind. This would bring out all the crazies, talk of reincarnation and spirits that would bring nothing but satisfaction to the madman orchestrating the horror show.

But before he could press send, a wobbly sensation under his feet stopped him, forefinger hovering over his phone. His whole body began swaying, like he was onboard a ship in the high seas.

"What the hell!" He grabbed the sink to avoid falling down, dropping his phone with a clatter on the floor and held on for the longest twenty seconds of his life. *Earthquake.* The realization made the hair on his neck rise. He held on until the room righted itself, a wave of sickening vertigo following immediately on the heels of the earth shaking, the cause yet to be determined. What did it matter if it was the worry over a natural disaster or the residue from the disruption to his system left by his physical assault? Either way something bad was up.

He picked up his phone, checked it was okay, then lurched from the bathroom, sweating from the throbbing pain in his leg.

"Everyone accounted for?" Chief Davis barked as he

stalked into the squad room, his deeply lined face more drawn than usual. The Ripper case had to be wearing on him, especially with the recent news.

Other than a few items having been knocked from desks and coffee spills spoiling keyboards, the half a dozen police officers in attendance all answered to the affirmative.

"About par for the course considering we're at the epicenter of a new serial killing spree without any science to back us up," Browne said.

"We'll catch him. No way can he elude us forever," Josh said through gritted teeth. It had been over a hundred and thirty years since the first murders. They had technological advancements on their side this time around that no law enforcement agency in the nine-teenth century could have imagined having at their disposal. Sure, it would take hard police work, hours of dedication and commitment as well, but it would get done. The killer would be flushed out.

"Yeah, but how many deaths will it take?"

The ominous tone in his partner's voice sent a chill coursing through Josh. He sent a quick text to Anna asking if she was okay. Then sent one to Zoe and Tom. He prayed they'd catch the evil bastard sooner than later, the deadline of September 8th a harsh reality that wasn't going away.

His phone dinged almost immediately. Zoe. She sent the message she was home, asleep when the tremors hit, but she was fine. Tom reported in next, letting him know he was on his way back, that he had intel about the suspect caught on video camera leaving the truck stop a few minutes before the murder. The good or bad news depending on if you were a cop or the killer, was the guy had an alibi that needed confirming, so they'd know one way or the other soon. If he was the murderer, they'd shut him down immediately. Josh prayed he was the bad guy even though Tom said his gut had serious doubts about his guilt. Anchor or any other town didn't need this kind of notoriety, much as the author of *I know Jack* might enjoy the limelight.

Where was Anna? He called her direct, ignoring the edit for using cell phones for personal purposes during work hours. They were into overtime so far by now, the department owed him a moment to check on those he cared about. Besides, all around him his fellow officers were calling home to check on loved ones.

"Josh."

The sound of her voice sent a wave of relief that hit him hard.

"Hey, love."

Silence on the other end. Then he realized he had let the word slip out without thinking and he inwardly groaned. The pair of them had managed to keep their relationship from never going past the sibling and best friends stage, the bond from living together in their teenage years holding strong. Always would. Not to mention they had recently bonded as tight as two people could not hitting the sheets when they enacted Wolf Pack Justice as their focus for working on cases, but that demanded professional distance as well.

"Sorry, the pain medication's making me loopy." He filled the silence with a lame excuse. "Where are you?"

"Just about to drive a friend home to my place. You remember Kelly Smith, Sonya's daughter? She needs a place to stay for a few days."

"What about her mom?" Then he remembered that Bear lived with them. The abusive asshole had taken up plenty of police time in the past.

"I'm working on it," she hedged, making him wonder all the more what was going on.

"What's the deal, Anna?"

"Sonja's finally ready to permanently kick his ass to the curb. I want to be there to make sure it doesn't backfire."

"Don't do anything until I get there. Understood?" Men informed by their partners that they are leaving them were the worst offenders for potential violence. Depending on circumstance, it can drive some men right toward the abyss. Ask any law enforcement officer how much they worry about domestic dispute calls and they will say they are always red flagged for danger.

"Anna! Promise me." He raised his voice and a few heads turned to stare at him.

"Okay. Meet me at Sonja's house. I'm headed there right after I drop off Kelly."

"You wait outside. You hear me?"

"Yes, Dad."

He hid a smirk at her sass. Anna. More heart than anyone he knew. She'd take in any stray mutt if she saw a need. But at least she'd come round these past few months. The death of their sister had left her broken, the only thing that brought her back was the mission to save others from a similar fate.

"That's *Mister* Dad to you."

"Sir, yes, sir!"

She hung up, leaving him shaking his head.

TWENTY

Anna pulled the GMC up in front of Sonja Smith's residence and shut off the motor. Kelly was safe and sound back at her house, settled into her own suite with Anna's Kindle for company. The girl loved to read, especially fantasies which explained her poor choices in life if she based any of them on the romantic leads in books that whitewashed the real world. No man on a white steed was coming for her, not at this time of history. Kelly would need guidance to avoid pitfalls like Leon and Gus. She could help with toughening her up, physically and mentally, but her sister Zoe was better suited to provide answers about relationships, one area Anna lacked experience in. No apologies.

She drummed her fingers on the steering wheel. *Where the hell are you, Josh?*

A loud shout from inside the house riveted her attention. Was Bear inside? Anna jumped out of the truck, shadowed by Friday, and pulled her Glock. Bracing it in both hands, she advanced toward the house, stopping in front of the living room window to look inside. No movement. She crept along the side of the house toward the back and peered in the small window of the wooden door. Bear and Sonja were both in the kitchen. His hands were locked around her throat and she was struggling to free herself. What the hell had gone wrong? Sonja was supposed to wait for her.

"Police! Open up!"

No faster way to get a response than to suggest a cop was at the door. A trick or two didn't bother Anna at all. She needed to get his attention in hopes of his lessening his hold of Sonja. The woman's face was turning blue, her limbs flaying about, then dropping helplessly to her sides.

Bear's craggy head turned at the sound of Anna's raised voice, his face a dark mask of fury. Instantly, she was transported back to her childhood. Her evil stepfather standing over her mom's body lying on the floor. His hands covered in her blood. The blows that rained down on Anna when she'd interrupted his murdering lust. She forced herself to push the image away, to see what was right in front of her. To escape the death echo.

Bear only grinned at her edict, a cut above his eye bleeding and obscuring his features, making him appear maniacal. She raised her foot, slamming her boot into the door. Once. Twice. On the third try, it flew open, splinters flying. She closed her eyes for a split-second to avoid injury. Friday came into the room as well, looking to her, waiting for her signal to attack. They had worked in tandem for months since he'd turned up on her doorstep one bitter cold night last winter, her training him on exactly how to handle this kind of situation. To wait for her hand signal.

"Stop or I'll shoot!" she screamed, her hands braced

on the Glock directed at the man. Sonja was so still, her eyes closed, her face puffy and pale. Was she even alive?

"Back off or I'll kill her." Bear pulled a knife, the glint in his reddened eyes demon-like as he held the long-bladed weapon in his right hand, the sharp point directed toward the poor woman's face. Sonja let out a weak cry, giving Anna hope. Alive.

Bear heard the sound. It took all his attention away from Anna for one split-second as he looked down at Sonja with satisfaction. He towered over the petite woman, his frame three times her size. Good. He made a wide target.

She shot Bear. Once in the head, once in the throat, and once in the chest. The knife clattered to the floor when it slipped from his lifeless fingers. He'd died so quickly he'd not been able to stab Sonja. Anna let out a deep breath. Sonja began to scream. Loud harsh screams that made Friday growl as he attached himself to the man's leg, dragging the body away from his victim.

"It's okay, boy, it's over." Friday dragged the man halfway out the back door before Anna could get him to let go. *Guess he wants to bury the trash.* It was then she started shaking. She dropped to the ground in the back-yard and hugged her companion. Friday huffed. Pleased to be part of the action.

"*My god.* Bear's dead." Sonja's rough voice, damaged by her near strangling, held hysterics.

Anna lumbered to her feet, about to comfort the woman. She was slumped on the floor, her lap cradling the blooded corpse of her former common-in-law spouse in the doorway. Her eyes were glazed with shock.

Sirens erupted in the distance. They promised a long night.

TWENTY-ONE

"A bit overkill to me, shooting him three times," Browne deadpanned, his expression on lockdown. Josh gave him a narrowed look. Anna gave him the hand signal. *I got this. It's okay.*

"You tell me what stops a killer holding a knife over his victim and her life hanging on by a thread? I had no choice. I asked him to stand down. He ignored the command. I killed him. End of story."

Browne shook his head. "Let's go through this again. Why were you even there? Weren't you told to wait for backup?"

Anna groaned. Twice wasn't enough? "I heard shouts coming from the house. I had to act. Fast. And it's a good thing I did. When I looked in the back window, his hands were already wrapped tight around her neck, her face turning purple, for fuck's sake!" Frustration boiled over. Why were they wasting time on this when a serial killer was on the loose in Anchor?

"Anna did what she had to. She saved Sonja Smith's

life by her quick actions. No different than one of us would do. You know this, Browne," Josh said.

"But she's not a cop. She should have waited for us to come on scene."

"You're insinuating it's better for a woman to die, then have a civilian save her over a cop doing the job? That's crazy. You should be thanking me, not harassing me for saving Sonja's life. I barely got there in time as it was. Another minute or two—" Anna shut her eyes, rubbing her temples, trying to dispel the bleak image. Bear's hands wrapped around Sonja's throat would haunt her without a doubt. The mind never forgot.

Browne narrowed his eyes, his mouth thinning into a rigid line. "Sonja's not singing your praises at the moment."

"Does she know I rescued her daughter tonight?"

"What? No one mentioned that," Browne said.

"They had Kelly intimidated over at the Yellowbird, cabin six. If you need proof, ask the new owner, Zeke Law. He had my back. Kelly's at my place now, safe and sound."

He had no comeback. Browne shook his head and lurched to his feet, the chair legs grating on the tile floor.

"Can I go? I need to make sure Kelly's okay."

Browne said nothing, exiting the room without a backward glance.

"You okay?" Josh asked.

Anna rubbed her aching forehead. "Tired and drained. I just need rest. If they're going to detain me, tell them to throw me in a cell so I can sleep. But someone needs to watch out for Kelly. What if Gus and Leon get wind of this? They're apt to put the pressure on her to make her do something stupid. She's smart, but she's also vulnerable." She prayed the carrot of college was enough to stop the worst from happening, but life did not come with a guarantee.

"They won't charge you, Anna. You only did what you had to do. Three bullets into a man trying to strangle a woman to death is not overkill. You want some water?"

"Why did she tell him so soon about leaving? I told her I'd help her, to wait for me to come."

"Why did you rush in and not wait for backup? Humans are not perfect, Anna. We're full of contradictions. Driven by emotions. Quit expecting things to always be logical and your life will go easier. We all make mistakes, do things that we shake our own heads at later. Can I get you something? Some water or a soda? A sandwich?"

She knew Josh was only trying to help, but every second stuck inside the police station grated on her. The place held bad baggage for her, hurtful memories of the time she was under suspicion for her sister's murder. Browne had been part of the team pushing her to confess to a crime she had not committed. Being questioned as a suspect while knowing you're innocent and grieving for the victim, it didn't get much worse.

"Some painkillers and water would help. But what would help more is knowing Kelly is safe."

"I'll see what I can do."

Anna's phone chirped. Tom. She read his text about his being back in town and on the way to her place. She quickly texted him back, filling him in on the facts. Then she called Kelly.

Breathing easier now after talking with Kelly about asking Tom to look out for her tonight and her agreeing to it, Anna felt some of the pressure from the day ease. She was running on empty. Maybe Josh could scrounge up something to eat?

But he came back with even better news.

"You can go home. We're releasing you for now," he said, re-entering the room with a bottle of water and some painkillers. He handed them over and she quickly dispensed with three of the white tablets, followed by half of the cold, soothing water.

"Thanks. Tom's on his way to my place. Just got the text."

"Right. And he talked to the suspect from the trucking company. We're checking out his alibi next."

"If nothing else, eliminating a suspect is progress. What about Ray Bendrick, JJ's significant other and pimp?"

"Cleared. Has a good alibi, shooting pool at Joey's Bar & Grill with a bunch of friends after hours. Half a dozen people vouched for him."

Damn. She knew they were both hoping one of them was the murderer, bringing an end to this terror building in Anchor. Anna had seen the news reports, and they didn't bode well. Scaremongering and speculation about a mythical entity revisiting the twenty-first century didn't help.

"Cross said there was nothing left at the scene from the killer found yet."

"How is that even possible?" In forensic science, Locard's principle made famous by Edmund Locard back in the nineteenth century holds that the perpetrator of a crime will bring something into the crime scene and leave with something from it, and that both can be used as forensic evidence. "The Sherlock Holmes of Lyon,

France, would beg to differ with Cross. Every contact has to leave a trace, right?" Disappointment washed over her as she accepted the facts. Cross was renowned. If he said the guy had gotten away clean, he had.

"Talk about shitty luck. Maybe we really are dealing with a ghost?" Josh scrubbed at his face; a gesture Anna always found endearing.

"No. I don't accept that. He has to have made a mistake. Something will show up. We'll get this guy. Or maybe it's a woman? But we will find them and lock them up for good." The pain killers she'd taken were going straight to work, clearing her mind. *Never give up, no matter how dark the moment, for it too shall pass.* A new message she'd been hearing these past few months joined the loop running through her brain. Good. She needed all the positive thoughts she could shove in there.

"Okay. I'm out of here."

"Be careful out there, Anna. This guy, he's good if he's got the entire department running in circles and confounding Cross. Keep your guard up at all times. Promise me."

"Don't I always," she quipped.

"You're one woman. You don't have to be a hero all the time."

"What fun is there in that?" Anna fled the room before Josh could come up with a comeback. She collected Friday. He'd been waiting patiently in the foyer, watching the doorway for her return. He got to his feet and joined her, his wise expression saying it all. *Men. What was a gal to do about them?* She tempered down her slight hysteria from events of the day which had since turned into an endless night, and the pair of them headed into the still balmy weather. A slight undercurrent of distrust lay not far away in her mind though as she remembered the earthquake. Did it herald the big one? Or was nature fucking with them, simultaneously sending out tremors, mimicking the ripple effect of the Ripper killings? Whatever it was, Anchor was at the epicenter, fucked either way if the case wasn't solved. Or if nature didn't give them a break.

TWENTY-TWO

Anna realized in all the brouhaha she'd forgotten to tell Josh of her concerns about Dr. Druitt. A sense that it would be a while until things settled down enough to warrant going to see the play, the good doctor was staring her in the face. But to hell with postponing the family barbeque! Zoe was pressing her to continue with it and she did want to have a talk with Cross, see what his take was on all this in an unguarded moment. He must be as disappointed as the rest of them about no forensic evidence left at the crime scene.

She turned down her street, relieved at seeing her other truck parked in the driveway. Tom was inside, protecting Kelly. How was the young girl doing? Anna hoped she was asleep. She didn't want to have to share the news about Bear with her tonight. What little there was left of it. Last she checked, it was only a few hours until sunrise. The first day of the Ripper killings had turned into the second day without her even noticing. Too much had happened and the urgent need to sleep overcame Anna as she and Friday shuffled through the front door of her new home. Two weary, deadbeat soldiers.

But it was not to be. Both Tom and Kelly got up from opposite ends of the sofa, making a beeline straight for her and Friday. Her companion had the good sense to skirt them and head for his blanket. Anna stayed trapped between the pair.

"What happened?" The question was asked in chorus. She held up one hand.

"Please, I need something to eat and drink before crashing. Give me a minute to catch my breath."

Tom moved off immediately, pouring her a stiff drink of whiskey before handing it to her.

"I'll make you something quick." He left the room, giving her much-needed space. But Kelly hovered, seeming unable to let her out of her sight.

The girl looked fit to explode, but she kept her mouth shut as Anna sat down on the sofa and took a slug of her drink. The strong liquor warmed her stomach and she took a deep, steadying breath.

Tom hurried back into the room and handed her a ham and cheese roll.

"Thank you." She took a few bites, washing them down with the booze. She shook her head, feeling two pairs of eyes boring into her flesh. Might as well get this over with.

"I was at your place tonight, Kelly. Your mom is fine, don't worry."

Kelly's eyes grew wider. "What did he do?"

"Far as I can tell, he didn't take well to the idea of your mom throwing him out."

"But you were there, right? She was going to wait for you to arrive."

Anna took another sip of the whiskey, feeling the

cares of the day slip sideways. But she needed to pull herself together and say what had to be said in the right way. Poor girl needed a proper explanation. It wasn't her fault Anna was exhausted to the bone. She couldn't bring to mind having lived a longer, harder day. Then she remembered finding Christine Gray's body on her property late last winter, driving for hours with Friday to take her to a proper burial ground, then falling onto the sofa fully dressed, too tired to even head to bed. That had been a night from hell. To say she was a magnet for bizarre and unforeseen circumstances that threaten to derail her life was to put it mildly. But no one got the better of Anna, she'd go the distance to right a wrong or bring the perpetrator to justice, even if that justice had to be handed out by her.

"She was supposed to wait for me, but something must have happened to speed things up. When I arrived, Bear already knew something was going on. I found the pair of them in the kitchen." She shook her head, swallowing the bile that suddenly rose in her throat. She set the whiskey aside. Maybe eating had been a bad idea. "It's going to be hard to hear this, but I found Bear assaulting your mom. He had her by the throat. She had even quit struggling before he grabbed a knife. I had to shoot him to make him stop. There was nothing else for it."

"What did you do?"

"I shot him three times."

"Is he alive?"

"No. He's dead."

A deafening moment of silence.

But then, out of the blue, Kelly was hugging her so tight she could scarcely breathe. "Thank you!"

The words were unexpected and brought tears to her

eyes. She blinked them away. This was not the time to indulge herself. Later, when she was alone, she'd have a good cry. But Kelly felt no such restraint, launching into a cascade of sobs and tears that tore at every nerve ending Anna had left.

Finally, the young girl swiped her nose on her sleeve and blotted the tears from her eyes with the wad of tissues Tom handed her. "Sorry, it was such a big relief. I really can't thank you enough. Now my mom's safe."

Tom gave her a look of sympathy.

"Time for you to go to bed, Anna. You look about ready to collapse."

Tom gave her a hand up, steadying her across the room and up the stairs to her second-floor suite.

"You going to be okay?" he asked. "Do you need something? Anything I can do?"

She shook her head, her stomach roiling.

"Call if you need anything."

Tom thankfully left her alone then, and Anna lurched into the bathroom, emptying the contents of her stomach in the toilet. After she rinsed her mouth, she felt better, and stumbled back to bed. Killing a man, justified or not, always upset her. She'd be more worried if it didn't. Taking a life is never something to be taken lightly, no matter how warranted.

TWENTY-THREE

SEPTEMBER 7—ANCHOR, ALASKA

The doorbell rang. Friday scrambled to his feet, trying to beat Anna in his imagined race to answer it. Her wolfdog always felt it was his duty to check out any new visitor first, making sure anyone who came in met with his express approval, though how he knew the difference between old friend and new at the door was anyone's guess.

"Make nice, okay? We want to make him feel at home." Anna caught a clear image of the pair standing on the front steps relayed on the monitor beside the door. It was connected to her newly installed camera system that covered every square inch of her new house and property for a hundred yards around the perimeter. No more taking chances. Her sister Zoe, and Cross, her sister's new boyfriend, stood waiting outside on the front step. Well, stranger matches had happened. But her gentle-natured sister with a man who autopsied bodies for a living was quite the shocker. Anna would reserve judgment until she had a sense of things herself, which was the main reason she hadn't canceled the dinner. The opportunity to observe for herself.

"It's Zoe and her new friend." Why she had a need to explain everything to Friday was anyone's guess, but she couldn't be alone thinking he understood every single word of her many conversations with him. The ancient wisdom glimpsed in those golden-brown eyes gave her pause more often than not.

They were early, but then family never needed to follow rules. Tom was out back splitting wood for the firepit he was intending to cook the steaks on for authenticity's sake, while Charlie couldn't make it. Josh was in the wind, busy working insane hours of overtime, uncertain if he could drop by, but promised to try. At midnight, the hands of the clock would roll over to September eighth, an infamous day in history. The day Annie Chapman met her fate in Whitechapel. After dinner, Anna and Tom intended to join those out on patrol. Not that they weren't already enough people on the streets of Anchor that a cockroach would have a hard time escaping into a crack. The only problem was no one was certain where the second event would happen. The section of town called Whitechapel was large enough to follow the same pattern as seen in England's notorious slum area at the turn of the century, but it wasn't the case in present day. The killer hadn't superimposed the crimes over the town's layout other than plying his murderous trade in a like-named area.

It had been a tough week for her town with no proof that pointed a finger decisively at any one suspect. Every lead had led exactly nowhere. The truck driver's alibi had panned out for the most part in that his girlfriend swore he was with her though the cops were still trying to poke holes in it, and there was nothing as yet to link Druitt to the crime. The stolen clothing had turned up zilch. Except for one chilling fact: four other outfits and assorted underskirts were missing. But other than the possible imprint of a ring that might identify the killer if it were found in their possession, there was no hard evidence of who had committed the heinous crime. The existence of the ring was being held back by law enforcement, as often is the case to help nail the culprit later. But the failure to name a suspect had led to wild speculation by the press causing Anchor to stay in a constant state of uproar. Patrols that she prayed wouldn't turn into vigilante posses, letters to the editor and to the police department. Even Anna had gotten some correspondence pushing her to consider conspiracy theories behind the killings. She shook her head and opened the front door to her visitors. She needed to set it all aside tonight, focus on the family for a few precious hours. After Tia had passed, she'd promised herself to spend more time with loved ones before it was too late. Tonight was the opportunity to prove it.

Zoe immediately held out her offering, her famous though rarely seen homemade dinner cloverleaf rolls like their shared mom Cindy used to make, her smile wide and endearing. Anna smiled. Her sister was pulling out all the stops, baking the special treat, though in all fairness she had hinted at them. They hugged first. Then Cross and Anna shook hands. Cross held an expensive bottle of wine cradled in his arm and managed a tight smile. Nervous, she'd bet. Even though they'd interacted a fair bit in the past, and she was grateful to him for his excellent work trying to defend their town, still, socializing was a whole other dimension.

"Thanks for inviting me," Cross said. Anna took the bread roll offering and left Cross to carry the wine.

"I'm pleased you could come," she said, trying to relax her face into a genuine smile. This guy could be her brother-in-law one day. Anna wanted the evening to go well nearly as much as she imagined her sister did. Zoe hadn't had many boyfriends over the years, so her spending time with a man held weight, especially if she was willing to bring him around family.

Cross followed Zoe across the threshold and took a quick look around. "Very nice. A well-situated fortress."

"I'll admit, I did go all out on security after someone blew up my house. A bit like closing the barn doors after the horse has escaped, like Charlie would say. Would you like a tour?"

"Yes, I've heard you have a war room?"

Zoe gave her a wink. Ah, the culprit. Of course, she knew how much Anna had invested in the special ops room that held all the precious, up-to-date gear for surveillance and cybercrime, a computer system that rivaled anything else available in the industry not to mention a weapon's safe that held guns and ammunition that would be the envy of the local police detachment. The room was her bastion against chaos.

"How about a drink first?" Tom said, coming forward to greet the pair. Anna had missed him slipping inside for a shower before joining them. She noted the damp hair, deciding in the moment it was rather nice to have a host by her side.

Friday remained silent and attached to her hip, not moving forward to check out the new guest. Well, at least he hadn't growled. Neutral was as good as it got for her wolfdog around strangers. A wariness in his eyes suggested it would take a fair bit for him to warm up to this particular interloper. Could he sense what Cross did on a daily basis? Perhaps the scent of death was ever present, something humans may not be aware of?

"A whiskey sour if it's not too much trouble?" Cross asked.

"I'll have the same," Zoe said.

"Coming right up." Tom took the fresh buns from Anna, being careful not to squeeze the package and strode toward the kitchen, obviously intent on helping out, freeing Anna to watch her sister and Cross interact. They seemed comfortable with each other, Zoe leaning in close when Cross made a positive observation about the living room. He walked over and admired a pair of paintings Anna had purchased from a local artist, one of a mountain scene with a skier perched at the top of the highest peak, ready to soar down through the pristine powder to the base. The other of a hand glider having just leaped off a cliff, a broad green valley with a meandering ribbon of blue river featured far below. Both made her feel exhilarated. Free.

"You like the sense of movement expressed in these painting?" Cross turned to her to ask.

"I do. It's the moment when everything turns into action. All the planning of getting to those locations, preparing to go through the motions of what it takes to get the job done, all of it happens in the *now*. No turning back. The bonds of earth are released for a short time. Humans don't get enough moments like that in a lifetime, brief as they are."

Cross nodded with understanding, as if he too felt that way. Zoe grinned at her, obviously pleased her sister and Cross had found some common ground. Maybe this wasn't going to be so bad after all? Still, a certain gangling of her nervous system made her cautious.

Much as she admired his work, he was a cold-blooded fish, having achieved a comfortableness with death Anna could scarcely imagine.

Tom came back with their drinks on a tray and handed them off.

Anna sipped her whiskey on the rocks and smiled at him with appreciation for his efforts. He looked good tonight, taking the time to have a shower and dress in a white shirt open at the collar with dark wash jeans. Anna wore a blue flowered dress, her hair blown out for once and even applied a touch of makeup. This past week with Tom in the house had gone all right, he was quick to help in the kitchen and he and Friday got along great guns. He had even cut down on his drinking, though after one visit to AA seemed to be all he could handle at the moment. Kelly had gone back to living with her mom, who needed her. The sense of domestic bliss Tom created was worrying her though. She was not wanting to ever lead a man on. She was far too independent to marry or co-habit for a long period; she knew it to the depths of her being. Once he had a new place, she'd be happy to be on her own again. But he'd been the perfect gentleman, helping with the case and making intelligent suggestions, never coming on to her. Perhaps she was a bit too full of herself, he may not have seen her as a possible hook up at all.

Anna refocused—she'd been drifting—and proceeded to give the pair a quick tour of her house. Cross was most interested in her war room, his eyes glittering with what she took to be envy as he took in the state-of-the-art equipment that far exceeded his own back at the office.

"Very impressive," he said. "Any other items on your wish list?"

"Now that you mention it, yes, I was considering putting together a DNA lab for testing criminal cases, cold and otherwise. Maybe turn it into a small business and provide employment. I haven't done all the background on it yet. Perhaps that's something I could consult with you about?"

Zoe's eyes lit up. She knew as well as Anna this could be just the kind of thing the two of them could bond tight over.

"It would be my absolute pleasure to help you. You would need DNA extraction kits, thermal cyclers, DNA sequencers, and PCR machines to start. You're looking at a PCR machine at the cost from twenty upward to fifty thousand, Thermal Cyclers between ten and thirty, DNA Sequencers ranging from one-hundred thousand all the way to half a million, LCMS or Liquid Chromatography-Mass Spectrometry pricing from one-hundred and twenty thousand to three-hundred thousand, and of course, Ancillary Equipment of all kinds, including centrifuges, pipettes, safety cabinets, and other necessary tools. All told anywhere from half a million to two million. There would also be annual operating expenditures. You must have deep pockets to be able to consider such a venture, though I have connections in the industry. I can look for the best deals possible and help with lab protocols, of course."

"Sounds like I asked the right person." The fact that he could rattle off all that would be needed to set up a ready-to-go lab for DNA testing off the top of his head, endeared him to Anna like never before. Blew her mind a bit, truth be told.

"That's my cue to go and put the steaks on," Tom said. He intended to grill the steaks on the grate perched over the old-fashioned woodfire filled with cedar chips for flavor. Friday would normally follow him at the word steak, but instead stayed protectively at her side. She absently patted his head for reassurance as she and Cross entered into a deeper discussion on the parameters of the lab she was now seriously considering providing for the town of Anchor. He was a wealth of information and Anna sat down and began taking notes on one of her top-notch computers.

They barely noticed when Zoe left to refresh her drink, so deep down the rabbit's hole they'd fallen in the excitement of actually going about the venture.

"I admire what you do, Anna, going after justice for victims," Cross said, looking up briefly from the notes he was assembling as they talked. "Just don't take it as far as that guy, Dexter, from the TV series. Not that I don't agree with him. Something to be admired there."

"Thanks, but I don't intend to. Not into torturing the perps, just eliminating them when necessary."

"Yes, you're known for that. Handing out frontier justice."

Tom popped his head in and said, "Dinner's ready."

His words broke the spell cast by the vision she and Cross were sharing.

"Thanks, Tom." Anna saved her own notes to a file and got to her feet. "Shall we?" she asked Cross, giving him a wide smile of thanks.

"A definite feast," Cross said with satisfaction as he sat down a couple of minutes later at the dining room table, surveying the handiwork of Tom and Zoe who had finished up while they'd talked in her war room.

"Thanks, guys. Sorry I got distracted," Anna said, finding a spot next to Tom.

The meal went off smoothly and Anna even found that she was to enjoying herself. The sensation was not something she'd experienced in quite some time and she savored every second of it. She knew all too well how quickly life could be ripped to shreds. But everyone seemed determined as well to forget what night it was. What might be looming in the background. Talk of the Ripper had been banned from the table, mutually agreed upon.

She raised her glass for a toast, dinging the side of it with a spoon to get everyone's attention.

"I want to say how very nice it is to have you all in my new place. Thank you for coming and breaking bread with me and bringing fun and laughter into my home."

"To your new home," Tom said, holding his glass up while the others followed his gesture. "May it bring you happy times and fill you with good memories of friends and family."

Everyone had a sip as the doorbell rang.

Anna excused herself and hurried to answer it. Where had the time gone? It was nearly midnight. She caught sight of Josh standing on the top step in the camera feed before opening the door.

"Josh. You came. Is everything okay?"

"Yes, nothing to report as yet. But I thought you'd be out on patrol by now?" he said with a frown. Guilt struck as she realized how much she'd been enjoying herself building a DNA lab on paper with Cross before breaking bread while her brother was out in the field working far too many hours. It showed most in his eyes, underscored by heavy shadows and red-rimmed. The sense of contentment the evening had brought on evaporated.

"Come in. I was about to change and go out. Have you eaten? There's lots of food left."

He shook his head, his jaw tight. "Not hungry. Is Tom still here?"

"Yes. So are Zoe and Cross. I'll go change. They're in the dining room."

Anna hurried up the stairs to her bedroom, yanked off her dress and pulled on a pair of jeans and a sweatshirt. She exchanged her footwear for socks and tennis shoes, then tugged her hair into a ponytail. Racing back downstairs, she found Cross and Zoe preparing to leave.

"Thank you for coming," she said to them, rushing to join them. "I'm sorry it's all over so quickly. We must do it again soon. And I will hold you to more consulting."

Cross nodded. "Anytime. Thank you for having us," he said and led Zoe out into the night which had turned cooler.

"We'll talk soon," she called out after them before closing the door. In the hall closet, she found a jacket and pulled it on.

"All set," she said, wondering what was keeping Josh and Tom?

But they strode into the living room looking normal, if rather quiet.

"How do you want to go about this?" she asked, checking the hall table for a flashlight and backup batteries. Friday was up already and waiting by the door, like he knew the schedule.

"I signed you up with me from Baker Street to Lockton Avenue. And Tom's partnered with Zeke Law over on Dorset and Spruce. Okay with you?" Josh said, his expression closed. Opposite ends of town. Must be what was left over after everything was divvied up.

Both she and Tom nodded. What did it matter, as long as they did their part? Though she had hoped that she and Tom might have partnered. She wanted to get his take on the evening with Cross. It would have to wait until tomorrow morning's recap over breakfast, provided the patrols kept the murderer from striking tonight. With half the town on patrol, surely that would be enough to stop the murderer in his tracks? Everyone was being supplied with whistles and some with air horns to draw attention to anything different going on. It might prove a noisy night, but anything to stop another woman losing her life.

"To sum it up, it's going to be a long night. If he follows the exact same pattern of the original killings, then it won't happen for hours yet. Sometime shortly after four-thirty and quarter to six is the closest timeline from past information. It was after Richardson's check of the yard where no body was spotted where he famously cut a strip of offending leather from his boot until John Davis did find her lying in the yard and called out to Kent and Green. Between those times, a couple of others reported hearing words. Albert Cadosch thought a woman said, 'No.' And Elisabeth Long heard, 'Will you?' from a male voice and an answer of, 'Yes,' from a female," Josh said, filling them in with the historical facts garnered from police reports written at the time of the original killings.

"But didn't Mrs. Long say she was certain she'd heard the brewer's clock strike five-thirty when she heard the short exchange between the man and woman? That shortens the timeline to after then and before quarter of six when John Davis was awoken by the chimes of the clock on Spitalfields Church when he found Annie Chapman lying in the yard?" Anna asked with an impossible-to-suppress shudder.

Before the others could speak, she summed up her theory. "A very short time period to do such harm to a human body. And yet, it did happen, making me wonder if he had anatomical knowledge, or at least butchering experience with a long knife? A noted surgeon of the day said it would take him close to an hour to inflict the same amount of damage." Anna had gone over this with Cross earlier in the week, but he was unable to say one hundred percent for certain that the man had anatomical knowledge, only that the knife was long, eight to ten inches was his best guess, and exceedingly sharp or well honed. She leaned more toward him knowing what he was doing if he could do such a thing so quickly.

"Depends if she was confused over which strike of the clock she heard, the half hour or the quarter hour? There's always been disagreement about the fact," Josh said. "And how long she had been dead before she was found because it was a cold morning and the doctor on scene admitted that with the organs exposed? It was a difficult call at best."

"Either way, we'll need to keep a sharper lookout starting around four o'clock. Who knows how the murderer sees it exactly? But maybe we'll get lucky, in the next few hours someone could notice something happening out of the usual," Tom said. "Make a pre-emptive strike."

"God, I hope so. We have to stop this madman, no matter what it takes." Anna didn't like to think how this second murder would be an escalation of the first, with body parts removed from the victim, but they had to stay aware of the monster they were trying to expose and take down. It didn't bear dwelling on though. This was the time for action.

"Brace yourselves, it's hell out there tonight," Josh warned as the four of them slipped out into the darkness, the sky clouded over and a white mist just beginning to rise, damp and clammy as hell. *Damn it, last thing anyone needed was a thick fog interfering with this night.*

TWENTY-FOUR

SUNDAY, SEPTEMBER 8, 1888—WHITECHAPEL, LONDON, ENGLAND

"I'd give you 5d for that bit of crocheting I liked. It would smarten up the front of my dress," Sarah said, sitting down at the table with a cooked potato she'd pulled from the pot on the nob. "You do crochet pretty."

"Too pretty to sell for that paltry sum. I'd hold out if I were you. It took you hours and hours, Annie," Mavis said, frowning at Sarah. Sarah ignored her, unwilling to look the woman in the eye.

Annie shook her head, swallowing a bit of warm potato. "Sorry, gave it to my sister up at Vauxhall today when she lent me some money. I got to get more thread anyway. I'm out, but my hook's still good." Annie coughed, holding her chest against the sudden pain.

The sound of footsteps made all the women look to the doorway. Annie groaned when she recognized the errand boy, knowing what was next.

"Deputy sent me to ask for your doss money," Evans said, pointing at her.

Annie lumbered to her feet. "I'll go and see Tim now."

She slipped into Donovan's office, waiting for the deputy to look up. "I haven't sufficient money for my bed. But don't let it. It won't be long before I have it."

"You can find money for your beer," he sneered. "But you can't find money for your bed?"

Annie hesitated in the doorway. "Never mind, Tim, I shall be back. Don't let the bed."

She spied Evans hovering nearby, no doubt there to escort her off the premises if she tried to hide out. No respite was ever given free, even though she'd been taken ill for a few days now. And over what? A bit of soap that could be had for a halfpenny. But Liza didn't have to be so cruel about it, punching her in the eye and chest, making it all the harder to earn her doss money. She followed John Evans, then he stepped aside. Annie slipped quietly from the lodging house into the cold, bracing night. At least there was no fog, making it a hazard to walk the streets. She tried not to think of the woman who had died scarcely a week ago, though everywhere she went there was talk of it in whispered breaths. Murder most vile.

The door Evans shut behind her sounded too loud in the darkness, and she shivered, wishing she had not bought the beer after all and could stay safely housed inside. Well, maybe she could borrow some boots and go hop-picking soon. Set a little aside. Not be endlessly chastised over needing a drink.

But she hadn't drunk much tonight. Sober enough, she thought, as she wended her way through Little Paternoster Row into Brushfield Street, before turning toward Spitalfields Church. She wandered for some time, not finding a punter up for it or a friendly face she could borrow off on the promise of returning the favor when she wasn't skint.

Tired, her chest still aching from the solid blow Liza had given in a fit of anger, she made her way over to Hanbury Street. At number 29 she was approached by a man, one she'd seen in the area before late at night. Only one weekends though. She stretched her lips into a thin smile, hoping he was the one.

She lay her hand on his chest, padded by a thick dark coat, shabby but of good quality fabric. He wore a brown deerstalker hat. He'd have a bob or two. "There's a bit of privacy to be had out back, gov, fenced and all. Everyone's still asleep." Once more she wished she was tucked in for night, warm in her bed. "We need to be quiet like. Mrs. Richardson has a lot of renters; some are up and about early in the day."

The man nodded. He dutifully followed her down the passageway to the small yard behind the house.

"This will do it," he said.

Annie was in the process of turning around to get her 5d he'd agreed to pay for their transaction when he grabbed her from behind. Before she could let out a yell of warning, his hands encircled her throat. He squeezed tight against her voice box. So tight she was unable to speak or breathe and sank to her knees in seconds. Her heart thumped wildly, as if it were about to take flight, like a tiny hummingbird's frantic beat. Darkness narrowed the scope of her vision, her body instinctively fighting to fill starved lungs with precious air. She felt life slipping away, her struggles useless against his strong arms, iron pinions clamped against her dying flesh. And with no time for regrets, she was rendered unconscious, left with no idea the blood that would soon drain from her body along with her name going down through the annuals of history.

TWENTY-FIVE

SEPTEMBER 8—ANCHOR, ALASKA

LeeLee Winter swept an armload of takeout boxes off the battered coffee table into a green disposable garbage bag, muttering to herself. Dried bits of food clung to the surface. She shuddered. She lived with a boatload of pigs. Disgust at the mess made her lips turn downward, adding years to her looks. Just past thirty, she looked a decade older with her too-thin body and already beginning to wrinkle skin. Where had her youth gone? She'd had plans back before she gotten hooked. Plans to teach little kids, maybe even go to college after she got her GED.

"You gonna go out tonight?" Jason asked pointedly as he sprawled on a ripped and duck-taped bean-filled chair. He was using again, needing his fix so badly he didn't care where or how he got the money to smoke the dragon. His usually glazed eyes were lucid, meaning he didn't have the goods to get high.

"Wasn't planning to. Do you not know what night this is? Read a newspaper, for fuck's sake."

Jason lumbered to his feet, his eyes narrowing dangerously at her.

"That's all a load of bullshit. For fuck's sake! No supernatural monster has arrived from the nineteenth century from England to visit the likes of us. You know where you're living, right? Nowhere, Alaska. People are so bored they're making it all a big deal when it was one only one old woman that died. You're safe to go out. If you like, I'll follow and watch." The last part was said grudgingly, as if LeeLee selling her body to get him drugs was an imposition of the highest order. "Come on, LeeLee. Everyone's out tonight. You'll have lots of opportunities and be home in no time. It's only a bit after four. Patrols will be going on until sunrise. We couldn't ask for a sweeter opportunity."

LeeLee dumped the plastic bag she was holding in the center of the floor, so angry she didn't care that some of the contents spilled on Jason's feet. He scrambled backward, his face turning beet red. A piece of coagulated cheese clung to one boot. She had to hide her smile at his discomfort. It was never wise to push Jason too far. But tonight, she was feeling the strain of the past week since that poor woman died. Murdered for going about her business. The anger pushed her to a new desperation. Maybe she could bunk in with Mike? He'd fancied her once.

"Fine. You clean up this mess then. I'll go and get the bacon."

A sudden sharp pain erupted across her cheekbone, and she gave a loud shriek. Jason screamed in her face, "Don't think you can say that to me! I gave you a place to stay when you were tossed out on the street. You owe me, big time, LeeLee."

She wanted to strike back but knew how that would end. How it always ended. Jason outweighed her, thin as he was, and was a hell of a lot stronger physically. Better to go out, and maybe, just maybe she'd run into Mike later. Test the waters. The idea gave her a flash of hope and she scurried into the small, dirty bathroom to get ready. A little makeup would hide the shadows under her eyes and a low top would attract any man. She regretted losing so much weight. Her boobs used to be bigger. Hell, her whole body used to harbor a fine set of curves. She supplemented their diminished size with a push-up padded bra. It helped, according to the mirror, and she left the half-boarded-up, shotgun-style house with a quickness to her step. Sure, it was pretty late for a hookup, but it was also the weekend. Maybe some punter, on a night when they were driving around endlessly looking for shadows would have the money. With a few bucks in her pocket, she'd head over to Mike's and suggest a little fun. Leave Jason's bony ass in the dust.

A sound in the backyard made her pause as she exited the bathroom. Were those damn raccoons in the garbage again? She slipped out the back door, the thick mist rising from the ground adding an eerie stillness to the night that seemed otherworldly. The cut-off feeling jangled her nerves, and she called out, "Anyone there?" She could only see a few feet in front of her, the cold mist laying clammy on her skin the instant it touched her. She couldn't even see the neighbor's house twenty-five feet away, so thick a soup had descended on Anchor.

The distant sounds of whistles being blown and

echoing in the darkness added an uneasiness that made the goose bumps prickle across her skin. Then an air horn blasted not far away, making her jump and gasp. She backed up toward the house, her heart beating too quickly and echoing in her head, deciding she didn't give a shit if the raccoons ate their fill. She wasn't taking any chances tonight. The rough ground proved a hazard, and her feet slipped sideways on the wet dew.

————

"Why fog? Tonight, of all nights," Josh shook his head, disgusted by the weather.

Anna's every sense was attuned to her surroundings, not that she could see fuck all. It was now after 0500 hours and the mist was only growing thicker. She understood dew point: the air was too saturated with moisture and water drops were forming. But why Mother Nature was adding to the danger tonight was anyone's guess. The thick atmosphere was claustrophobic, moisture clinging to her skin and hair.

She whispered, "Karma's off. Feels like the universe is pissed or has abandoned us."

Josh snorted. "Some asshole's out there, making damn sure of it."

He had not been the best of companions tonight, or actually, make that morning. Sunrise wasn't far off. But she couldn't blame him. He was exhausted from a week of little sleep and long hours on the job, likely running on nothing but adrenaline and caffeine.

A sudden blast of a nearby air horn made Anna lurch, clutching at her chest. "Those damn things. If it's another cat or dog or raccoon..." She left it hanging, angry at herself for being startled for the umpteenth time. You'd think a person would be used to it by now. It had been happening regularly for hours. The shrill whistles weren't bad, though more frequent. She pitied the canine population. Seemed everyone's imagination was jump-started by being on patrol. She wouldn't let herself dwell on what it hopefully was preventing.

Then the crack of a gunshot nearby stopped them both in their tracks.

"What now!" Josh took off running, stumbled over something on the sidewalk in his haste, before righting himself and slowing down. A cop's instinct was to run toward danger while most civilians bolted in the opposite direction.

Anna raced right alongside him, praying she wouldn't take out a kneecap or face plant.

They arrived on scene, breathless and bruised from stumbling over cracks and debris strewn on the sidewalk invisible in the thick soup, only to discover a red-faced man standing over a garden statue of a winged angel. One wing was blown entirely off, like a bad movie plot. A director sending a clear message that no angel was safe in Anchor.

"Sorry, I thought I saw something. I didn't mean for it to go off," the man said, his voice shrill. Josh confiscated his gun and deactivated it, pulling out the clip. Then administered a verbal warning.

A loud shriek rented the air, so close by to where they stood the hair on Anna's neck prickled, the sound slamming into her. A wolf howled in the distance and Charlie and Friday came to mind. How were they faring? She'd dropped him off when her friend begged for some company on this long night. Anna had insisted she either stay home or take the day off. Charlie could no more take a day off work than shave her big Texas hair, so she'd stayed home. Smart. With all the itchy trigger fingers tonight, someone could get killed. As it was, one man had tasered his friend, mistaking him for the killer. Josh had called it. A night from hell, straight out of Dante's Inferno.

TWENTY-SIX

The house that Anna and Josh raced toward now in the fog was a well-known crack house on Baker Street. Josh banged on the front door, its peeling paint and rusty hinges a testament to the neglect no doubt exhibited to a greater degree inside. He drew his gun and shouted out, "Police! Open up!"

Anna pulled her Glock, two-handing it, trying to suppress her heavy breathing.

The door was suddenly yanked open and nearly pulled off its hinges. A disheveled, thin man in his late twenties to early thirties stood there, his ragged shirt covered in dark splotches that looked like blood, visible in the light shed by a low-voltage bulb. The desk lamp minus a covering was perched on a rickety table beside the door. "She's dead, man. Really dead." He appeared in a daze, staring at his hands as if they didn't belong to him. He absently wiped them on his shirt, only managing to spread the blood around even further.

"Where is she?"

"Out back, on the ground. I found her. She's…she's cut up bad. Real bad. Oh fuck, what the hell."

"Are you armed?" The man stared at them uncomprehendingly.

"Hands behind your back," Josh instructed.

Anna didn't wait but scurried past the pair, intent on the backyard.

"Anna, no! Wait!"

But it was too late, she'd already opened the squeaky door to find the victim lying prone on the ground, an exact copy of the second event long ago in Whitechapel. The poor woman with her head laying toward the steps and her body, knees up, facing the alley, had dark blood pooled all around her. Even in the fog, Anna was close enough to see her throat was cut ear to ear and some internal organs were lying on her shoulders. The macabre image made her lurch backward and sink to the ground a safe distance from the body, not wanting to pollute the crime scene. She didn't touch anything, but rocked back and forth, trying to make sense of things.

The impossible had happened. Even with the net cast by the multitude of residents of Anchor dutifully patrolling the streets, the murdered had found his victim. Killed and butchered again. Blame it on the fog or blame it on lack of foresight. But all she knew was someone was going to pay for this heinous crime. *Be aware, crazy Jack, Anna Hale's gunning for you.*

The next hours vanished in a haze of police protocol. The sense of dislocation followed Anna home and into her kitchen where she found Tom brewing coffee and making breakfast. She poured herself a cup and slumped into a chair, eyeing her house guest over the rim. Though she'd thought she'd never want to eat again, the fragrance of the bacon sizzling in the pan made her stomach rumble with need. Her mind might be in turmoil, but her body required sustenance.

"Have you read the newest letter?" No need to ask what letter.

"Not yet." Anna pulled out her phone while Tom used tongs to remove the strips of bacon from the frypan and lay them on a paper towel.

"Dear Boss, Saucy Jack again! He promised to make his next appearance on September 8th and so he has, his reanimated spirit living in yours truly as you have already been informed. Take note of how very sharp my knife was when I applied it so diligently to her diseased flesh. I precisely ripped into that creature who prowled the dark streets, spreading her vile exploits on an unsuspecting public. I thought to leave some trophies by her side this time to prove my point. You should be thanking me for protecting all of you from her foul exploits, inviting the unwary into her filthy lair. Death reeks as well as evil should. Jack the Ripper. PS. Expect this to continue until I finish cleaning up Whitechapel. No need to thank me. We have a double-date soon enough if memory serves me correctly. September 30th. No catching me now!"

Anna lay her phone flat on the table, powering it down. She'd eat what she could, then sleep a few hours. Disgust at the ego of the killer made the bile rise in her throat and she swallowed some coffee to dispel it.

"He couldn't even be bothered to write an entirely new letter. Some of the statements are nothing but an amendment or correction to the last one. He's taunting us," Anna said. She watched Tom turn over the eggs in the same pan he'd fried the bacon in. Cholesterol was the least of their problems.

"He got off lucky. If it hadn't been for that thick fog, someone would have seen something sooner. Bad luck on our part," Tom said. He plated their food and set a full plate down before Anna and one for himself. "Eat. Your body needs it."

Anna managed a few bites. "It's good. Thank you." She set down her fork and finished the last of her coffee. "This whole thing, it's so much worse than the crimes from 1888."

"How so?"

"Because after reading everything I can get my hands on, including social media accounts, it appears most likely a madman did the original crimes. Like Aaron Kosminski. A lot of people peg him for the 1888 murders, and if they're right, then it makes our murderer someone capable—without the excuse of insanity or the passion of the moment—of deliberately and diabolically killing and butchering women in a precise pattern to mimic the old crimes. Only trying to prove he cannot be caught? What kind of motive is that?"

"When you put it like that, yeah, he's the worst of the worst." Tom cleared his throat. "So what's the plan?"

"I'm going to grab a few hours of shuteye." Anna rubbed at her gritty eyes. "This one is vastly different from the first victim's in a number of other ways. No video. The fog was so thick no one could have seen anyone escaping the backyard, even covered in blood if they wore dark clothing and kept to themselves. Jason Sunak, the man the victim lived with appears to be telling the truth. We found him covered in LeeLee Winter's blood, traumatized by what he saw. But he had no telltale cut marks on his hands." She didn't need to tell Tom that knives tend to slip once coated in blood, injuring the murderer. "No motive to kill her. She'd gone out to make some money to buy drugs. He admitted to punching her once in the face before she went out, as incentive." Anna winced, clenching her hands around her coffee cup. Much as she despised the guy, wanted it to be him, he didn't look right for the murder. Jason had been needing a fix and too shook up by finding the body, seemed incapable of making up a story with the few brains cells still functioning after years of poisoning himself. The man would undergo close scrutiny anyway, and would probably be asked to undergo a polygraph test.

"What about the ring imprint? Did Cross give any indication?"

Anna shook her head. "Not yet. The face and neck were so covered in blood. No way to tell until he washes the body. He's scheduled the autopsy for this morning. We should know soon, but I did notice that her forehead had something cut into it, same as before. Best guess, an A.C. for Annie Chapman, the original victim. He even tried to take away their names, the bastard. Obliviate their very existence." She stopped to draw breath and think. "We need to stay focused on Dr. Druitt for now. After seeing him in that play—" Something she'd finally gotten around to doing. "He had the look of a madman down too well. And he painted that Sickert reproduction. Find out where he was last night and see if anyone saw him around the time of the killings to verify his exact whereabouts? It's a place to start."

"Sounds good. I'll join you in that sleep." Then Tom realized how it sounded and added. "In my own bed of course."

"I'll help with the dishes first." Anna got up and began to clean away the remnants of their meal. She wished

Friday was home, she missed their morning routine, but Tom's company helped.

She stopped mid-action of putting their cutlery in the dishwasher. "Maybe there's a drug connection? I mean, I don't see a local dealer having the wherewith of the mastermind behind this case, but if there was a beef, a rivalry between gangs, maybe making the crimes look like the Ripper's is just a smokescreen?"

"Okay, but what's the motive?" Tom asked.

"Say they're sending a message of how easy it is to kill off their livelihood? You know, the women they're using to earn the money to buy drugs," Anna answered.

"Kind of far-fetched and convoluted, but anything is possible at this point. I mean the whole idea is so insane, recreating crimes that the murderer does not want to be caught for. We could snoop around. Check it out tomorrow. Visit a few known drug dealers."

"Sounds good."

In short order the dishes were placed in the dishwasher and the counters cleaned.

"Thank you for the meal. Wake me if you hear anything," she said. She left the room and trudged toward the stairs leading to her suite on the second floor. It would be a minor miracle if she could sleep, but she had to try. Last thing she needed was to be weak when she had to be strong.

TWENTY-SEVEN

"We got three weeks to solve this or—" Anna left it hanging as she drove the GMC down the street toward city hall. The damned so-called double event hung over the town of Anchor like a blood-soaked death shroud. The town's mayor had called an emergency meeting tonight, the day after LeeLee Winter's murder. Tom had joined her for the drive over, the pair of them invited personally by the mayor's office. Josh would most likely already be in attendance, the lead detective on the case. He'd been less available to Wolf Pack Justice since the murderers had begun. Not his fault. It was his job to serve and protect. Anna appreciated any word or help he could offer, while she and Tom went their own way, tracking down and investigating leads. The cops needed all the help they could get on this one, no squawking about territory and jurisdiction without the blinders and self-imposed limits of politics.

"Any word from Cross yet?" They'd been working the Druitt angle all day. He couldn't be ruled out as yet and was first up to bat. The theory of a drug war a far distant second. Druitt had been on patrol for a part of the evening, partnered up with a woman, Sarah Jenkins, who had been only too happy to complain that she'd been abandoned when he'd taken his leave around three in the morning. She'd ended up joining another group to extend her stay, not wanting to walk alone. Who could blame her with a madman on the loose? He had to be hiding in plain sight, thinking himself safe behind the mask of sanity. The good doctor's logical excuse was a caseload of patients to see today. But who could vouch for him from that time he left Sarah until the murder? They'd tried to interview his wife, but she'd overreacted to their inquiries, unwilling to say anything at all.

"Cross might show at the meeting." Anna had hoped to catch him beforehand, ask him about the ring imprint, but he hadn't returned her calls today, just texting to say thanks for the dinner. She got it. The pressure was on, for all of them.

"I've a good mind to break into Druitt's office. See if I can find something incriminating. If the ring is in his possession—" She left that thread hanging as well. Also unspoken the possibility that he had one of her internal organs, the uterus and part of the bladder missing from the recent victim. Who did she blame? The original murderer for his atrocities, the copycat killer for his attending to every detail possible in the twenty-first century or society for its unending interest in the case, never letting it die a truth death. Did it matter in the end? Nothing had changed her opinion that the herd needed culling. Badly. And she was making it her mission to see that it was.

"I didn't hear that," Tom quipped. "How can I help?"

They made a quick plan for later, then she parked the

truck a block from city hall, every spot taken near the packed entrance.

Anna spotted Josh walking with a slight limp out one of the double doors of the municipal building as she and Tom hurried along the sidewalk. The wound on his calf was still giving him grief. The problem with muscle wounds is they have to be used to keep a person mobile and it slows the healing process, especially leg muscles. Then Josh being Josh, he'd never give in and give his body a break. She understood, she was made the same way. He stopped and lit a cigarette, his hand shielding the flame in the slight breeze, leaning against the black wrought-iron railing of the staircase.

"When did you start smoking again?" she asked by way of greeting as they joined him. He'd been proud of quitting a few months back.

"Within hours of the second murder," he said. His expression bleak, his thousand-mile stare firmly in place. He took another puff, then snuffed out the butt in the provided receptacle a few feet away.

"He'll be caught soon," Anna rushed to encourage him, her heart aching for his pain. "Too many boots on the ground to avoid it. And the town's too small for him to evade us forever."

"He's clever, he's resourceful, he's obviously planned this for years. How could such a person have landed in Anchor of all places? That's what I keep asking myself. It can't be just the coincidences of the renaming and the book release. It's something more, something I'm missing."

"Something *we're* missing, buddy. You're not alone in this thing," Tom reminded him.

Josh let out a sigh. "Yeah, there is that. What have you two been up to?"

Anna quickly filled him in, avoiding mentioning their plans for later. Much as Josh would do all he could to help them, still, he wore a badge.

"Druitt's alibi needs to be securitized under a microscope. Don't worry, it will be," Josh promised, his tone dark. "We should all meet up for a drink later."

"Yeah. Good idea. We need an hour or two after the meeting, then we'll be home," Anna promised.

Josh didn't ask what they were going to do and they didn't volunteer the intel. An unspoken bond existed between the members of their elite group.

"Let's head in. Going to be interesting how this meeting unfolds," Tom said, echoing Anna's thoughts.

Every chair in the conference room was occupied when they arrived a couple of minutes later. The trio stayed standing along the back wall, observing the crowded auditorium. There had to be nearly four hundred people in attendance, most busy talking among themselves, a buzz of anticipation charged the room. The press was well represented as well, local and national reporters took up a number of seats. Cosmo Chapman whose book, *I Know Jack*, was proving a best seller, was surrounded by his admirers. His smug look when he saw Anna standing in the back of the hall grated. But she had to admit, she'd leafed through his book and the writer had at least taken the time to get his facts straight. He hadn't proved exploitive of the victims, but instead stepped up and shared some of their stories.

The new mayor, John Wells, chosen to replace Buck Duffy who had infamously murdered his own wife and lover and kidnapped Zoe, rose to his feet and moved to the microphone. Mayor Wells was a middle-aged man and former business owner, his ginger hair attesting to his freckled face, lined from too much sun. He looked a bit too much like a ventriloquist mannequin for comfort, but his unflappable manner was legendary, his earnest demeanor endearing.

"The meeting is about to start. If everyone will please quiet down and take a seat, we'll get on with things. I want to keep this short. I'll read my statement first, then the Chief of Police Davis will speak, and finally the press will be allowed to ask one question each, and one question only."

Wells cleared his throat. "I would like to thank Detectives Pace and Browne for their role in investigating these heinous crimes and the entire Anchor Police Department for their full cooperation in working alongside the mayor's department in efforts to solve the murders. Early this morning, the body of LeeLee Helen Winter was discovered at a residence on Baker Street. The deceased was found in the backyard, with injuries similar to the second crime that occurred on September 8th, 1888. The one of Annie Chapman."

A voice rang out. "Is it true her forehead was cut with the initials A.C.? Was she also strangled first like Julie Ann Johnson?"

Wells frowned. "If you would hold your questions until the proper time, it would assist the orderly progress of this meeting. Now, I'm going to turn this over to Chief Davis, and he can give you the latest update on the case."

Chief Lloyd Davis stepped to the podium, his expression sober and his jaw set in stone. His reputation was on the line. Two killings meant a serial killer. And the murderer had made his intentions clear right from the start. No doubt the FBI would be taking an interest soon, possibly sending an agent from their Behavioral Investigations Unit. The intel from this case was unique in the annuals of history and would no doubt be talked about for years to come. Unfortunately, just like the perpetrator most desired. Why do such an evil thing? Anna had a background in criminal profiling, one of the many tools in her wheelhouse she thought necessary in her quest for justice.

"I will be brief. I can share that the department is focusing all its resources on investigating the murders. And if you want the facts of the actual killing…" Davis grimaced with distaste. "All you need to do is read an autopsy from historical records and you will get a complete snapshot of what happened. The medical examiner, Dr. Cross, has assured me, both crimes *exactly* mimic the original crime scene with the exception of leaving the initials of previous victims on the women. His report is due shortly and will be shared with the proper parties. In the meantime, rest assured, this is our number one priority. And we'd like to thank the residents of Anchor for all their assistance on the night in question. We hope to move forward with the same level of help for the days and hours ahead as we bring the murderer to justice."

Davis stepped back from the microphone as the mayor spoke again. "We'll now open the floor to questions."

"Was the clothing similar, the pocket torn, and were their items left beside the victim? The small piece of coarse muslin, the small-tooth comb, a pocket comb in a paper case, and the two pills wrapped in a bit of envelope with the letters, 'M' and 'Sp' visible, postmarked London, Aug. 23, 1888 and a soaked leather apron lying a few feet away?"

The press had done their homework. Fair enough,

the facts of the original slayings were readily available in books and online communities.

"Yes, that is the list given to me minus the leather apron," Mayor Wells said.

"Have the FBI been informed?"

"They are aware." The terse answer spoke volumes.

"I'd like to ask Detective Pace a question," a reporter, Sasha Perkins, working for the Anchor Free Press, said.

Josh hated public speaking with a vengeance. Anna gave him a look of sympathy and the sign language gesture for *you got this* before he stiffly walked toward the front of the hall, hiding his limp from view.

"Is it true that you are part of Lone Wolf Investigations? An investigative team that goes beyond normal police purview? A group of like-minded individuals headed by your sister Anna Hale and assisted by ex-military personal, Tom Jackson? And furthermore, has been involved in the deaths of suspects before they can even be arrested?" she hissed.

The shock and sting of the words washed over Anna like an icy cold shower. Sasha Perkins had a vendetta against her agency, ever since her brother had been caught in a sting operation Anna had uncovered involving photographing teenage girls changing and using the facilities in a local restaurant bathroom. He'd been given a suspended sentence for his crimes and probation when he'd turned state's witness. This reeked of revenge.

A few heads swiveled and the seated audience members took in her and Tom standing side by side. Nothing like being outed at a public townhall meeting. This was a rare event, a public meeting of this magnitude with a host of fellow press surrounding her, the perfect opportunity for the journalist.

"And your point is, Miss Perkins?" Josh asked, too much of a gentleman to point out her vendetta and family connections. "Because you must also be aware that the shootings of the suspects have been investigated and cleared by the department."

"With this case being what it is, we welcome all help," Chief Davis stepped forward, speaking and settling the matter.

The mayor was about to add something else when a man strode in the door with a loud bang. He marched down the aisle like he was on parade, commanding everyone's attention with his no nonsense appearance as he made his way to the front. From his black suit, black tie and snowy white shirt in contrast to the sea of camouflage in the audience to his buzzcut and deeply tanned skin, his look screamed law enforcement. "That's good to hear, Chief Davis. Special Agent Jack Decker of the FBI at your service, sir."

To his credit, Davis shook his hand and nodded with approval. "Welcome aboard."

Decker shook the mayor's hand, then Josh's next, leaning forward and whispering something in his ear. Josh liked what he heard, allowing a small smile to escape.

Anna glanced at Sasha Perkins, noting the look of chagrin on the reporter's face. The young woman turned a bit more and locked horns with her, her anger clearly visible. Much as it was a cheap shot, still, Anna had some sympathy for her. Family defends family.

TWENTY-EIGHT

Anna was frustrated. She needed to know about the strange imprint on the first victim's skin. She was certain the chain-link mark had been caused by a ring worn by the murderer. Had it occurred again? Her research on the availability of the jewelry suggested it was a common item, readily available online. It wasn't much, but so little evidence existed it had to be taken seriously. She pondered the limited evidence of the case as she and Tom waited outside the doctor's office, parked a few doors down waiting for the right moment to do the night's deed. They'd finished their takeout burgers and were drinking coffee, pretty much tasteless in her opinion. Just fuel to keep going. She needed to start taking care of herself better, or at least eat something green.

"Where the hell is Cross?" she finally exploded, feeling the urge to go home. She needed an intensive session beating up the boxing bag in her newly installed gym. Anything to take away the sense of helplessness she was currently experiencing, not able to save a woman from undergoing such a horrible, tragic death. She could only imagine how frightened Julie and LeeLee had been in the final moments leading up to their deaths. Tears stung the back of her eyes and she blinked them away.

"I imagine he's inundated with calls. And now the FBI," Tom said, looking up from working on a file on his computer.

"What are you working on?" she asked, drumming her fingertips on the steering wheel.

"Studying photos of townspeople at local events, seeing if I can spot anyone wearing the kind of ring you mentioned the killer wore. No luck so far. Most people wear smooth bands or diamond-encrusted ones. I thought we might get lucky." Tom shrugged, his expression pensive.

Anna's cell phone dinged and she picked it up off the dash, frantically checking the incoming text message. Cross. Finally. She read the brief statement and turned to Tom who was staring at her, waiting for her to speak.

"Yes. Same MO He wore the ring again."

"Good. That's a solid lead."

"He won't be aware it left an imprint. The police are keeping that information secret. If we can find anyone wearing the style of ring, we can place him under tight scrutiny. Prevent another killing."

"I think we can head in now," Tom said. "Everyone's gone home."

Tom was right. The streets were deserted, as if people wanted to be safe at home after dark. Good, if everyone followed that directive, there'd be no more killing. But why should one madman hold her town hostage? It grated on Anna's last nerve.

She started the non-descript van she'd bought out of the area for surveillance work and drove off the parking lot and into the alley, parking near the back entrance to the doctor's office, one of a handful of businesses in the Yellowhead strip mall. Tonight she'd attached a temporary peel-off sign to the driver's door, the name of a security company printed in typeface to explain their presence to anyone chancing by. She and Tom were both disguised, wearing dark clothing and baseball caps pulled down low over their faces. Donning a medical mask and plastic gloves, they disembarked from the vehicle. Time to go to work.

In less than thirty seconds they were inside—Anna in possession of the security code from a little online sleuthing—and headed for Druitt's office located behind the reception area desk. The new toys she considered tools her instant millionaire status had bought were far reaching and soon she'd be in possession of enough AI resources to power a small planet, artificial intelligence being of keen interest to her. Okay, that was a slight exaggeration, but more importantly, was Stephen Hawking, right? Would we as slow to evolve, fragile biological creatures be superseded by supercomputers? Could it spell the end of the human race with everyone out of a job or dominated by a sentient entity thousands of times smarter than us not limited by the need to sleep or eat? Or, with enough control exhibited now, could we prepare the human race for an enviable future? Anyway, she looked at possible future scenarios, the fourth industrial age was going to have a major impact on everything and everyone she knew. Part of her was exhilarated by the potential while another part was scared stiff of the downfalls not yet thought of or understood. But if data was the new oil, then surely it could help drive criminal investigations, maybe even recognize psychopaths before they do their evil. Or could Jack the Ripper be caught using AI? She had plugged the scant facts of the copycat case, but nothing had been spit-out more than her own mind had come up with, so maybe computers taking over was a bit far-fetched. Yet.

Anna took a deep breath, as riveting as the subject was, she forced herself back to the present. She had a job to do. The confined space in the medical office was still a maze of patient files in the old-fashioned folder format located on pull-out shelves, the middle-aged doctor preferring to consult a handheld chart over a virtual one. She found it comforting after her mental dive into the deep waters of AI and the future. She understood the need for many to hold an actual book in their hands over the use of electronic devices.

"You ever get a little time, I'd appreciate a tutorial on how you do that," Tom whispered.

"How's that?"

"The easy access key you seem to come supplied with at backdoors we need access to."

Anna snorted. "Sure. And you can teach me how to persuade trucking companies personnel to give up the goods."

"It's all good looks and charm, baby."

"Well, you got that covered. And don't call me baby, sugar plum."

Her words seemed to take Tom by surprise and he gave her a sideways look.

"Why, Miss Hale, I didn't think you noticed."

She ignored his taunt. If there was one thing she was learning working alongside Tom and Josh it was lightening up and not take herself so seriously while simultaneously giving everything to the case at hand. She led the way to the back and Druitt's personal corner office. A tidy space, almost obsessively so, spartan and dustless in the dimmed evening lighting. A four-drawer file system, a cleared off desk and a happy photo of his family taken in front of a Christmas tree with everyone wearing matching sweaters. Even the dog. Dr. Druitt stood mid-center, widely smiling. Did the mask hide his real persona? Seemed so hard to believe, the man looked relaxed and comfortable in the picture.

The murderer would definitely be obsessive about control, an organized serial killer. It had happened before. Dr. Shipman came to mind and his motive being greed. The bastard even forged wills. Dr. Druitt, on the other hand, didn't appear to have any financial incentive. What could possibly cause him to do such a thing? To risk his future? His family's well-being? Anna had no answers as yet, only questions. Perhaps they'd never know the why. But if they could find positive proof he was the monster behind the slaying, the least they could do was catch the evil bastard and hang him high in the town square as a warning to others to stay the fuck out of Anchor.

The file cabinet was locked, but a quick jimmy of the flimsy lock produced results. Anna rifled through folders neatly labeled. Nothing out of the ordinary. The second drawer provided no clue but when she opened the third one, three hard cover books stood out: *I Know Jack* by his nibs Cosmo, a tome by a far more famous writer naming the artist Sickert as the Ripper, another by Donald Rumbelow, a respected author on the case, and *The Complete History of Jack the Ripper* by Philip Sugden. It didn't make him guilty. Many people studied the case obsessively, being an unsolvable mystery. Hell, even her sister was a bastion of knowledge. But it was a small red flag on the play.

The best drawer turned out to be the last one she

checked. It contained his work laptop. She held out her find to show Tom. He'd been busy sleuthing through his desk and looked up at her whispered call.

"Nice," he said.

"Break into this baby, plant a bug, and we can watch what he's up to back in the war room in real time."

He pursed his lips. "Remind me never to leave any of my electronic devices laying around for you to find."

"Ha, too late for that," she mocked, laying the computer on the top of the desk and getting straight down to work. She attached a device that would shoot out his password, bypass the operation system, and lay down an excellent bit of programming software that would end any expectations of his having privacy for the foreseeable future. She had no ethical concerns about it. If he wasn't doing anything wrong, then nothing could be found. She just wished she had equal access to his home computer.

"I'm an open book," Tom said.

"No nudie pics or dark web connections?"

"No. Hmm, this looks interesting." Tom pulled out a black soft-sided leather journal from the bottom desk drawer he'd pried open and a brown deerstalker hat worn by a man some thought Jack the Ripper back in the day. The journal itself was six inches by eight, demonstrating heavy use, the fabric distressed. The cap looked older yet, a relic of a bygone age. She set the laptop back exactly where she'd found it and closed the file cabinet drawer, joining Tom.

She held her penlight over the book as he began rifling through it. Her heartbeat began to increase as she read a couple of entries written in a perfect hand, a marvel in itself if it didn't discuss the deeds of a madman. The sentences and paragraphs were devoted to discussion and analysis of the Ripper killings of 1888. The book was decades in the making, the entries going back over twenty years.

Could this be it? Was Dr. Druitt their guy? The thought that the medical man she'd known for years could be the monster made her stomach roil. But even this wasn't enough unless he confessed somewhere inside these pages. To be one hundred percent positive of his guilt she needed to find the ring because all they had to date was entirely circumstantial evidence. Then, and only then, could she throttle a confession out of the bastard. They both took a moment to capture the evidence on their phones. It would be best to leave the hat in place and have Josh get a search warrant.

A slight noise made them lock eyes. Was someone there? She slipped the journal into her waistband of her yoga pants at the curve of her back to keep it hidden, then gestured with one hand for them to move over to the doorway.

She peeped around the edge of the doorframe but the hallway was clear leading toward the reception area. She shook her head to let Tom know nothing could be seen. They stood close together, actively listening. Anna could feel Tom's warm minty breath on the back of her neck below her ball cap and it sent a flush of heat through her body. He had a thing for breath mints, always chewing on them. She shrugged it off, not needing the distraction. They waited for several minutes, silent statues in the dimness, but nothing further happened.

Must have been an airduct or something shifting in the building. Her mind began to plan ahead. They'd be on Druitt like white on rice going forward, his every move scrutinized. She also needed entry to his home when it was empty to check for the ring. Now that they had the first two locations for the murders, a map of Anchor may produce possible spots for the so-called double event. But on second thought, that would be taking an awful big chance pinpointing his next murder site. More likely he wouldn't go that route. Whatever, she'd do everything in her power to prevent another murder from happening. Hopefully by September 30th they'd have proof positive of Druitt's guilt or innocence. Or have another suspect in custody. Anna was too smart to let herself be blinded to other potential leads, but circumstantial facts were adding up and not in the good doctor's favor.

Anna and Tom crept down the hall, every sense alert in an effort to avoid surprises. But in short order, they exited the building and sped away. After a few blocks of driving, she pulled onto the side of the road and got out to pull off the fake business sign, throwing it inside the van for safe keeping.

"Now what?" Tom asked as she jumped back into the driver's seat.

"Now we set up a schedule of surveillance."

"And Josh?"

"We have nothing definitive yet. Let's hold off until we've read the journal. Hell, there might even be a confession within those pages. Then we can tell him about the hat."

"What about chain of evidence? Can't he just deny and say he was framed?"

"Do you think he's headed to jail for these crimes if it's proven without a shadow of doubt that he's the new Ripper?" Anna scoffed, then sighed. "Okay, soon as I've photographed it, I'll put it back. Then the cops can find it as well."

TWENTY-NINE

Anna honked her horn outside Charlie's place and the front door of the small cottage was flung open in a nanosecond. Charlie must have been watching the street. Friday came trotting out first, immediately followed by Charlie. She had a large rolling suitcase in one hand and set it down on the top step to lock the door.

"Looks like we got company," Anna said, giving a solemn nod. "Best part of that explosion was getting a bigger place."

"Only you could find the bright spot to being made homeless," Josh said with a wry grin.

"Hardly homeless. Charlie took me in, even though it cramped her style."

"I appreciate you taking me in. I intend to find a place soon as I can find the time," Tom said.

"No rush. I'm enjoying the company." She didn't look at Tom when she said the words, just got out of the van and helped Charlie with her bag. And the fact that both of them had slowed their consumption of alcohol was an added bonus.

"I can't stay in that house alone with a murderer on the loose," Charlie rushed to say. "My skin's crawling like I got ants dancing all over me! I jump at every little noise and I've already lost half my best dishes. They keep slipping from my hands. I hate to bother you, but you did say anytime."

Anna gave her a long hug. "And I meant it. I love company, you know that. I can never pay you back for all you've done for me. Between keeping the business afloat when I fell apart to allowing me to stay here for months when my new place was being built—well, I owe you big time, Charlie, and I'm happy to be able to open my home to you now."

"Thank you. But it was nothing. It's what family does for family."

Charlie settled into her seat behind Josh and Friday sat in the one beside her after a friendly greeting.

Anna got back in the driver's side and was about to pull away when her phone rang. She answered it, noting the number. The Yellowbird Motel.

"Anna, it's Zeke Law."

"What can I do for you, Zeke?"

"I have a situation."

"Can it wait till morning?"

"It involves that young girl, Kelly Smith, that you rescued?"

"That *we* rescued," Anna corrected him. Josh was staring at her now, eyes narrowed.

"Well, I did what I could."

Zeke's self-effacement endeared him to her.

"I'll be right there soon as I drop by my place." What had happened that would drive Kelly back to the Yellowbird? It didn't make any sense. Anna had held out the best carrot she could offer, a chance at a good future doing what she wanted. Was she more hooked on drugs than she'd realized? Well, this time, she wasn't taking chances, the girl was staying with her. Charlie and Tom would help to straighten her out. Zoe too. She was an expert on addiction.

"What's up?" Tom asked as she ended the call.

"Gotta help out a friend."

"Tonight? It's after midnight."

"I don't abide by the clock. People need help when they need help."

"True. I'm coming with you."

"I was hoping you'd help Charlie settle in?" Anna suggested. Tom didn't know Zeke and she wasn't certain how well it would go off. Zeke might take offense or maybe Tom would get his back up? But they were both former soldiers, they had experience at situations that others couldn't even imagine. Made the pair of them highly valuable in a world where others had gone soft from easy living.

"I'll be fine. I don't need y'all to settle me in. I can do for myself, thank you kindly," Charlie piped up from the back seat.

"Fine."

The drive home was quick. Charlie made fast work of clamoring out of the van, collecting a key from Anna, and waving them off, Friday standing by her side. In short order they were headed out again.

"I should look into getting Charlie a dog," she mused.

"Who is this Zeke Law?" Tom asked, interrupting her thoughts on what kind of breed her friend would prefer.

Anna filled him in on the facts as they raced toward the Yellowbird. "Not certain what the deal is, but my intention is to bring Kelly home with us. Tonight."

"With all that's going on in this town, she's probably overwhelmed and started using to forget what the deal is," Tom suggested, his mouth flattened in a firm line.

"Yeah, I hear you. It's crazy shit. The sooner this monster is caught, the better." Anna pounded the steering wheel. "We have to find him!"

"It's not your fault, Anna. You care more about this than anyone I know. You'd move heaven and earth to help someone. You are not responsible for other's choices."

Anna swallowed against the tightness strangling her throat. Tom knew her better than she'd realized. She'd been so certain Kelly was going to be fine. Bear was dead. Her mom was safe and had made amends. What the fuck had happened?

The town was under a lot of pressure. Too much stress created by one psychopath hiding in their midst. Anna felt a sudden urge to get herself a large bottle of whiskey and drink enough to forget the world and its problems for one night. But that wouldn't solve anything. Just give her a bad hangover and dim her wits. Something she needed more now than ever. Sharp wits. This murderer was the worst of anyone she'd stalked. Leaving such an empty trail behind him like some kind of supernatural predator. If it wasn't Druitt, who the fuck the will o' the wisp lurking in Anchor?

Anna sped onto the parking lot at the motel, the van's back wheels kicking up choking dust from the loose gravel.

"I'll check in with Zeke. You watch to see if anyone leaves, okay?"

Josh nodded.

She hurried to open the office door and strode

toward Zeke, standing pensive behind the counter. Spying her, he grabbed his Remington .308 from under the counter and joined her. If possible, he looked even more mountain-man tonight. His dark beard and hair a testament to lack of grooming or care. But he smelled clean, the fresh odor of soap waffling off him.

"Looks like you were already onto something tonight, by the dark clothing and headgear."

"Yeah, following some interesting breadcrumbs. How many of them out back?" she asked, hand resting on her side hostler that held her Glock. It helped to ground her. The stiffness at her lower back reminded her she hadn't removed the journal as yet.

"Three guys, two girls. Cabin six."

"I've brought a friend to help as well. Tom Jackson. We work together on cases. Former military. Same as us."

"Good. The more the merrier. Not that I intend to entertain this crew." Zeke grimaced with distaste. "A bunch of druggies strung out of their damn minds. Place stinks to high heaven. I visited them earlier to warn them to keep the noise down. That's when I spotted your girl."

"Thanks for the call. I thought I had it handled, paying her tuition to college, but something must have happened."

"Willpower and the body don't always agree. Might take a few times before it gels. But don't give up."

"Don't intend to. Okay. Let's haul ass." Anna strode out of the office. Tom joined them, Anna made a quick introduction, then the three of them marched toward cabin six. Time to rescue a kitten. At least this was something she could do, disappointed as she was with the fact Kelly had once more placed herself at risk. A frisson of fear stuck her when Kelly's name suddenly rang a bell. Mary Kelly. The most horribly mutilated of the Ripper victims. She stumbled, nearly tripping on the path, righting herself while forcing back the terrifying image she'd viewed online of the body of Mary Kelly. An image that had haunted the world for over a century. No. It won't happen. She refused with every fiber of her being to let it. If she had to lock Kelly in a room on November ninth, so be it. Better yet, lock down the whole town. But she could well imagine the screaming that would come from a curfew edit in notoriously independent Anchor, Alaska.

"You okay?" Tom asked.

"Yeah."

"I'll head around back in case someone tries to leave," Tom said. He strode from view, vanishing around the corner of the building.

Zeke knocked on the door to the cabin, holding the shotgun pointed at the ground. "Open up, it's the owner."

It took a few louder bangs, but finally a guy who looked like he could use a good long shower and some eyedrops to relieve his red-rimmed eyes, poked his head out and demanded in a winey belligerent tone that didn't bode well for his immediate future. "What's the matter now? We're being quiet."

"I have someone here who needs to speak to Kelly Smith. Get her now."

The guy scratched his head, like it was rocket science. "Kelly Smith?"

"Pretty girl, wants to be a clothing designer. Ring any bells?" Anna said, stepping up and narrowing her eyes at the guy.

"Oh, you mean K." He stood there, looking pleased

with himself he'd figured out the puzzle, until Anna redirected his focus.

"Yes, get her. *Now*. Tell her Anna Hale wants to talk to her."

"Fine, fine. Hang on a sec." He slammed the door in their faces and shouted. "K, some lady wants to speak to you."

The cabin was silent for a few seconds. Then the door slowly opened, revealing Kelly. She wouldn't look anyone in the eye, but stared at her feet as if they were the most interesting thing.

"Kelly, it's Anna. I've come to offer my help. Are you okay?" Anna worked hard to keep any judgment from her tone. She didn't want to scare the girl. But if she refused to cooperate, all bets were off.

"I'm fine. Quit worrying about me."

Her tone said she was anything but fine.

"I do worry. You know what's been going on in town, right? That women are being murdered?" Anna stepped it up a notch, unable to keep the worry and concern from coloring her tone.

"Yeah, I know. I'm not dumb. I stay away from those places." Kelly picked at her thumbnail, tearing off a strip of skin.

"But how can you know which places to stay away from?" Anna pointed out. Kelly had no answer for that.

"Does your mom know you're here?" Anna asked.

The sad young girl shook her head, a tear rolling down her cheek. She swiped at it, then sniffed.

Anna lowered her voice. "Come and stay with me, at least until you're feeling better. I'll talk to your mom."

"Don't tell her I'm using again." Kelly took a step backward, like she was going to slam the door shut.

"I won't, I promise. But you need help, Kelly. I can get you all the help you need. Please, come home with me."

"One of the guys saw him, you know."

The words were spoken softly, but the realization of what the girl was saying hit Anna in the solar plex. "You mean the Ripper? Someone you know saw him? What did he see? What's his name, Kelly?" Anna moved forward involuntarily and took hold of the girl. She needed answers.

Kelly tried to pull away, her eyes glazed by the drugs in her system. "Let me go! I didn't see anything. And the guy who saw him, he won't talk. He's scared. Keep out of it."

"Who is it? Kelly, listen to me. Women's lives are at stake here. You must tell me!"

But the young girl clammed up, her mouth etched in a rigid line.

Anna glanced at Zeke. He gave her a pointed look to stand down.

"Okay, how about we get you to my place? You can sleep it off there. At least I'll know you're safe, even if that leaves all the other women in town hanging out there, a possible victim of a madman." She laid the guilt on.

Kelly looked down at her feet and scrubbed the toe of her tennis shoe in the grass beside the cabin. "His name is Squirrel, okay. Ask him what he knows."

"Squirrel?" Zeke said, his expression suggesting he was not impressed.

"His real name's Todd, but he hates it. One time, he got kicked in the nuts on a job and the name stuck. He also likes to collect things. Stuff most people would throw out."

"Okay, good to know." Zeke visibly winced.

What is it with guys and their balls? "Okay, we ready?" Anna braced herself.

Zeke yelled out, "We need to talk to Squirrel. The rest of you can stand down."

The inside of the motel grew quieter. Then some shouts sounded out back of the cabin. Twenty to one good old Squirrel had tried to escape and Tom had nabbed him.

THIRTY

"What the fuck!" Tom shouted. "You bit me!"

Zeke took off first. Anna hated to take her eyes off of Kelly but she had to help Tom. What if he was being swarmed? Or one of them had a knife? Hell, one of them could even be the Ripper.

"Please, *please* don't go anywhere, Kelly. Just wait here. I'll be right back," she implored the young girl before racing off, following in Zeke's footsteps.

Rounding the corner, the first sight she was confronted by was of the pair of them wrestling on the ground. The guy that most likely was Squirrel had a bloody nose. A skinny asshole, his eyes looked like a mad dog's as he held onto Tom like his life depended on it while Tom worked to subdue him. Hopped up on drugs, the guy squirmed like an octopus, all flailing limbs. It would be funny, if he hadn't been bit by him. A human bite was a serious matter.

Zeke finally managed to grab hold of the idiot by the scuff of the neck, pulling him off her partner. He shook him hard, not letting go, his feet off the ground.

Tom clamored to his feet, before checking out his hand.

"Hope you're up to date on your tetanus shots?" Anna asked. "Sorry about all this."

"Fucker came out the window and landed right on top of me. The bite hurts like a bitch. If he has AIDS or something else equally bad, he's going to live to regret it. Bad enough Josh lost a chunk of flesh to a real dog, but this is *way* out of line."

Squirrel was still punching and kicking at thin air, trying to dislodge Zeke. What kind of anger-fueled drug concoction was the guy on anyway? "Secure the shotgun," he instructed Anna.

She reached down and picked it up from where Zeke had abandoned it to help Tom, making sure the safety was secure on the gun and leaned it up against the cabin wall out of reach of Squirrel. Then she pulled out a couple of zip ties from her jacket pocket. "We're going to tie you up if you don't stop moving around, Squirrel," she warned. She needed to check on Kelly and get Tom to a hospital. ASAP.

Tom slugged the idiot in the face and finally he went limp, dangling from Zeke's hands. Anna couldn't blame him, being bit would probably incur a number of future checkups, uncomfortable and fraught with worry.

Anna quickly clamped Squirrel's hands and feet together, securing them with the white plastic ties. "We need to be sure this is Squirrel. Then interview him. I'll get Kelly." Anna took off at a quick trot and breathed a sigh of relief when she nearly ran the young girl down as she rounded the corner to join them.

"Is that Squirrel?" Anna asked, pointing him out, laying a gentle hand on the girl's thin shoulder. Tom had the druggie propped up against the back of the cabin. He appeared to be coming around, moving his head side to side.

"Yeah. What happened to him?"

"He bit my partner who will probably now need to undergo a series of shots. Does Squirrel have any medical conditions?"

"I don't know." Kelly looked nervous, like a starling about to take flight. Anna kept her hand on her shoulder, just in case.

"It's okay. We only want to talk to him. Find out what he knows."

"Let me talk to him. I can calm him down," Kelly offered. "We get along okay. He likes me."

"All right."

Anna led the girl over to the trio.

Kelly stopped in front of Squirrel; her expression surprisingly compassionate as she crouched down to talk to him, face to face. "Please tell them about what you saw. Do it for me, Squirrel. The guy needs to be stopped. What if it happens to someone we know?"

He looked at her, blinking rapidly, his breathing ragged. Anna could instantly see the effect the young girl had on him. His face cleared and he nodded before speaking, "I saw him, mostly from the back. He looked kind of big though."

Anna's heartbeat increased and she stepped closer, her gaze glued to Squirrel's bloodied face.

"Tell us *exactly* what you heard and saw. Start at the beginning," she demanded.

Squirrel didn't look at her but stared at the ground. "I was going to stop by, see Jason. I needed a hit, real bad man. I walked in behind their place."

"On Baker Street?" Tom asked.

"Yeah, down the alley. I was just coming up to the

fence. It was foggy. Hard to see any kind of distance. But I heard this loud thump, like something had fallen against the fence. I stopped and decided maybe to go around the front instead."

"Did you?" Anna asked.

Squirrel shook his head. "No. The fence had these cracks, so I crept up to it see what was going on. More squishy noises. Some kind of weird sucking sounds, like, well, I can't really describe it."

When LeeLee was getting butchered. Anna tried to dispel the gruesome images, needing to concentrate. She dug her fingernails painfully into the palm of her hand to ground herself.

"I looked through one of the wider cracks with one eye, quiet like." Squirrel looked terrified. "It was awful, man. He was stabbing at her, pulling stuff out of her and throwing it around. All wet and bloody. Like a horror movie on steroids. I wanted to run, but I was afraid to make a sound. Maybe he would come after me next?"

"Could you see who he was stabbing? You said *she*."

"LeeLee, it was her. I got a glimpse of her face," Squirrel said the name softly, his Adam's apple bobbing up and down as he swallowed. "They were only a few feet away from where I was standing."

"What was he wearing?" Anna asked.

"I don't know. Dark clothes. A funny hat and a long coat. I couldn't see his height, he was bent over at the waist, crouched down like. God, it was awful. What if he had turned around and seen me staring at him? The fence had a broken gate. He could have been on me in a second. I'd be dead too."

Anna pulled out her phone and showed him a photo of the deerstalker hat from Druitt's office.

"Like this hat?"

"Yeah. Weird." Squirrel sniffed, his nose was swelling up and making his voice muffled now. Had he seen the doctor?

"Could you see any of his hair? Did he have a knife?"

"I didn't see his hair, just the hat. And yeah, he had a long blade. I saw it when he raised it up high to strike each time."

"What hand did he hold it in? Left? Or right?"

"His back was mostly to me." Squirrel stopped to think about it, as if he were trying to picture it in his mind. "I think, right-handed?"

"Did he make any sounds?"

"No."

"Could you see his feet?"

"Black shoes."

"Modern?"

He shrugged. "I don't know. Can I go now? That's all I saw. Honest."

"How old did he look to you?"

"Older than me."

"Middle-aged? Older?"

"Not sure. He moved fast like a cat." Squirrel shuddered, no doubt the image sharp in his mind.

"What did you do next?"

"I left."

"You didn't think to call the police?" Zeke demanded. "Punch in 9-1-1 and get the woman some help?"

Squirrel had nothing to say to the accusation. Even Kelly gave him a look that suggested his cowardness was beyond her understanding too. He looked down, whispering, "It was too late, okay? She was dead. Any fucking idiot could see that." Tears filled his eyes and he sniffled again.

"You said *mostly* his back was to you? Did you catch a

glimpse of his face? Did you recognize him?" Anna asked.

Squirrel shook his head. "I didn't know him at all. I saw his profile mostly. Yeah, kind of his face for a second or two."

"Did he have a big nose? A scar? Jowls?" Anna pressed him for details, beyond pleased with what she had gotten him to admit to.

"No. What's a jowl?"

"Saggy skin around the jawline that comes with age. Makes people look older," she explained.

"No. His face was more like it was carved out of a rock. Pale-like. Spooky. He didn't look really old. In his late thirties or forties, I guess."

"Keep all that in mind, Squirrel. You can work with a sketch artist. They might bring out more details. It's worth a try." Even a side view of the killer was a whole lot more than they had until now. Dr. Druitt had a youthful face for his age, no jowl line yet. And one full shot of his face, if the sketch artist could draw out more details, would be more than was ever known about the original Ripper.

"Who's your family doctor?" she asked.

"Don't have one. I hate going to the doctors. Them and their fucking pills." Slightly hypocritical.

"I take it you're into self-medication?"

Squirrel shrugged, not answering her question.

"Untie his legs, Anna. Time to haul his ass to the station," Zeke said.

"I want a lawyer. I'm going to sue all of you. This is harassment." Squirrel was back on the defensive.

"Buddy, you're damn lucky I didn't slug you into next week," Tom said, effectively shutting him up.

A human bite definitely outranked a bloody nose in anybody's book.

"Let's go," Anna said. She kept a close eye on Kelly, taking her hand as the four of them trooped over to the motel's office. She leaned in and asked, "You okay?"

"What? Yeah, a bit fucked up." Kelly rubbed at her forehead with her free hand. "I need to sleep."

"Soon as we get to my place, you can sleep, rest, whatever you need, okay? Just hang in there while we deliver my partner to the hospital. He needs treatment."

Two partners bitten in less than two weeks. A stranger case had never existed to Anna's mind. But they now had an eyewitness. The monster was real, not a phantom of imagination driving those in town to twist the madman into another legend that would out last all those alive today and possibly for generations. With the lack of evidence left at a crime scene and the few facts known, the supernatural slant was somewhat under-standable. However one looked at, this was a much-needed break in the case and she was proud of her team for uncovering it, even if it had been partly luck and being at the right location. What was it real estate devel-opers say ad nauseum? Location. Location. Location.

THIRTY-ONE

In front of the motel's office, Anna turned to Zeke. "Thanks for your help. You need any assistance with the idiots still messing up in cabin six?"

"Nah, I got it. You got your hands full. Now that you've rescued Kelly, again, I'll call the cops on them. They're all using. Won't be hard to find drug evidence in the cabin. Let me know how you make out, okay? With everything. I'd like to know. Kind of feel sorry for that young girl. She's mixed up right now and damn lucky to have you in her corner."

"Don't know about that, I couldn't stop her from using, but sure, I'll call you. Thanks again." Zeke Law was turning from a stranger into a man she'd like to call a friend. He had stepped up again. Called her first, was instrumental in helping her team get their first real break in the Ripper case.

Tom, Kelly, and Squirrel were already inside the van when Anna climbed in the driver's side. She gave Tom a look of sympathy sitting in the front passenger seat. "You okay?"

"Not fond of needles, but yeah, I'll be fine. If that asshole isn't diseased?"

"I'm not diseased!" Squirrel protested from the back seat. Kelly was busy trying to wipe the blood from his nose, wetting a tissue and dabbing at it. He whined with pain but let her finish the job. Though his feet were free, Anna had left his hands secured. She didn't trust him for a second and no way was he getting out of reporting what he'd seen. He was a valuable witness. The evidence was piling up for Druitt and she fairly itched to read the diary.

"You'd better not be," Tom warned. Anna glanced at his hand. He had already flushed the wound with water, but the bite was still weeping, the flesh around the wound dark. It was going to leave a hell of a bruise.

"Hospital first, then I'll take his nibs to the station. Can you wait a little while, Kelly?" she asked, checking the girl in the rearview mirror.

"Yeah, sure."

"My arms hurt. Can't you take these stupid things off?" Squirrel groused.

"We can't take the chance you might decide to run off again," Anna explained patiently, pressing her foot down harder on the gas. She'd already checked that all the doors of the van were locked. "Your testimony is of vital importance. You might be the only one who has seen him." She appealed to his vanity, hoping to keep him pacified enough to cooperate at his upcoming interrogation. No doubt he'd be kept at the jail for hours, housed inside a small room. Not like she hadn't had experience in that direction. About the third time you were asked to explain events was about the moment all the luster wore off. Add being a suspect to the list, and well, it sucked.

"You're important to the investigation now, Squirrel, might even get a TV appearance out of this."

"Yeah?" He perked up. "Do they pay for shit like this? Hell, I'll bet they do."

Squirrel was more than pacified at the idea, giving Anna good reason to believe he'd cooperate.

Anna parked in the lane in front of Anchor Hospital Emergency, jumped out and rushed around to open Tom's door to assist him.

"No need to come in," Tom said. "Deal with that asshole first before he changes his mind. Or loses it again."

"I'll be back soon as I've delivered him."

"No rush. This could take fuckin' hours." Tom gave a wry smile and strode away, careful to hold his hand cradled close to his chest, and passed through the electronic door into emergency. Gone in a flash. She'd be far less easygoing herself if she was sporting a human bite. Damn Squirrel for his overreaction. And lack of compassion for the human race. If he'd not been such a coward and come clean sooner, they'd be one day closer to preventing another murder. She gritted her teeth to keep her thoughts inside, and not undo all the good she had managed to keep the idiot in line long enough to deliver him to the law and got back into the van.

Back on the road with the pair huddled together in the back seat, Anna nodded in time to the country and western song with the peppy beat coming through the sound system. The movement kept her focused, gave her mind some freedom as the rhythm quickened her blood. Kept her from climbing into the back seat and throttling Squirrel.

Anchor Police Department was relatively quiet when she pulled into the parking lot. How long it would stay that way when the news leaked out they had an eye witness was anyone's guess. Anna didn't care who got credit for finding Squirrel, more happenstance than good sleuthing techniques, but it was satisfying anyway to march the young man into the station.

With Squirrel in tow, she hurried to deliver him to Josh, bypassing reception. She'd left Kelly in the van against her better judgment, but the young girl refused to go in and promised to wait for her. She had to trust her word, hard as it was.

"Anna, what are you doing here?" Josh stood up abruptly at her arrival at his workstation, his limp barely noticeable. Other cops milling about the room eyed the pair of them, giving Squirrel squinty-eyed looks, no doubt his reputation proceeded him. He bounced from foot to foot, seeming unable to stand still, his hands still bound behind his back.

"Squirrel here witnessed LeeLee's murder."

You could have heard the proverbial pin drop in the dead silence that accompanied her statement. Anna could feel the hushed breaths. This was huge. Biggest break in the case she knew of to date.

"Is that right, Squirrel?"

Ah, Josh knew the kid too.

"Yes, and he wants to help nail the bastard."

"Will I get a reward?" Squirrel looked hopeful, like he'd found a money tree with both hands ready to pluck some cash.

"There's no reward being offered."

Squirrel didn't like her brother's answer and shuffled back a step.

"But his information will be valuable and bring the attention of the media, right, Detective Pace?" Anna prompted him.

"News agencies or magazines may pay you." Josh went along with Anna's assessment.

"Okay then."

Crisis averted. Anna spoke up, "Tom's at the hospital and I have to take Kelly to my place. Do you need me for anything?"

"What happened to Tom?"

She gestured at Squirrel. "Ask him."

The three of them had gathered a crowd, surrounding the desk with cops. Anna had to swallow her anxiety. She still loathed being in the station, memories from past interrogations of her when she'd been a suspect still rankled. But she kept it at bay, thinking of the greater good.

"Okay. I'll catch up with you later."

Anna turned and hurried through the throng of law men gathered around them, needing to get back into the fresh air. See Kelly situated. She felt the diary's borders pressing into her spine, a constant reminder of its importance. She strode out of the station, intent on delivering Kelly before heading back to wait for Tom.

Outside the building, she took a deep breath and a moment to center herself. A rarity in her experience. The scents that she associated with fall were already tingeing the air, the fragrance of fallen leaves and flowers turning brown, a rich loamy odor that hit before the snows fly. She took a look around, a real glance for a change, not just as a waystation as she rushed about doing her job or checking for threat assessment purposes. She could see Kelly from where she was standing, slumped in the front seat now. The caragana bushes that lined the spacious property had turned to seed, their pods bursting to prepare for the next generation. Golds and reds were patchworking the landscape. It was the time she liked best. When everything had come to fruition. Was this it? Would Squirrel be able to identify the murderer? Could the case be close to being solved? She sent a silent prayer to the universe she imagined holding their collective breath. Or maybe it was more like, same old, same old. Fix one problem and two more pop up. Well, fuck it, she'd stomp on all the fires she could. *Never give up*, that was the ticket.

THIRTY-TWO

Anna escorted her new charge up the sidewalk to the house, keeping an eye out for any unexpected developments. Since her home was blown up a few months back, she was always skittish about not checking things out thoroughly before entry. The alarm system hadn't been tripped or her phone would have notified her of an intruder. Anyone visiting her property for that matter would set things in motion. She still had her suspicions about Dr. Molly, the therapist that didn't do much for her anxiety, but increased it with her vendetta. In her mind, she thought she had reason to. Anna had shot and killed her brother, Elvis Strobel. The notorious Black Rose Killer.

"You can have the same room as last time. Towels in the bathroom and the sheets have been changed. Frig is full. Can you hang tight while I see to Tom? He'll need a ride home from the hospital."

"Is he still staying here?"

"Yes. Do you have a problem with that?"

Kelly quickly shook her head. "No, just wondering if you guys, you know…"

She left it hanging. Anna ignored the bait.

"And my friend Charlie's also staying here. She doesn't feel safe right now." But if they had a lead, arrested a suspect, that would change. Too bad Anna had little time for socializing at the moment. She'd love to have another dinner party with all her new roommates. At that instant, she realized, she'd been lonely of late. It had been months since Tia's death. Her sister had been staying with her at the time of her murder, and they had enjoyed those precious few weeks together. She pushed the unwelcome thoughts aside. She needed to stay focused, not become ineffective due to depression. She'd experienced bouts of sadness since her mom had been murdered when she was a teenager. Best cure. Getting on with things.

"Do you take in any stray that asks?" Kelly muttered, giving her a look as if her nose were out of joint.

"It's called paying it forward. Though in the case of Charlie, more like backward. She took me in when my house was blown to smithereens."

Kelly startled, looking around with worry. "That can't happen again, can it?"

Anna could have screamed with frustration at the slip. Why the hell had she said that? If the girl took off again, it would be her fault.

"*Never*." Anna almost gave herself whiplash so vigorously did she shake her head with denial. "I made sure of it. Every security device known to man, and some no ones heard about has been installed. State-of-the-art. Safe as Fort Knox." Anna took a deep breath. "Thanks for your help with Squirrel, by the way. He wouldn't have said what he did if he wasn't doing it for you."

Kelly gave a tired smile. "Yeah, he's okay. When he's not messed up. We used to date, but, well, you know."

"Things changed," Anna finished for her. She needed to keep the young girl talking, work on creating a bond that might withstand cravings. Or was that just a pipe dream, knowing the dreadful statistics for rehab failures? Less than twenty percent of those in outpatient programs maintain complete sobriety for an entire year. Talk about heartbreaking for families and an unimaginable tragedy for those afflicted.

"You dating anyone?" Kelly came right out with it this time.

"No time for dating. Now, promise me you'll be here when I get back? There's a madman on the loose out there Kelly, I want to keep you safe until he's caught. You understand? He could be anybody." A madman or the most cold, calculated bastard the world had seen since, well, no one worse came to mind. Except maybe a child killer.

"Aren't the cops close to catching him? I mean, the FBI's here, right? That's got to help."

"In a perfect world. But he's a slippery bastard. No evidence left at the crime scene, which is a miracle since we have the medical examiner on our side who's one of the best in the business." Damn it, with all the forensic science available at this time in history, why was it so damn hard to nail a suspect? Anna wanted to blame Cullen Cross, but she knew he was working day and night in efforts to solve the case. He wanted to catch the evil bastard as much as anybody, she imagined. She put him back on the list of people she wanted to see soon. A check-in, face to face, was warranted to see if he had anything he was looking at on the backburner he hadn't shared yet. Anna was more than willing to step out on a limb and help him anyway she could. Offering her services was just the ticket to see him.

"You should go. You're trying to catch him too, right?" Like Kelly could read her mind, she gave Anna a sturdier look and made a gesture, placing her hand over her heart. "I promise, cross my heart, to be here when you get back. Good enough for you?"

"Thanks, Kelly."

Anna made a quick list of people she wanted to see today. A trip back to the theater to check in with Eileen was in order as well.

"Be back soon," she said. Anna strode out of the house, wishing she could barricade the house. She did have a way, a system she'd had installed that brought down metal barriers over the windows and secured the doors, but that was for emergencies, and might frighten the girl more than help her. She'd have to trust Kelly at her word.

She drove her favorite GMC half-ton out of the four-stall garage this time, feeling somewhat certain Kelly would stay put. She drove her souped-up truck down her lane, headed for the hospital. But first a quick detour to see Cross.

Parking in back of Cross's office, she was about to disembark when she spotted the M.E. in the light of the streetlamp headed toward the dumpster. He threw a green trash bag inside the metal container, then caught sight of Anna. He looked surprised to see her but gamely came over to meet her when she got out, jumping down from the running board of the truck. She had to admit to some surprise at seeing the medical professional throwing out his own garbage. Didn't they have a cleaning crew for that?

"Anna. Didn't expect to see you so late." It was late,

nearly three in the morning. Nothing good ever happened at three a.m., at least according to Sergeant Carter, her mentor. No kidding, good people get bit and murderers run amuck. "You didn't get my message?" Cross looked exhausted and she felt guilt for coming by to bother him. But she needed to look him in the eye and see if he was holding anything back. Any clue as to what he was thinking would help. A sense of frustration was gaining hold of her and she tamped it down with difficulty. She was exhausted and mistakes were too easily made.

"Just feeling desperate, you know. Anything worth sharing, Cullen?" She chose to use his first name. He and Zoe were dating which meant informality was the new reality moving forward. If this was the man her sister wanted, then she would make darn sure to get along with him, so she had to tread lightly, hard as it was.

He shook his head, though he didn't meet her steady gaze at him, his eyes shifting to the side. *Fuck*. He did know something. Something vital. "What is it? What are you not telling me?"

"Okay, I did find a fiber on the victim's clothing that wasn't a match for anything else she was wearing and it came from an old garment. Minutes ago. No time to report it yet, you're the first to know."

"This is good news." A rush of adrenaline followed. Maybe it would be a match for the hat? "Good work, Cullen."

"Just got to keep slugging it out. Nothing else to do."

The guy didn't seem very excited about his find. Probably too exhausted. Of course, he didn't know about the hat they'd found in Druitt's possession. Forensics was a vital part of uncovering a suspect. Even if Squirrel's information pointed at someone, they still needed to prove the man could have done it. Science could nail the bastard to the barn wall as Charlie would say.

"How's it going with the FBI?"

"Phttt. About as you'd expect. Double checking everything I do or say."

It explained his mood. Cross was too good at his job to need anyone looking over his shoulder.

"Doesn't make your job easier. You're good; you don't need scrutiny. We're lucky to have you in Anchor. You could make a name for yourself in New York City."

Cross stood a little taller at her compliments, less exhausted. "Yeah, thanks."

"Quid pro quo. We found an eyewitness today. A guy who saw the crime as it was happening through a gap in the fence."

Cross looked stunned at her announcement. Then recovered himself quickly. "A real coup, Anna, well done. Do the FBI know yet?"

"Probably. We hauled the witness to the station over an hour ago."

"Who saw the crime? What did he see?"

No reason not to share the intel that Anna could think of. "A local druggie called Squirrel. He described his clothing. Even caught a glimpse of his face. They should be able to create a sketch from his intel."

"That is an unexpected development."

"Quid pro quo going forward?" she prompted him.

"What?" He looked distracted now, his mind so far away she almost felt the need to wave her hand in front of his face. A few more uncomfortable seconds passed and then he blinked when she did make the motion. "Sorry, did you say something?"

"I was making a suggestion that we share intel from here on in?"

"Huh," was his brilliant comeback.

"Are you getting any sleep at all?" Was Cross breaking down under the strain? It had to be a heavy burden to be the man everyone was looking to for answers. The pressure to know all kinds of expert avenues open to analysis from a victim's standpoint at a crime scene. He had to keep abreast not only of blood and tissue advances but weaponry, bullets, fibers, paint chips, poisons, drugs, hair, teeth and fingerprints. And he was a one-man show with a part-time assistant. Not like a big city with a team at his back.

He gave her a rueful look, running a hand over his hair to smooth it. "Not much. Never ran up against so many dead ends. This guy is good, brilliant even, at not leaving much trace evidence, Locard Principal aside. If only a blood sample could be found."

"How can that be? He was throwing stuff all around, according to our eyewitness. Wouldn't that be more likely to contaminate things? Leave his own blood or hair?"

"You'd think so. He must have gotten off damn lucky. Didn't cut himself or drop hairs. Nothing to link him unless you catch him with the clothing in his possession that shed that one fiber."

"But we do know the clothing was stolen?" She wanted to tell him about the hat they'd found, but it had to go through a proper chain of evidence first of getting a warrant. She couldn't jeopardize the case, even for Cross.

"Not of much help, I'm afraid. No CCTV at the museum or the theater production. Now if this happened in London, England today, that country is very well covered by CCTV. The Ripper would never get away with these crimes again there. The killer chose his geography all too well."

"Well, at least now we have an eyewitness." Just thinking of the leads Squirrel's testimony could bring brought on much-needed hope.

"There is that."

Cross didn't sound as elated as she felt. Probably too damn exhausted.

"Anything else, Anna?" he asked pointedly.

"No, I'll get out of your hair. I need to head over to the hospital. Pick up a friend." Should she tell him about the journal? She decided in the moment to hold off, until she'd read it. Maybe there wasn't anything inside that would matter other than Druitt was interested in the case, like millions of others.

THIRTY-THREE

Anna's premonition about the diary turned out to be spot on. While she waited for Tom in the waiting room of the hospital, she read through the journal until her eyes crossed and her head nodded from exhaustion. But all she discovered was a man who made laundry lists of the five mutually agreed upon crimes of Jack the Ripper from 1888 and juxtapositioned them against the most mentioned, reasonable suspects of the current day. Nothing in it she didn't already know. Or personal about Druitt. Other than she found he'd written a short poem about the Ripper. But no confession or anything incriminating between its covers.

She threw down the black book in disgust. She was no further ahead now than before she broke into his office. Then she remembered the deerstalker hat. She was losing it she was forgetting about that piece of evidence that could yet prove vital. If the fiber found on the victim matched the hat in Druitt's possession, that should be enough for the cops to bring him in and interrogate him in hopes of gaining a confession. But she should put the diary back first to add to the trail of evidence. If Druitt had confessed within those pages, it would have been game over. But no such luck. All hopes lay with Squirrel now, that his sketch would bear fruit.

"Hey, Anna. You shouldn't have waited up. I could have hiked it over to your house or caught a ride with someone. You must be exhausted," Tom said, suddenly standing over her making her startle. Her radar was faulty tonight. She hadn't felt his presence until he was right on top of her. Her former mentor would chastise her soundly for that. *Always be alert. Always be watching.* Not that Tom was dangerous. But she had never needed to be on her A game more.

"Spent the time reading the diary. Nothing whatsoever illuminating about it though, sad to say."

"Shit. That is too bad. I had hopes for it. Are we putting it back tonight?"

Anna took a good long look at Tom. He was worse for the wear than she was.

"What did the doctor say?"

Tom grimaced. "Usual bullshit. Shots, tests, and a waiting game."

"Sorry about that. It sucks."

"Well, at least we got an eyewitness out of it. What's next?"

"Let's go home. The journal's a dud other than it shows his interest in the case like a million others. Now the hat will prove useful if there's a fiber match. Cross found one tonight that's not from the victim's clothing. Josh needs to know about it and get a search warrant."

"Good news. But can't skip the middleman, eh."

"No, not this time." If only Druitt had confessed within the pages this thing would be all over. A visit in the middle of the night to the good doctor would not go astray. Lure him out and take him down after making him confess. The idea buoyed her up and gave her hope. This could all be over soon. No going down in infamy as the second illusive Jack the Ripper, doc.

The pair of them shambled out of the hospital together and headed over to Anna's vehicle.

"We missed having that drink with Josh tonight," Tom said, climbing inside the GMC.

"You in any pain?" Anna thought to ask. She did need to put the diary back into position. Tonight. But she'd do it alone. Tom needed to rest more than she did, recover from the bite.

He shrugged. "Not really. Just didn't like that Squirrelly critter getting the better of me. He'd better be cooperating now or so help me…"

Tom left the threat hanging and awkwardly buckled himself in with his good hand, the other bandaged.

"You did good. Nothing to fault yourself for. The guy was high on drugs. No easy way to deal with it."

"At least we got a few weeks before, well, you know."

The horrifying reality looming over everyone's head was the double-event scheduled for the end of September. If in fact the murderer was following past crime lines and there was every reason to believe he was. No, she couldn't accept the idea, instead she focused on catching him long before that.

"I pray it's enough time to track him down." Anna took a couple of deep, slow breaths, realizing she was breathing too quickly from the exhaustion and stress. She needed to start taking better care of herself. Right, soon as this case was solved, she promised herself to do better.

"It will be. I've got every faith in our ability to smoke him out."

The idea of smoking him out bore instant fruit for her. "Yes, smoke him out. Like they did back in the day. Dress-up policemen to lure the guy."

"Back in the day they could do that because of all the long gowns and bonnets that helped to hide identities. Today not so much."

"Yes, but this time we use real women, not policemen. If we haven't nailed him before September thirtieth, then we recruit some women that are into martial arts or defending themselves and send them into the fray. Decoys. Smoke him out. Then if he goes for one of them, she can pull a gun and end him once and for all. Self-defense."

"Anna, no, I don't want you pulling that shit again. The last honeypot sting was enough to take ten years off my life. I'm half gray now."

"It might not come to that. And you're not going gray. Keep it in the back of our minds for now, all I ask."

Tom grunted, obviously not agreeing with her. Maybe it wouldn't come to it, but she'd be ready. Her mind went over the list of potential women able to handle themselves well enough. Be prepared to take the risk. But no one came to mind.

THIRTY-FOUR

Squirrel exited the Anchor Police Station, jittery though hyped up from the sense of approval he'd been given by the cops for coming forward. It was a new experience for him, having good things said about him. And he had remembered more of the guy's face than he'd expected to. Working with the sketch artist they'd called in especially to assist him had made him feel important. And watching the drawing come to life from his words was exhilarating. For once he had been somebody everybody wanted to talk to. Not just a druggie low-life given short shift or called names and vilified.

He turned down the main roadway leading toward the north of town, wishing he had someone to call and pick him up. Kelly would be the person he would most want to meet up with but she was with that PI now, unavailable at the moment. The town felt deserted, like people were hiding inside or safe and warm in their beds. He envied them. He'd never had a chance. Foster kid through and through. Tossed around by the system until they spit him out like a piece of garbage.

But maybe it wasn't too late? Tonight, he'd done the right thing and been rewarded for it. Hell, he might even get an interview or a magazine article out of the deal. Some real cash. He could go back to school. Learn a trade. He had been good with his hands in high school when he took shops. Had a real knack for fixings things according to his mechanics teacher. Once he'd even got a snowmachine going everyone else had given up on. Yeah, he could become a recycler of old, abandoned things. Save shit headed to the dump. Too bad somebody wouldn't pay for his story right now. Then he could stop at the twenty-four-seven convenience store and get a hotdog and some candy. Nobody had thought to offer any food at the police station, but the pop had gone down fine. His sugar cravings came back thinking of it. But he was skint. Spent his last money to party at the motel tonight and his so-called friends were all tapped out.

He shivered as the coolness of the damp dew of night began to penetrate his thin hoodie while he spun dreams in his head of never having to worry about paying for a roof over his head or food in his belly. It was going to be a long, lonely walk to the Yellowbird. He hoped the others still had the room and hadn't been tossed out by that do-gooder Zeke Law. If not, he was going to be shit out of luck. End up sleeping down in the small encampment down by the river again. That would be his last choice. Last time he'd been there someone's tent caught fire and all hell had broken loose. The cops came and arrested people. And it wouldn't look good for him to be seen there. He was going places now that was for damn sure. This was his big break. That fifteen seconds of fame everyone talked about. He had to parlay that into something good, earn some ready cash.

213

Tomorrow he'd look into his choices. Start on the right path.

A vehicle suddenly turned on its headlights a short distance away, blinding him as it turned onto Main Street. He shaded his eyes and stumbled closer to the Anchor Real Estate office window. Asshole. But the black SUV drove right on by him, leaving him stranded in the darkness with only the streetlamps for company. A fox screamed in the distance making him shudder. At least it wasn't a wolf. He was scared of wolves and coyotes. Yeah, and mountain lions. Those bastards could sink their claws into you so fast you'd never know what hit ya.

He began to walk quicker in efforts to keep warm and distill the unease of being all alone with a fucking murderer on the loose, turning the corner onto the stretch of Cariboo Drive that led past the crematorium. He glanced at it now across the open field, quiet and silence, a monster with its tall smokestack often belching its contents into the sky. A sober reminder that he wasn't going to live forever. What would death be like? He'd overdosed once and been brought back with Narcan, but he didn't remember anything at all. No bright light or someone to greet him on the other side. Probably all fucking bullshit.

The blinking neon sign of a yellow bird in a few strategic positions that made it look like it was flying came into view. A few hundred yards now. A skip and a jump.

He began to half-jog toward the motel, focused on having some snacks and pop if the greedy bastards hadn't eaten all his stash. Then another set of vehicle lights blinded him, suddenly pulling out and coming in his direction. He veered his path closer to the ditch, giving the black SUV ample space in case the driver hadn't seen him yet. He could never remember which side of the road he was supposed to walk on, facing traffic or away. But then the driver zig-zagged closer to his side of the road. Was the asshole playing chicken or did he really not see him? He windmilled his arms to draw attention to the fact he was there. Not much light along this stretch, no cameras either. A real no-man's-land.

A fox began to scream again making the hackles rise on his neck. The vehicle was bearing down on him! He jumped sideways in an effort to leap away from it at the last second, stumbling on the coarse gravel and twisting his ankle painfully. As it gave out under him the thousands-of-pounds machine hit him point-blank, throwing him up and over the hood before he bounced backward and careened off the road. Bright flashes blurred his vision. He tried to crawl away, but his broken body wouldn't cooperate.

A car door slammed. Then a face hovered above his own, a pale shape in the darkness.

"Help me," he whispered, trying to reach out toward the shadowy figure, face hidden by a hoodie and dark clothing. Instead, the man grunted and swung a baseball bat at him. It connected with his skull and darkness swept over him, leaving him abandoned in the ditch.

THIRTY-FIVE

Anna pulled up behind the medical offices once more. She shut off the motor and rubbed her aching head. Dawn wasn't far off she noted through bleary eyes. One last job and she could rest her weary head on her longed-for bed. But putting the journal back was important. She wanted the search warrant she prayed would be forthcoming to find all the evidence. And if the deer-stalker hat was a fiber match for those found on the victim, they'd be in the home stretch. Meaning the good doctor would be up the proverbial creek without a paddle. A profound thought struck her. A man who had given twenty years to the citizens of Anchor was about to have his reputation torn to shreds. How could this be? What signs had they missed? Anna let out a deep breath. As much as she wanted this nightmare to be over, to protect any future victims, to see it end this way made her sad.

If the fibers matched, was there any other way they could have gotten on the victim? Was this the hat Druitt used in the play? It did indeed look similar to the hat she'd seen him wear to reprise his role in the production of *Doctor Jekyll and Mr. Hyde*. The irony was not lost on Anna. One more nail in Druitt's coffin.

She slipped from the van and entered the back door, still under the pall of melancholia. Soon citizens of Anchor would be up and about and she needed to get home without being seen. Nothing appeared disturbed since her and Tom's earlier visit, making her breathe easier as she rounded the corner into the doctor's private office. Opening the bottom drawer of the desk, she replaced the journal. There. The die is cast.

Why did she feel guilty then? Maybe because doctors willing to come to work and settle in Alaska were hard come by? Especially in small towns, general practitioners were worth their weight in gold.

The somber mood followed Anna home and didn't leave her during the few remaining hours before she had to rise again and enter the fray. Even so, she was the first one up and had coffee and breakfast started two hours later than normal making it more of a brunch than anything before Tom strode in, fresh from a shower. Friday lay on his kitchen matt, waiting patiently for the bacon to be ready.

"Morning. Smells darn fine." He smiled and she returned it as best she could. Considering yesterday's brouhaha, Tom seemed in fine spirits.

"Hey, what's up? You look like someone stole your thunder."

"They can have my thunder if they could solve this case and not have it be the loss of a doctor in our town." She'd already texted Josh the results of the search, fessing up to her illegal actions. He didn't seem concerned about legalities, more about results. He promised to find a way to get a search warrant, but that was hours ago and she'd heard nothing since.

"Ah, yeah, I hear you. We're going to have to put the journal back today."

"Done."

"You should have let me go with you." Tom stopped mid-action of pouring himself a cup of extra-dark roast coffee. He took a sip and his eyes opened wider. She'd chosen the heavy caffeine fix, needing all the help she could to get a spark of energy back.

"I was in better shape than you. Seemed the thing to do." Anna removed the strips of bacon from the frying pan and placed them on paper towels to drain, poured off the excess grease, then stirred in eggs and began to fluff them as they cooked. A full country breakfast to face the day was in order. Leaving the eggs to stay warm in the pan, she donned oven mitts and pulled a full tray of golden-brown homemade biscuits from the oven. She placed them in a basket and set it on the table.

Charlie walked into the kitchen followed by Kelly and both made a beeline to the table, grabbing for a biscuit each and yelping at the slight burns to their fingers. The young girl even let out a giggle. Steam rose off the buttermilk staple as the women broke the treats open and applied a layer of butter that instantly began to melt. The contented smiles on both their faces at first bite warmed Anna's heart and some of the darkness lifted from her mood. Friday moved to her side and she handed over some of the bacon, making him chuff a thank you.

Tom picked up the bowl of scrambled eggs. Anna turned off the stove and followed with the plated crispy bacon, sitting down at her usual spot. Her soul's burden lightened more watching her friends eat and joke around. This was what life was all about. Providing for people she cared about. The moment reminded her of her precious mother and how hard she had tried to provide a decent home and food on the table and how terribly she'd been hamstrung by the brutal man she'd lived with. A man executed only a few short months ago. A day that would live on in infamy when he'd left them to burn alive on the kitchen floor by setting the house ablaze. He had also been the catalyst for Tia's murder when Anna had been in Texas for the execution and Tia was taken by the Black Rose Killer. She blinked away a sudden rush of tears. Damn it. What was the matter with her? She was more emotional than usual right now. She steadied herself by imagining a calm sunny beach with the water gently flowing toward the distant horizon. A sailboat caught on the wind riding the ocean's current, its sails white and puffed, a testament to man's ingenuity. She'd read about the visualizing technique online and barring therapy that she had no use for since the Dr. Molly fiasco, it was all she had. But it did help. Some.

"My turn tomorrow."

Anna blinked and the sandy beach with darkness hovering at the edges disappeared. "Excuse me?"

"To make breakfast," Charlie said, raising her perfectly trained eyebrows at her.

"You're on."

"What's the deal for today, boss?" Tom asked. He'd eaten his fill and looked at her over the rim of a white porcelain cup with the Lone Wolf Investigations logo of a solitary wolf. Time to upgrade the swag. They were a full-fledged pack now. She needed to ask Charlie about designing a new one. She was an amazing illustrator and had created the first one.

Her phone dinging alerting her to an incoming text and stopped her from answering him.

She read Josh's message in near disbelief.

> We have the hat & a fiber match. Druitt arrested half an hour ago. Turn on your TV.

Anna jumped up from the table, her heart thumping madly, rushing to hit the remote button that switched on the kitchen set. And there was Dr. Druitt being led out in handcuffs from his office, his head hanging down to avoid the cameras, shoulders slumped. Not unexpectedly, it was a full media circus. Microphones and reporters are jockeying for a prime location to get the best photo op. Did they have the right man? Please, please, don't let this all be in vain.

She had a hard time with people being exposed on the news until there was a proper conviction in a court of law. Seemed to her that just the very fact someone is seen on social media even without solid proof being accused of a crime was enough to ruin lives, no matter the outcome. No one remembered the verdict, focusing more on the suspicions of guilt as if the mere hint was enough to convict someone.

But she comforted herself with the fact that a fiber match was a solid piece of evidence. Especially with it being found locked in his desk drawer with the diary. All they needed now was the ring. And likely it would be found at his home. She could only pray they'd find it soon. Then she could lay this all to rest. In some ways it was anticlimactic, but it meant also that a suspected killer was off the streets. Maybe Anchor could return to its former glory. Sure it had its foibles, but she had to believe it had a solid heart.

"Dr. Druitt was arrested?" Charlie looked aghast, her hand on her throat. "He's my doctor. He didn't do it. Please, tell me this is a mistake. Anna? Tom?"

Anna winced at the shock obvious in Charlie's voice, the coffee and food souring in her stomach. Yes, this was going to tear lives apart. Druitt had a wife and two children. She licked her lips. "Sorry, Charlie, I should have warned you. There was some evidence found that points toward his possible guilt."

"What evidence? What did he do?" Charlie's troubled eyes pinned her to her seat.

"A journal was found and a deerstalker hat with a fiber also found on at least one of the victims. Sorry, Charlie, the police had to bring him in for questioning. If he's innocent, he'll be fine. But they would be amiss not to look into it."

"Oh Lord, this is awful. How could this happen? Bad enough that a funeral director was a serial killer—" She caught Anna's wince and amended her words, "Sorry Anna, but this, this is beyond horrible. To think a man of medicine capable of such a thing." Charlie shook her head.

"I saw Dr. Druitt once," Kelly said, biting on a fingernail. "What if he remembers me? What if…"

"Don't go there. You're safe here." Anna got up from her chair and went around and kneeled down, placing her arms around the young girl, feeling her body quake with fear. "It's okay. If he did do it, he's off the streets now and can't hurt anyone else."

"You don't sound that sure," Charlie commented, narrowing her eyes at Anna.

"I'm pretty sure, but until he confesses and they find a final piece of evidence that nails the case, I remain open minded. Hopefully we'll know for certain soon." Anna got to her feet. "In the meantime, I think we should take a small break, recharge our batteries and reassess our options and priorities. There's a lot of missing people in Alaska and they deserve to be found."

"I agree with Anna. I'm going to work from home today now that we don't need to continue surveillance on Cross, using your awesome new computer system to do some research. Will you be working in the office today?"

"I'll head in with Charlie. At the very least, I want to work with her on creating a new logo for the business." Anything to get their minds off the current situation while they waited for more information.

"A new logo?" Charlie asked in surprise.

"There's more us of us now. Thought it was time to change it up and make the pack idea more apparent."

"I see what you mean." Watching Charlie shift gears behind her beautiful sky-blue eyes helped Anna to focus in on what mattered. Keeping her people safe and secure from one hour to the next. But she'd be damned happy when this waiting game was over and Druitt was confirmed the killer. Or even if he wasn't and could explain the fiber being on the victim from a hat in his possession, then she'd have a mandate to keep sleuthing.

THIRTY-SIX

But soon as Charlie and Anna arrived at Lone Wolf Investigations a horde of media descended on her place of business. The pair of them had to press through the bodies, trying to reach the front door.

"Is it true that you had a big hand in nailing the suspect for the two Ripper killings, Dr. Druitt?" Sarah Perkins asked, microphone at the ready.

"No comment." Anna pressed her lips together. She barreled her way through the thong, tugging Charlie along in her wake. Where in the hell did she get the information? It couldn't have come from Josh. Well, some had always had it in for her in town, never believing apples fall far from the tree. And the bastard wasn't even her real father. Not speaking ill of the dead wasn't a concept she embraced. Just because you died didn't make you an instant saint if you were a devil in real life.

Charlie looked ruffled and stormed to the bathroom to tidy her big Texas hair and regain her composure.

Anna locked the front door and closed the venetian blinds against the mob.

"People have lost their damn minds," Charlie grumbled coming back into the room and sitting down at her desk.

Time to regain control. "I'm thinking a grouping of three wolves, one dead center looking the viewer right in the eyes, the others looking outward to the left and right, giving the sense of security in all directions," Anna suggested. "Maybe a couple of shadowy ones looming in the background."

"Oh, that sounds good. Let me grab some paper." Charlie began to sketch the image quickly, her pencil flying over the pad. "And do you want Wolfpack Investigations or Wolf Pack Justice as the new moniker?"

"I'm thinking Wolf Pack Justice in larger print and Private Investigators in smaller print underneath. Black and white, no color."

"Okay, give me an hour or two and I should have something." The phone rang on her desk and she grimaced. "Or not." She picked up the phone and said, "Good morning, Lone Wolf Investigations." Then she rolled her eyes and covered the mouthpiece. "I forgot already."

Anna laughed. "All good things take time."

Her phone rang as she walked into her office. Kelly's cell number popped up on screen.

"Anna, Squirrel's not answering his cell. He *always* answers it when I'm calling." The words rushed out of Kelly; the panic obvious.

"Calm down. Maybe he's turned it off so he can sleep. He was up late being questioned last night."

"No, he hardly sleeps. I need to go and look for him. Can I borrow your truck?"

"I have a better idea. How about we look together?" Anna's stomach folded in on itself with worry. Something was off. The prime witness and only witness to the Ripper case was missing.

"Can you come home now?"

"I'll be right there." Anna hurried back into the outer office, her anxiety adding momentum to her step. "I have to go. Kelly's upset that she can't contact Squirrel. He's not picking up."

"Go, I'll lock the door behind you. I'll be fine. The hyenas will find someone else to bother. As my mama loved to say, *their cornbread ain't done in the middle*. And if they bother me, well they'll find out there are a hundred ways to argue with a southern woman and all of them will get you dead."

Anna snorted at the crazy sayings and braced herself for another onslaught. Half the crowd was still milling about outside her establishment. Okay, best to pull the bandage off in one jerk. She opened the door and stormed through it hitting the key fob at the same time, making the crowd part like the Red Sea. She clamored into her truck and locked the doors. Last thing she needed was uninvited company.

Ten minutes later she pulled into her driveway. Kelly was already waiting out front and she jumped in soon as Anna hit the brakes, phone in hand.

"Where does Squirrel normally hang out?"

"On Baker Street. He bunks in with Eddy Mosely when the pair are getting along. Sometimes he stays in the encampment down by the river. Couch surfs with friends."

"We'll try Eddie's first. What's the number?"

Kelly recited the street address and Anna made a quick U-turn and sped back the way she came.

"Is Tom still home?"

"Yeah. Why? You thinking I should have asked him to drive me? Fine, let me out."

"No, of course not." Anna reminded herself to be careful. The young girl was overly sensitive at the moment, most likely looking for any excuse to do a runner. Last thing she wanted to do was drive her away. "I'm glad you called me first."

Kelly didn't look convinced, picking at her thumbnail. "I'm sorry, okay. I know you mean well. I'm just, well, worried. And not sure of things."

And edgy coming down off the high no doubt. The poor girl was only trying to buy relief from her shitty life, taking drugs. But that was over now. How to make it sink in that she could have a good life was Anna's next question? Or were the drugs hiding an underlying mental illness?

"Life doesn't come with a handbook. It should. But I've always found answers in quotes about how to live well. Letting go of the past is key. Understanding the effects on how you see things. Perspective is everything. *We can have any world we imagine.*" And if only she'd take her own advice. One day at a time, trying to keep the monsters at bay, imagining a brighter future with evil eradicated. Problem was she knew that could never happen. Each time she hit the mole on the head, like the whack-a-mole game the town sponsored every summer during Anchor Fun Days to raise funds for community events, someone even more corrupt popped their head through the hole. And their town's dot on the map was infinitesimal in the scheme of things, meaning she could well imagine what other larger centers were dealing with. *Don't go there. Mind your own town. Your own state.* She forced her thoughts onto higher ground.

"Any world we imagine, eh." Kelly looked thoughtful. "Then I want to live in one where everyone is kind to each other and people share things equally. Like that's ever going to happen. People are so damn greedy about money."

"You can be part of that. The kindness part anyway. But remember to protect yourself as well." Anna was out of her depth now. She couldn't deny that many people worried about money. The world was divided by haves and have nots. But her focus for years had been on getting justice for others, not worrying about money or what it cost to do business. Hell, she was using a vast part of her inheritance in efforts to save the world from itself. Not on ways to live better like designer clothes or spa days. Anchor's a blue-collar town, filled with people working on oil rigs and in factories, some still mining. No place to wear fancy clothes anyway. And seeing the world as a tourist held no charm for Anna. Not when there was so much to keep her occupied at home.

"How do you do what you do? You kill people, right?" Anna swallowed. "Only when I have no other way."

"But you put yourself in situations where bad things happen."

"Not always by choice. Bad luck seems to follow me around. But I feel a solemn duty to try to make the world a better place by catching one bad guy at a time. What-ever it takes." Where was this conversation headed? Kelly was all over the map, her mind still clouded by her recent blowout. Damned drugs.

The young girl frowned, one of her legs hopping up and down. "Even if it hurts someone else? What if Squir-rel's been hurt or worse by the guy? You know, the Ripper? You made him go to the cops and give a statement. He's seen the guy, right? Maybe the Ripper found out and did something about it?"

Kelly narrowed her eyes at Anna, the accusation clear. Anna had asked her to get Squirrel to talk to the police, promising him goodwill and cash. The fact he'd been more or less bribed wasn't sitting well now.

"We don't know that. Squirrel could be holdup somewhere. Let's not buy trouble." Anna's stomach took a dive, her breakfast sitting uneasy. *Please don't let that be true. If the Ripper somehow got to Squirrel and he turns up dead, I'll lose this girl to the streets.*

Silence.

During the drive to Eddy's small rundown house where they found him asleep and pissed at his roommate over some infraction, Kelly kept her own council. No Squirrel. But Kelly wouldn't leave until she spent some time with Eddy grilling him on the night before and tidying up the place so that Squirrel wouldn't come home to absolute chaos. Anna let her have her head, the girl was all over the map today, so upset she needed to blow off some steam.

"I'm sorry about all this," Anna said, her throat tightened by worry as they finally got back into her truck to drive down to the riverfront encampment. Was she responsible?

"It is what it is as my mom would say."

But the time spent at the homeless camp on the Anchor River bore no fruit either. No one had seen Squirrel in a number of days. Not since before the party at the Yellowbird. The campsite was about what one would expect, all left over things, broken down and thrown away by those with other choices. It would disappear come winter. Had too. It was damn cold in Anchor when the snow flies.

"Where else would he go?" Anna asked as she shepherded a distraught Kelly back up the half-overgrown path to her waiting vehicle. Kelly shook her head and climbed back in, buckling her seat belt.

"Just drive. I gotta think about it."

Anna's cell rang and she pulled to the side of the road to answer it when she recognized her brother's number.

"I'm afraid I have bad news, Anna," Josh said without a greeting.

"Is it about Squirrel?"

"Yes, how did you know?"

Anna closed her eyes, unable to look Kelly in the face.

"What about Squirrel?" Kelly half-shouted, her tone shrill in the small space.

"Kelly and I are out looking for him right now. What's the news?" Even as she asked, the cold, hard reality gripped her like the man with the sickle pressed his weapon to her neck.

"He's been found dead. Hit and run."

THIRTY-SEVEN

"Where?" Anna asked.

Kelly had grabbed her forearm, her fingers dug in so tightly Anna could feel her nails drawing blood through the thin cloth. But the small wounds were nothing compared to the one opening in her soul. Every death took a part of her with them, the good and the bad. How long until she had nothing left? Wasn't running on empty equivalent to being an assassin? The thought sickened her, made her intent on experiencing each and every death, no matter how painful. Or deserved. Even the Black Rose Killer had broken off a small piece. Very small though, she had to admit.

"Near the crematorium out on Cariboo Drive."

"Where Tia was taken. No cameras then. Any witnesses?"

"None found yet."

"Is Squirrel okay?" Kelly asked, her face stark white with worry. She looked about to burst into tears.

Anna slowly shook her head. "I have to go. I'll call

you back, Josh." She turned to the young girl. "I'm sorry, Kelly. You're going to need to be strong now."

The girl began punching her arm, tears streaming down her face. "He's dead, right? You killed him. You killed Squirrel. It's all your fault!"

Anna had nothing to say to the accusations as she absorbed their impact. Yes, she had gotten him to tell the police what he knew. But she had never thought the killer would harm a witness. It didn't fit the stereotypical Jack the Ripper case. It was a modern invention. In a weird way, the murderer had made a mistake. Played a different hand that the original crimes. What did it mean? Or had someone else killed him? Maybe a drug deal gone bad? Or maybe it was an accidental killing, hitting him on the side of the road in the dark. Cross should have answers soon.

"We don't know who killed Squirrel as yet, Kelly, or if it was anything but a terrible accident. It could also be a drug deal gone bad."

"You'd like that, right? Someone else to blame." The girl descended into a fit of weeping and all Anna could do was wait it out. When she tried to take her in her arms to comfort her, she'd swatted her away. Finally, the sobs died down and Kelly dried her eyes on her sleeve.

"Take me to my house. Mom needs to know. Squirrel stayed with us one summer."

"Your mom took Squirrel in? That was good of her."

"You're not the only do-gooder in town."

The charge hurt more than she could say. Was that how people saw her? As only doing good things to make themselves elevated? The idea made her physically ill. It had never been her intention to do that. Never. Where had the wonderful girl gone that wanted to go to college and better herself she'd met recently? It was like Kelly was two different people. She'd switched into a whole other mindset in such quick order it made Anna's head spin.

"I do care about people, Kelly. And no one needs to know when I do something to help others, okay? I'm not shouting it from the rooftops. Sure, it makes me feel good to help, but I'm not broadcasting my actions as something to be admired. I just want to help you have a better life. Get opportunities I didn't have growing up or my mom." Anna desperately tried to explain herself, worried to death Kelly would be forever lost if she didn't step in. End up dead in a ditch like Squirrel. Was his death her fault? She couldn't go down that rabbit hole right now. She had to focus on the one she could save.

Kelly shook her head. "I don't know anymore. But quit trying to help, to buy people off."

"Maybe later, after you've had a chance to think, talk to your mom, maybe then you'll at least consider my offer? You have a talent, a real gift. You need to develop it, go on to bigger and better things. Think of me as a conduit. I want and expect nothing in return, okay? No one ever needs to know you accepted help from me. I like it better that way."

She shrugged, back to picking at her nails. One of the hardest things Anna ever did was to drop her off at her mom's a few minutes later, knowing that she might not see the young, talented girl anytime soon, though she could keep tabs on her with the newly installed tracker to her never-out-of-her-hand phone. Something every parent and friend could use, a lifeline to a loved one. She made a promise to herself. She'd give her a few days to get her head straight, then try again. Nothing else for it. Squirrel's death had come as a shock, to both of them. And Anna wouldn't rest easy until she got to the bottom of the mystery and brought the culprit to justice. Legal or otherwise. She knew she wasn't like other women. Perhaps her past was to blame. Or maybe it was just the way she was born. Either way she had a job to do and doing it was her only salvation to keep from feeling overwhelmed with doubt and grief.

She headed for home. Time to bring Tom up to speed. They both needed to look into Squirrel's background more closely. Find out who he had pissed off in the past. Thank goodness he'd had time to help the department with a sketch before he died. Did it look anything like Druitt?

She texted Josh, asking him to scan the drawing Squirrel provided and send it to her and Tom when he got a moment. She knew he was run off his feet. And now they had another case to solve. Was Squirrel's death an accidental hit-and-run or not?

Her phone dinged when she parked in her driveway and she quickly opened the attachment Josh had sent, staring at the pencil drawing of the suspect on her phone. Did it look enough like Druitt to convince a jury of his peers? Problem with Druitt was he had no defining facial characteristics. No mustache or beard. Not overly fine-featured or coarse. He could be the man in the scanned image or one of thousands of other men. Would Squirrel have picked Druitt out of a lineup? Good question. And one they would never have an answer to now.

Friday greeted Anna at the door, followed closely by Tom.

"Where's Kelly?" he asked. "Did you find Squirrel?"

Anna chewed on her lower lip, not happy with the news she had for him. It was only late afternoon, but she was hungry and thirsty, running on empty.

"I need a beer."

"Did you have lunch?"

She shook her head.

"Let's eat in the kitchen. I was about to make myself a sandwich."

Anna grabbed a bottle of Coors Light from the frig and popped the lid, sitting down on a chair in the breakfast nook. She liked the view of the backyard from the cozy spot. When they'd re-landscaped after the explosion, she'd planted a small orchard of apple trees, duly fenced in to keep the deer population from decimating them in the early spring when food was scarce. Instead, she'd made a feeder for them a good hundred yards from the house where they came to feed once a day. The heavily burdened trees were in full fruit mode now, ready to be hand-picked and preserved in the freezer for the winter. When would she ever have time to do that?

Tom pulled a loaf of whole wheat from the bread box and lay the slices on two plates. Then he doctored them up with mayo and mustard, before adding ham slices, cheese, lettuce, and tomatoes. He deftly sliced both even with one damaged hand though she knew better than to interfere with him doing the job, any job. Tom was nothing unless it was fiercely independent. He added a scoop of potato chips and carted them to the table along with a beer for himself.

"Thanks."

He waited until she'd eaten the first half, fed Friday a few choice pieces of ham, and was starting on a second beer before he inquired, "Hard day?"

Anna sat back and took a long pull on her beer. Time to pull the bandage off. "Squirrel's dead and Kelly blames me. She's back with her mom."

"Aw, well you can't blame yourself for that. It's her

right to go home and be with her mom. You can only be there when she asks for help. Trust me, I know."

Tom did know. He was speaking from experience with his sister Laura who had been using drugs before she died, trying to make it in Hollywood. He carried more than his fair share of grief and guilt over her death. That damned city of lies, taking in innocents and chewing them up for trying desperately to reach for an impossible dream. Tom and Anna shared a look of such intensity she had to look away first and pet the top of Friday's head. Tom continued to voice his opinion.

"What happened to Squirrel? The guy was living such a pristine lifestyle too. Hard to believe he'd get himself into any trouble."

She snorted out a mouthful of the beer, then blotted her mouth and chin with a paper napkin. This was why she liked this good, solid man. His amazing ability to segue into clever views on life in a split-second. "Apparently that pristine lifestyle comes with complications. He was killed in a hit-and-run last night."

"As much as I detested his way of fighting," he said, raising his freshly bandaged hand. He'd even pulled a pair of thin plastic gloves over his hands to make the sandwiches before disposing of them. She appreciated his thoughtfulness. "I hate to think of him dead. He did try to make things right at the end. The drawing doesn't help much though, could be anybody. Mr. Average Joe."

"I wonder how they're making out with Druitt? If only he'd confess, life might get back to some semblance of normalcy again." She worried that it had been rather too easy to break into his work office and gather evidence. What if someone did it in reverse? Planted evidence. The journal and books could be easily explained away by a good lawyer, but the hat, not so much.

She was about to voice the thought when her phone dinged. Incoming from Josh. She turned the phone so that Tom could read his message as well.

Druitt's protesting his innocence. No confession.

"We might as well get working on Squirrel's case. And for that I'm afraid we need to talk to Kelly. Find out his drug connections. Who he had a beef with?" Tom said without looking her in the eyes.

"The lovely crew from the Yellowbird. We could start there," Anna suggested. "I'll text Zeke and get any names and addresses he was party to." She fired off the text while Tom went about cleaning the table off. She glanced up at him. "I should be doing that with your bad hand."

"It's not so bad, just a bit stiff. Worse is the worry about his leaving any gifts behind."

Anna winced. Her phone pinged almost immediately. "Tom has two names for us. Kash Geller and Snake Johnson. One home address on Baker Street. Near where Squirrel lived with Eddy Mosely. They all bunked close to each other." Makes sense though why party at the motel if they were all from the same town? Maybe it was a bit nicer than their cribs or the two girls wouldn't spend time with them there? She could only imagine how much time was invested in housecleaning. Kelly had tried to do something with it today, but it was mostly a lost cause.

"What about the girl? There were two girls there."

"I'll have to ask Kelly for her name." Anna dreaded the asking, but it had to be done. She decided to text her instead, wondering if that was the coward's way out. But it was also quicker and maybe less stressful for Kelly. To her credit, Kelly answered immediately and she shared the name with Tom.

"Hope Parker."

"Nice name, compared to Squirrel and Snake."

"She lives near Kelly as well. Let's hit there first."

"So I'm invited. Are we taking Friday?"

Friday immediately got to his feet, tail wagging, an expectant look on his furry face.

"Looks like. I could use the moral support today. It's been a tough one."

THIRTY-EIGHT

Anna knocked on the screen door of one of the few three-storied Victorian style houses left standing in town. One of the original homes back from Anchor's hay days, it had been turned into a rooming house by owners back in the thirties. Now it contained a few apartments, often taken by oil workers.

She knocked a second time. Tom stood by her side as did Friday. Anna wasn't taking any chances. Two members of her team had been bit, she didn't intend to be the third.

"Hold on, I'm coming," a female-sounding voice shouted from inside. The woman came into view sans dog. Anna breathed a sigh of relief.

"Yes?" the middle-aged appearing woman asked through the screen door. She had short gray hair and wore a loose-fitting top and jeans over her considerable bulk. She glanced at all three of them in turn, her lips pursed.

"I'm Anna Hale, a private investigator and this is Tom Jackson. We work together. I was wondering if we could talk to Hope Parker? Her friend Kelly Smith says she lives here?"

"I've heard of you. Hope's my daughter. What's this all about?"

"She was seen at a party at the Yellowbird recently. We want to talk to her about her friend Squirrel who was also there."

"Squirrel? That pain in my ass? No need to talk to Hope about him." The woman crossed her arms. "Hope needs to stay as far from that low life as possible. She's grounded. We got a murderer on the loose in Anchor and that stupid girl thinks to go partying? At the Yellowbird?"

"Squirrel died last night," Anna cut through the bullshit.

"What? How?" Shock slackened the woman's face.

"Hit and run. We need to talk to Hope. She might be able to help."

"You'd better come in. But the dog, if that is a dog, stays outside."

"Of course." Anna gave Friday a look of sympathy and a hand gesture to go back to the vehicle. She'd left the window open on the driver's side so he could either jump back inside the cab or use the truck box.

"You don't have a dog yourself?" Anna asked as the woman unlatched the screen door.

"No. Can't abide them. Messy, dirty creatures always wanting attention."

Tom and Anna shared a grimace but followed the charming woman into the living room.

"Wait here. I'll get Hope."

Anna perched on an overstuffed sofa and Tom chose a straight-backed chair. The room looked well lived in, the furniture worn, but the place was spotless. No dust on the coffee table or end tables and the rug looked newly vacuumed. The scent of an artificial air freshener lingered in the air.

Heavy footpads on the stairs alerted them to company. A few seconds later a nineteen or twenty-year-old girl with an attitude only a teenager or someone barely out of their teen could muster, came into the room with a cocky look, her hair sleek and shiny, framing a heavily made-up face. She gave Tom an expectant look, but had flat eyes for Anna. Anna had to keep herself from giving the game away and instead nodded solemnly.

"Hope. I'm Anna Hale and this is Tom Jackson. We work together at Wolf Pack Justice as private investigators. Has your mother shared why we're here?"

"Something to do with Squirrel?" Hope frowned. She didn't know or was hiding it well. Most likely Kelly had already told her, if not her mom.

"Yes. We have some bad news about him."

"He's dead, right?" A small crack opened in the chilly surface but she pressed her lips together and shook her head, as if trying to dispel the image.

"Yes, I'm sorry, but he is. A hit and run last night."

"What's it to do with me?"

"You were seen at the Yellowbird the night Squirrel and your friend Kelly were there. We were hoping to find out more about his friends? His connections? Any light you can shed would be of great benefit."

"Just like Squirrel's shedding light was of benefit to him?"

The girl wasn't pulling any punches.

"Squirrel stepped up and did the right thing."

"Got him killed."

"Maybe, but it could be something else. Did he have

any beefs with his dealer for instance? Or another supplier? I'm not looking to bust anyone, but to get to the truth of it. We aren't even sure if it was an accident yet, but I'm looking into all angles."

Hope shook her head, her mouth downturned. "There's nothing to tell. And you won't get anything out of Snake or Kash either. Waste of time. It's the Ripper behind all of this. Everybody knows that. Some detective you are."

Okay, time to try another tactic. "Yes, it could be the Ripper, Hope, and it may well turn out to be the case. But if it is someone else, I want justice for Squirrel. *No stone unturned* is my motto. I'm certain you want justice as well, right?"

The girl shook her head, her expression closed off. "I got nothing to add. And I gotta be places. I got an evening shift to cover."

"Hope, I have a sister, Laura. She died earlier this year. And I had to know what happened to her, no matter how painful the truth was. So, please, if there's anything you can think of, call this number. Your friend Squirrel deserves as much." Tom got up and handed the girl a business card. "My personal number's on the back. Call anytime."

She eyed him sideways. "Sure. Maybe you like to party too?"

Tom's rugged good looks obviously appealed to the young girl. And maybe the fact he smelled good and didn't leer all over her like most of her male friends, Anna suspected.

"I work a lot. Not much time to party, Hope."

"You need to get out more," Hope suggested.

"Maybe, but I need to find out what happened to your friend even more."

"Right." Hope tucked his card into her jeans, with a promise and a smile.

Ten to one she'd be calling Tom. Soon. Maybe it would help and she'd spill something useful.

"We'll see ourselves out," Anna said, standing up. This was headed nowhere. It didn't seem much worth it to interview Kash and Snake, but it was all part of the job.

Hope shared a smug smile. Well, whatever it took. She trusted Tom. Knew him well enough to be able to say with one hundred percent certainty he'd never party with such a young girl, no matter the enticement.

THIRTY-NINE

As expected, the rest of the interviews turned up nothing. Snake was as cooperative as his name suggested while Kash was too strung out to be of any use.

"Might as well call it a day," Tom said.

"I have another idea. It's not that late," Anna said. She'd been thinking about the truck driver and his alibi. Had the police considered another possibility? "No stone left unturned, right?"

"Exactly my thoughts. If it turns out we're done with the Ripper case, Druitt proves guilty, there's another case I want to ask Cross about I'm thinking needs a closer look by the team. Soon as he's done with Squirrel and the FBI mosey on down the road, of course."

"Yeah?" Anna left Whitechapel in the rearview mirror and drove out to Cariboo Drive, headed for the Yellowbird to follow up with her hunch. "Cross. What case?"

"Back when he was working forensics in Fairbanks, he investigated the death of a young woman, a well-known local prostitute found dead with her throat cut at the local dump."

"But we're trying to find missing persons that there's hope of finding alive."

"I'm getting to it. It's the sister of one of the women gone missing in the area, one of the cases you handed me. I wouldn't have known about the death of the sibling, but I thought the name was familiar and investigated it further. That's when I found Cross had worked on the case."

"Was it solved? Did they catch the murderer?"

"No. The murderer had gotten away clean. No DNA or even fibers found on the victim that were a match to anyone on file and there were no clear suspects. No witnesses. A perfect murder in that no ties existed to the victim due to her profession. And then about six months later, the sister turns up missing."

"So Cross wasn't able to solve it. One of his few failures," Anna mused. "How can he help you now?"

"The sister was also known to have recently entered the trade so she might be alive somewhere, scared to go home and took off for parts unknown. Cross might be able to shed some light on things. I think it's worth a try. Something could turn up. The family needs answers, both parents are still alive. They had two daughters, one confirmed dead. If there's even a slim chance of bringing them closure on what happened to the other sister, I want to find it. And if I can find her alive…"

Anna could hear the simmering passion in Tom's voice as he left his wish for finding the woman alive hanging in the air. "Good work. Yes, by all means investigate it further." She swung the wheel of the half-ton, directing it onto the motel parking lot, keeping a sharp eye out for trouble as the truck bounced over the incessant potholes that desperately needed filling. But gravel cost money and Zeke no doubt was on a shoe-string budget.

"The Yellowbird?" Tom asked.

"I want to check on something. The alibi for the trucker. We only have the word of his girlfriend that he was with her at the time of the first murder."

"I thought we were past that? Druitt's in jail and looking to be arraigned soon. Didn't the police look into it as well?"

"Mostly. But something's niggling at me. His ex-girlfriend likes to party. I just want to check the night in question. My old friend George Stubbs, who owned this place before Zeke Law, had this place closely monitored. Should be easy enough to check the night of August thirtieth for answers if Zeke's left the system in place?"

"Have they found the ring yet that left the marks on the two victims? My head was so buried in the Amanda Tayor case, that's the name of the missing woman in Fairbanks, I forgot to ask."

Anna shook her head and killed the motor of the GMC in front of the motel office. "No. The search of the residence turned up exactly nothing." It bothered her as well. The ring would nail the case. What if it never turned up anywhere? But if they got a confession out of Druitt, it wouldn't matter. Enough forensic evidence existed to at least put him close to the victim at some point.

"You coming in?" she asked.

Tom shook his head and pulled out his iPad. "Now that I got the green light for the Amanda Taylor case, I want to zero in on a few things."

"Suit yourself. Coming Friday?"

Anna held the door open and Friday padded into the office first, looking happy to stretch his legs.

"Evenin' Anna." Zeke Law looked up from his stool as she drew near. He was perched behind the scarred reception desk, keyboarding away on a laptop. He closed the lid and stood up to greet her. He was looking good, appearing freshly showered by the dampness of his hair and the scent of soap that wafted in the air. A far cry from the former owner, George Stubbs, who wasn't a fun of dry skin judging from the lack of washing. "How ya doing?"

"Good. Just came by to check on something."

"And here I thought it was because you missed me."

"You thinking to flirt with me?" She smiled at his comment. Friday growled.

"I'd best be careful around you until your companion approves of my patter." Zeke chuckled. A good sound, it resonated in a positive way.

"Best defender a gal could have." She gave Friday the hand signal to stand down.

"What can I do for you?"

Anna explained her needs, hoping Zeke was amenable.

"For you, Anna, sure. The cameras are still active and connected. And you made it just in time. The storage is for two weeks only. After that you'd have been up the proverbial creek without a paddle. Come into the back and you can watch it now." He turned to glance at her. "If the girlfriend didn't check herself in, which is the most likely scenario, otherwise the cops would be aware of her lying, then she snuck in. Even though it's only a few hours of timeline, still, it's going to take a while to check all that footage from ten cabins."

"Yeah." The fact that Tom was waiting in the truck and it wouldn't be fair to keep him cooped up there too long, she wavered on the best thing to do. "I'll do a quick check now, then come back alone tomorrow, if that's okay?" She did the math in her head and realized that tomorrow might be too late. Storage was only for two weeks. "No, I'd better do it now. I'll send Tom home with Friday. He can pick me up later. It might take most of the night to check that amount of storage."

"Whatever works for you. You can bed down here if you get tired." Zeke pointed out a sofa nearby the desk that held the monitor with all the camera feeds. The couch had a handy afghan laid over the back. A decent setup with the coffee machine still on, the scent making her mouth water.

Decision made, Anna went back to the truck with Friday tagging along. She opened the door for her companion and he jumped in, settling down on the back seat. "I'm going to be awhile. Go on home and I'll catch a ride later."

Tom frowned. "You staying the night?"

"I need to watch all the footage. Why?"

"Nothing. Just wondered. It's a lot of trouble for something that may turn out to be a complete waste of time." Tom didn't look her in the eye but closed the iPad and made to get out of the passenger seat. She backed up to let him disembark, and he strode around the front of the truck to the driver's side door. "Be careful, we hardly know the guy," he warned before clamoring inside.

What was his problem? "I need to settle it in my mind and this is the only way I know how." Sure, she knew she could be obsessive about a case, digging for the truth. But better that than following the footsteps of those choosing to only see evidence that proves their case and ignoring anything else.

FORTY

"Shit. There she is, Leeann Marko, Brad's ex." Anna groaned, rubbing her aching eyes. Nearly 0500 hours in the morning and she was about done in, but her hunch proved one hundred percent correct. The ex was cheating on the cheating husband from Fairbanks, or at the very least partying without him. So, the truck driver's alibi didn't hold water. Part of her was elated to find new evidence while another part of her worried about what it would do to the Ripper case. It may lead nowhere, but then again, it could be important. Didn't mean the truck driver did the killings, but he'd lied, which bore looking in to. *Brad Sorenson, you got some explaining to do.*

Anna made a quick copy of the evidence and sent it by email to her personal address, CC'd Josh and Tom, and decided to call it a night.

"What is it?" Zeke rubbed his eyes as well, waking up from the sofa he'd dropped down on a couple of hours ago. He pushed the afghan off of himself and sat up, yawning. "Did you find it?"

"Sure thing. Leeann Marko, the ex-girlfriend, was here the night of the first Ripper murder, not with the cheating husband."

"Good work."

"You snore by the way."

"Always do when I'm exhausted." He took her comment in stride. "This place takes it out of me. A shit load of work still needs doing."

"I owe you one." Guilt struck for keeping Zeke up half the night. "Thanks for helping."

"No problem. Need a lift?"

"I could call someone. Save you the trouble."

"And wake them when I'm already awake and capable?"

"Okay then." Zeke looked very capable himself, standing up and stretching, the shirt pulling tight over his six-pack and biceps. Her mouth watered, and it wasn't for coffee this time.

He grabbed his keys and they strode out into the fresh morning air, leaving the stuffy office behind.

"Sweet time of the day, when everything is possible," Anna remarked, looking to the east to see if the sun was preparing to light the world for one more day. A wolf howled off in the distance and she froze, listening, the sound mournful and gut-piercing. Something was off. Bad karma at work. *Be warned, packmate.*

"What is it?"

Anna shivered. "Someone walked over my grave."

Zeke gave her a piercing look. "Pay attention. Intuition's a powerful thing."

"I always do." *Risk assessment: high.*

Zeke gestured at an old Ford half-ton parked near the office, battered from more than a decade of service. "She may not look like much, but she's got a heart of gold."

249

"Most important thing, I've always thought."

"Yeah, me too." Zeke grinned at her and opened the passenger side door for her. Anna slipped inside, not too bothered by his chivalry. Sometimes it was nice to remember she was a woman. Too often she submerged her needs in her efforts to solve a case. It left her damn lonely on long, cold, wintry nights.

He closed the door securely behind her and went around to the driver's side.

"I owe you for all this. I'm thinking buying you dinner soon? If you have someone to fill in for you?" She'd watched him put a closed sign that read be back in thirty minutes on the door when they'd left. He might not be able to afford full-time help.

"I'd like that. I think I can scrounge up someone to take over for one night."

Anna's phone pinged and she pulled it from her pocket. When she read the words, she nearly had a heart attack. As it was, she broke out into a cold, clammy sweat. Adrenaline sluiced through her, making her tremble with the shock at the news from Josh.

Druitt committed suicide tonight. Hanged himself.

"What is it? What's wrong?"

She barely heard Zeke over the tinnitus droning like wildfire popping the seed pods of Jack Pine trees in her ears. Her fingers were shaking so hard to key in a question for Josh it took all her concentration.

She asked:

Did he confess?

No. Maintained his innocence right to the bitter end.

Anna pounded the dash with one fist. Damn it! Now her hand hurt too.

"What? Talk to me, Anna."

"It's Dr. Druitt. He committed suicide tonight. No confession of guilt." She used his professional moniker, feeling in death he had somehow earned it. If only he had confessed, she could rest easier.

"I pity the cops. Someone dying on their watch cuts to the bone," Zeke said, rubbing a hand down his face.

"All too true."

They both sat there in silence for a moment, absorbing the shock.

"There's something else that bugs me about this case," Anna mused, talking out loud as much for Zeke's benefit as her own.

"What's that?"

"For such an organized killer—to be at this point in his so-called career—he must have done something like this before. Killers don't start off this good at the job. They work up to it, each killing increasing their ability to do it exactly the way they envision it. There should be earlier murders or even a victim left alive."

"Makes sense. What are you thinking? I can see those gears shifting away in that brilliant brainiac mind of yours."

"Yeah." Anna let a small smile at the compliment escape before slamming back to earth remembering what had happened tonight. A family torn apart by a husband and father's death. She had no right to feel anything but sadness. "My partner, Tom Jackson."

"The guy who was bit by Squirrel right here at my motel the other night? Terrible thing about his death. And now the doctor. I gotta wonder what kind of town I moved into. And to think I thought it would be a calm sort of semi-retirement compared to going to war. Turns out I was wrong."

Anna pressed on. "Tom's investigating—well he's just beginning to work on it—a case involving a woman murdered in Fairbanks, her body left at the dump with her throat cut. But her sister has also gone missing, leaving some hope of finding her alive. Maybe the guy operated there first?"

"How long has this Dr. Druitt lived in Anchor?"

"Far as I know, all his career. But Fairbanks's only a few hours away. He could have slipped up there for a day or two. Carried out the murder."

"It's certainly worth looking into. But I'd best get you home. You need to sleep, beautiful."

Zeke started the old half-ton and the vehicle fired to life, purring like a top. He patted the scarred and faded dash with affection. "Like I said, she doesn't look like much, but she'd got a good heart."

Anna barely heard him over the roaring in her ears. Something wasn't clear as yet. And she had a bad feeling about the case. The way she always felt before the other shoe dropped. She rubbed at her roughened neck, so long ago burned by her wolf talisman leaving its imprint in her flesh from the fire that consumed her mother. She wore it still. A reminder of where she had come from. What she had to do.

She finally registered the name Zeke had called her and gave a very unladylike snort. "I'm a long way from beautiful. Scarred inside and out."

"Maybe that's what makes you beautiful? Rising like a phoenix from the ashes."

"You a poet now?"

"What? You never heard of a warrior poet?"

She didn't want to encourage him any more than he already was from their night of working together. "Anyway, just so you know, I'm not looking to hook up with anyone. Not now. Not ever."

"A woman on a mission. Right?"

"Correct. Someone has to be there for those needing justice."

"And that takes up all your time, twenty-four-seven? You can help others without becoming a martyr, Anna."

She shrugged, not up for debating something already settled in her mind. She'd spent the night tied to the computer screen, now she was running on empty. She let her silence speak for itself. In a few minutes Zeke pulled up in front of her new house.

"Nice place," he commented, leaving the motor running.

"Thanks for the ride. I'll call you about dinner, okay? When things settle down."

He turned his deep brown, expressive eyes her way. "Good. I'd like that."

She managed a half-smile and opened the truck door. It protested with a loud squawk, its long years of service showing in its bone structure. She knew how it felt. She was about used up tonight. And she still had Druitt's death to absorb.

The house was quiet as Anna slipped in the front door, not wanting to wake anyone. Friday came up to greet her, a welcome sight.

"Hey, still awake, huh?"

He chuffed a greeting, his tail wagging and followed her up the stairs. She felt like her own tail was dragging on the steep steps. It had been an exhausting night. If she could catch a few hours of shuteye, maybe she'd get a better perspective on things? Right now, she felt off-kilter. Otherworldly. Squirrel and Druitt's deaths had left her running on deficit. A buoy drifting on the waves with no land in sight. But having Friday join her was some consultation. The pair of them laid down on her queen-sized bed and she absently stroked his rough-edged head.

"You doing okay, boy?" she asked him. Of course he was, everyone spoiled Friday.

He snuggled in closer and closed his eyes.

"Yeah, time to rest."

She closed her eyes and passed out.

FORTY-ONE

Anna punched the bag again in a one-two faster than the eye can see maneuver, feeling the satisfaction burn along her biceps and in her shoulders. The action took her mind away, focused her on the physical sensations. The ground beneath her feet. The sore muscles of her shoulders and arms, the jarring of her spine. The head rush of light entering her brain. The power of being physical was a gift in itself.

She swiped the sweat from her eyes with one boxing glove, blinking against the sting of the salt and halted the workout to have a half-bottle of water. She'd woken up, still in a funk she couldn't seem to shake. Why did Dr. Druitt kill himself? The unanswered question pressed at her. Inspiration hit in the moment. Yes, she needed to see footage of his interrogation. She was excellent at gauging when someone was lying. It would help alleviate the guilt is she could see what happened. What was said. If he was hiding something.

Anna tugged off the gloves and tossed them on the workout bench. Then grabbed a towel to absorb the sweat, placing it around her neck, before heading for a quick shower. Dressed in comfortable capri pants and a loose-fitting white blouse a few minutes later, she slipped into the war room. The weather person had promised warm weather today, unseasonably warm for September. She should take advantage of it, get out for a good long walk with Friday, but first she had some footage to scrutinize. Druitt's interview.

She brought up the feed on screen and placed headphones over her ears. She didn't want to miss one nuance. Micro-expressions mainly, and some tells from body language and voice inflections, told the truth and were directly tied to the limbic system, one of the three main sections of the brain, the one so hardwired into our human past when freeze, flight or fight were the only options. Hell, they still were for the most part, considering how dangerous the modern world was and not getting any better judging by the news. Whereas our "lying" brain, capable of complex thought and amazing intellectual ideas, the neocortex or new brain, is the least reliable part of humans, more than capable of deceiving others. And doing it often. Which meant Anna was far more invested in watching for those one-fifteenth to one-twenty-fifth of a second "tells," when the truth broke through the surface. She watched the footage intently, so absorbed she didn't hear Tom enter the room a few minutes later. It wasn't until he set a mug of coffee in front of her, the delicious fragrance soaring in her direction, that she looked up to see him standing by her side, fresh from his morning shower.

She paused the video and tugged off her headphones.

"Morning, thanks for the coffee."

"I heard about Druitt." His expression was reserved,

almost relaxed, but a slight tic under his left eye told the story. It bothered him too.

"Yeah, it sucks. I'm trying to get a read on him."

"Was he guilty? Hiding something?"

"Don't know yet. I wish I had a better baseline on him." She took a gulp of the coffee while Tom slipped into an office chair beside her. "I also want to visit Fairbanks today. Check on the case you mentioned, Amanda Taylor. You're going to speak with Cross today, right?"

"Hmm." Tom drank some coffee from the second cup he'd brought along.

"What?"

"How did last night go with Zeke? Did you discover anything more about the trucker? You certainly got home late enough." He was studiously staring at the frozen computer screen and she couldn't see into his eyes, but there was a slight edge to his tone. Jealousy?

"Yeah, his girlfriend was busy partying at the motel in the night in question, meaning his alibi is for shit. I'll pay him a visit while I'm in Fairbanks as well."

"I'll go with you."

"No need. A long drive gives me time to think."

"But it's my case. I want to follow up on it."

Tom didn't ask for much and he was right, it was a case he was passionate about. He should be there.

"Okay, give me a couple of hours then we'll head out."

But two hours later, Anna was still undecided about Druitt's guilt or innocence, and she shut down the feed with disgust, backing out of the police department's computer system without leaving a breadcrumb trail for their IT guy to follow. The doctor was a hard man to read. Perhaps it came about due to his having to report hard news to patients and he'd learned to keep his emotions in check, but it made it darn difficult to know what the guy was thinking. Not that he was glib, more like he was reserved, careful of his words. If only they'd had the chance to hook him up to a polygraph. But he'd died too soon. Footage of the hanging didn't exist. Anchor Police didn't have cameras in the bathrooms where he'd managed the feat. It was an older jail that needed replacing, but the city budget didn't half cover the expense. Maybe now they'd be able to make a better case for it. Too late for the doctor.

Unsettled by the not knowing for certainty the doctor's guilt or innocence, Anna exited the war room and hurried to the kitchen to grab a snack. She about collided with Tom, exiting the room.

"Oops, sorry," he said, grabbing her arms to keep her from tumbling over. The maneuver brought the pair of them in close proximately, sending a flutter of excitement through Anna's body. Awkward.

She brushed him off. "It's okay. I was lost in thought and moving too fast as usual."

"I've already packed some food and water for the journey. Figured you'd be hungry."

"Good guess." She was always hungry. Hungry for truth, hungry for justice, and now apparently a roll in the hay wouldn't go amiss. Not that she was a nun, though she had been living without for so long it was second nature to turn away from temptation. Pretend it didn't exist. But from the micro-expression Tom's face exposed, his pupils enlarging and nearly taking over the colored irises, she knew the tale. He was as interested as she was. Pheromones. Nothing more. Nothing less. Can't control all your biological urges with default human biology at work. Though nobody smelled as good as Josh, which was a whole other story.

"Learn anything more about Druitt?"

"No. The guy is an enigma." Anna watched Tom pick up the carryall of food he'd prepared as she reached for a few bottles of chilled water from the fridge.

"The press doesn't seem to think so. They're crowing about the case being solved this morning and how the new Ripper wasn't nearly as clever as he thought he was. Lots of back patting going on. Hope it doesn't come back to bite them in the ass," Tom said with a grimace.

"Everyone's guard will go down now. No more patrols, even though the date for the next killing, September thirtieth, is only three weeks away."

"You worried about it? Do you really think the doctor would kill himself without protesting his innocence with every breath? I know I would." Tom's expression turned righteous, defiant, his body language screaming fight, not flight. He was a good man to be teamed up with.

"I think Druitt was a realist, an intellectual man who had come to be idolized by his patients. He saw the forensic evidence, the fiber that linked him to the killings on the famous hat, his obvious interest in the 1888 murders, and his being in the play that was actually debuting in London at the time—I still can't believe that remarkable coincidence—and he accepted the inevitable. He was going to be charged, his family was going to go through hell, his stellular reputation in tatters, and he made the decision not to go through the shame of it all. As to whether he's guilty, unfortunately, only time will tell. If we don't get another letter issued, bragging that we didn't catch him this time, maybe it's over? Until October rolls around, I'm keeping my guard up."

"Please do. The thought of anything happening to you, Anna, well, I don't want to go there." Tom's expression shifted to one of concern for her well-being.

"Nothing's going to happen to me or to anyone I care about."

They'd reached the front door now and they both stepped outside in the warm sunlit day. A certain shift in the air current as the pair of them walked along the cobblestone sidewalk that ran in front of her new home drew Anna's attention. A sense of being almost in a bubble of time, cut off from normal sensation and transported to another moment. An image exploded across her vision. Of a woman lying dead, her throat cut and her face horribly butchered made her gag. She stopped in her tracks and took deep breaths, trying to dispel the frightening image. It had come on so fast, like nothing she had experienced before. A premonition?

"What is it? What's wrong?"

Tom dropped his bag and took her by the shoulders, staring intently at her.

Anna shook her head. "I don't think this is over."

FORTY-TWO

"So, there's no official citizen patrols tonight, no safeguards just in case?" Zoe asked. She was in Anna's kitchen helping her prepare for the dedication ceremony of Tia's Place, the dog sanctuary the three siblings were financially supporting together to honor the memory of their beloved sister, Tia. One of the town's veterinarians, Georgina Mann, was also helping by connecting it to her practice and providing vet services. Zoe's new boyfriend, Cullen Cross, was joining them later, still wrapping up at the office even though he was his day off. The man was a human dynamo, helping other departments across the country now that things had settled down around Anchor.

"No, nothing official among the residents." The Amanda Taylor case had come to a standstill as well. Anna and Tom's visit to Fairbanks had turned up no definitive connection anyone could prove to the Anchor crimes and the Amanda Taylor case of the victim being left with her throat cut at the town dump. Thirty-nine stab wounds in total though she was not eviscerated—a word that made Anna shudder with horror every time it came to mind. Two pertinent facts, the date of the killing coincided with a case from 1888: The Bank Holiday Murder of August sixth of Martha Tabram at the George Yard Buildings site, her body found on a landing by another tenant. And she was mutilated in the same way.

Anna had made the discoveries about the two sisters and was certain they held significance, even though the death was not connected to the canonical killings accepted by most contributed to the original Jack the Ripper. Had it been the practice run that had led to the later killings in Anchor? There was no connection to Druitt either. Unfortunately, Amanda's sister Christine was still missing but presumed dead by local law enforcement. Tom still had hopes of finding the sister alive, but Anna had grave doubts.

Tom had found a place of his own and had moved out over a week ago. She missed his presence and especially his culinary skills. But it was time. A big man like Tom Jackson needed space. Not to mention he was becoming a distraction, though he could never hold a candle to the torch she would always carry for Josh.

Squirrel's death had since been ruled an accident by Cross and no suspects found to date. Nothing getting completely solved was wearing on Anna. She kept feeling the other shoe was going to drop any second.

"You need to keep your guard up tonight, sis," Anna added. Tom, Josh, and Anna were intending to keep a careful watch on the town until the early morning hours, along with a handful of neighbors they'd managed to persuade to forgo a night's sleep to help. The Anchor

Police Department had authorized extra officers on shift as well.

"Everyone's so certain that Dr. Druitt did it."

"Everyone wants to *believe* he did it. Helps them sleep at night."

"But you don't?" Zoe turned from her sandwich making task to stare at her, her beautiful blue eyes troubled. Even though it would have easy enough to have the event entirely catered, the siblings had decided a personal touch was required. Tia would have done the same. In fact, was always the first person to volunteer to help out at any event that needed her help. She'd loved to bake and make crafts that always brought in funds for town groups, volunteering her time whenever and wherever she was asked. Her Christmas contributions were highly sought after, especially her handmade tree ornaments. Just thinking about it brought tears to Anna's eyes she blinked away. Today was going to be rough enough without getting maudlin.

"The jury's still out." In point of fact, a group of twelve had never been convened due to Druitt's suicide. "Until tomorrow rolls around, we can't be certain." Then maybe, if nothing happened, *please God let it be so*, then everyone could breathe a little easier. No doubt there had to be others wondering and worrying in town, still on the fence about the doctor's guilt. Someone could have planted the hat. But no break-ins had been recorded by the security company. If the women had died by another hand, the unsub would have to possess similar skills to Anna to go undetected. Not impossible, but not likely either.

"There's been nothing from him in the press," Zoe said, stacking the completed sandwiches into a plastic carryall.

263

"He might be playing opossum. With everyone's guard down, he can strike again with impunity."

"You are pretty paranoid these days, sis. Just sayin'."

"You reckon?" Anna gave a snort of laughter. "But it's the only way I can feel I've done everything within my power to stop anything more happening to this town or my family." Neither of them needed to mention how Anna blamed herself for being away the day Tia was taken by the Black Rose Killer.

"How did your dinner date with Zeke Law go?"

"It wasn't a date. It was a thank you for allowing me to use his tech equipment and keeping him up all night. Least I could do." The dinner had gone about per par, a bit too much drinking and no action on the play. Anna had made certain of it by going home alone.

"Does he know that?" Zoe smiled, raising her eyebrows.

"I've always made it clear I've got no time for romance. How about you and Cross? Crossed any lines yet?" Anna teased, studiously finishing boxing up the lunch for the event. She decided to eat a sandwich to avoid getting hungry during the event in case she was too busy and stood with her back to the counter eating it, watching her sister.

"Clever, Anna." Zoe blushed, her lips quirking into a smile. "But yeah, I like him. Quite a bit as it happens. But it's early days. We'll see."

"If tomorrow rolls around uneventfully," Anna said. "Then we need to have him over again. Though his being so taken by you hasn't helped his track record any. He found so little forensic evidence on the Ripper case." Anna shook her head in pretend wonder. "He seems to be losing his touch. I wonder who's responsible for that distraction?"

Zoe ignored her dig and asked, "Did he send you the specs for the DNA lab set up? He said he was going to."

"Not yet. But it's been a busy time." What was that about? She had expected him to have sent them as well, he'd seemed so gung-ho. Anna glanced at the clock. "We should be going."

FORTY-THREE

12:15 A.M. SEPTEMBER 30—ANCHOR, ALASKA

"Kelly! Door!" Sonja Smith shouted over the loud knocking, busy pulling the tray of chocolate chip muffins from the oven while ducking the onslaught of heat threatening to frizz her newly styled hair. Her heart rate increased, thinking of her date in less than an hour. It had come out of the blue. All hush, hush and quite intriguing. A romantic tryst set up for the same time they'd met two weeks ago while out walking their dogs. She could thank Diva for it, her blue-eyed husky dog always wanting to be let out after midnight into the backyard. But this time, she'd taken off, the gate being off the latch, someone having bumped into it or forgotten to close it, Diva in hot pursuit of a squirrel. She'd gone after her, nearly bumping into the man in the back lane.

He was such a gentleman too. All apologetic about running into her when it had clearly been her own fault. Nice and tall, just how she liked her men. Not overly physical like Bear. She crossed herself, thinking ill of the dead. A part of her would always be grateful to Anna Hale for saving her life, but she did miss having a man around the place.

The man had shared a love of breath mints too, offering to share his pack of wintergreen mints. He smelled nice as well, a tidy well-dressed man, a bit unusual for the outskirts of the Whitechapel neighborhood. One day she hoped to raise the funds to move out of it, but her job at the local drugstore paid for shit.

The knocking continued, louder, and she cursed. Kelly was notorious for encasing herself in headphones and ignoring the world. Something they fought over on a regular basis. She set the muffins aside and took off the oven mitts. Then marched to the front of the house, glancing at the hall clock. It was nearly midnight. She didn't have time for this.

She yanked the door open and found herself face to face with Anna Hale.

"Anna, what a surprise. Is something wrong?" Sonja glanced up and down the street, but everything appeared normal. Well, as normal as any other day in the rundown neighborhood.

Anna shook her head, her expression so Anna Hale. Determined and concerned. "Nothing to report so far."

"What is there to report on?" Sonja frowned.

"Ah, you've forgotten. This is a notorious night in history. 1888, Whitechapel, London, England," Anna prompted her.

"But that's over with. You helped nail the killer. It was all over the news, well, still pops up. A doctor yet, doing what he did." Sonja stepped back. "Would you like to come in for coffee? I made muffins." Hopefully she wouldn't stay too long. But the woman had saved her life and helped her daughter. She did owe her common courtesy.

"Sorry. I'll take a rain check though. I only wanted to look in on you and Kelly. She's home?"

"Yup, up in her bedroom. Too lazy to answer the damn door."

"Good. That puts my mind at ease. You're looking nice, by the way. That's a gorgeous blue dress."

"Thanks." It was on the tip of her tongue to mention the new man in her life, but Anna's phone rang.

"Oops, sorry, I gotta take this one."

"No problem. You stay safe as well." Sonja closed the door, breathing a sigh of relief. Just enough time to freshen up and then she'd nab Diva to head out for a walk in the back alley. She didn't want to miss the opportunity to meet up with her neighbor. Who knew, it might lead to romance. And she'd always trusted people who loved dogs more than those who didn't. Bear hated Diva and look how that ended. She shuddered and pushed the gruesome thought aside, rushing to reapply her lipstick and grab Diva's leash.

FORTY-FOUR

3:25 A.M. SEPTEMBER 30—ANCHOR, ALASKA

"What was that?" Josh asked, stopping to listen as something clattered to the ground nearby. He and Anna were making up one of the seventeen teams comprised of residents and police officers volunteering to patrol till dawn. They had convened at 1100 hours, acting as the eyes and ears of Anchor with extra boots on the ground. Other than an earlier fiasco when Rick Bowness's flare gun had fired off by accident bringing everyone running an hour ago, it had gone off without a hitch. Maybe they would get lucky and no one would be harmed tonight?

"Sounds like a metal garbage can lid fell off." Anna shivered in her light fall jacket, wishing she'd brought along a hat and warmer gloves. It had turned colder in the past hour, draining her enthusiasm. But hope was rising in her as well. Maybe the monster was truly gone? Dead in his jail cell. Because shamed or not, she could not make sense of an innocent person killing themselves. Hell, if she were accused of a crime she had not committed, she'd be protesting her innocence all the way to the Supreme Court.

A large creature came lumbering out of a yard, barreling toward them, not twenty yards away.

"Damn, that's a black bear!" Josh pulled his gun and held it braced between his hands, ready to shoot if it did not veer off. Anna followed suit, her stare never leaving the unpredictable creature.

Black bears in town were not unheard of. Dangerous creatures if one got between them and their cubs, but otherwise they tended to leave people alone in the fall after a summer of feasting on wild berries and fish. Wild packs of dogs were more of a problem. Anna had rescued Friday during a purge this past winter when he'd come to her place to hide out and found her, something she was grateful for.

Fortunately, the creature decided not to tackle the humans and headed across the street in the direction leading away from town. But not before it had been exposed in the light of a glaring street lamp.

"Was that blood on his muzzle?" What were the chances of it being red paint at this time of night? "It looks wet too."

"Crap, I hope not," Josh muttered, holstering his gun. Anna slipped her Glock back into place as well. They'd made their way back to Sonja Smith's street in a circular route, her house now less than half a block away, meaning they were now on the outskirts of Whitechapel, the eastern edge of town. A terrible feeling of dread came over her and Anna began to run, a loud drumbeat echoed in her, demanding answers.

They followed the path they'd seen the bear exit from, using their flashlights to check the ground for any blood spots. Nothing obvious, though the darkness and running full bore didn't make their job any easier. They rounded the back of the house next door to Sonja's, headed for the alley. Her heart rate increasing alarmingly, making it harder to breathe. Anna kept her glance directed at the ground, shifting her focus back and forth across the narrow trail. It was covered with scant gravel and debris from litterers that used the area as their personal garbage dump.

A shape suddenly emerged in the glare of her flashlight, laying on the dirt behind Sonja's, near the rickety fence. *No.* A woman lying face up, blood obscuring her face. Who was it? Sonja or Kelly? Or someone else? A strip of blue peeked out from under a thick black skirt. Was it the same dress she had admired on Sonja earlier tonight? The sharp stench of feces and blood made her stomach recoil.

Anna came to a halt, incapable of movement, her feet refusing to come any closer to the body. She crouched down on the gravel. Her breathing was rapid and uneven. She worked hard to regain control of all her senses, pushing away the panic that erupted. Josh moved between her and the victim, obscuring her view while leaning over to check.

"Who is it?" she managed to ask, her voice strained.

"I'm not sure. It's hard to tell with the injuries. No ID."

"Who does she represent? Elizabeth Stride or Catherine Eddowes?" Anna had to know. The initials of the 1888 victim would tell the tale of what had happened to her. What her eyes refused to see at first glance.

"There's so much blood I can't say. But judging by the injuries, it must be Catherine Eddowes. Goddamn it, the bear has contaminated the body. Are we ever going to catch a break?"

The atrocities of what had been done to the woman, having the worst of the mutilations inflicted of the women murdered made Anna's heart lurch. And then to have a bear come upon her. She pressed a hand to her chest in hopes of calming it down. Last thing she needed now was to have a heart attack. An operation to close a small hole in her heart years ago left her aware of being careful though she had never allowed it to stop her from doing anything that needed doing. In fact, it probably had her thinking in the opposite direction. If time was shorter for her, she needed to do all she could while she still had the chance.

"Fuck," Josh said, then used his radio to call it in.

"*A will o' the wisp, are they real or insane?*" she whispered, reciting the line of poetry from a poem about the Ripper she'd read in the back of Druitt's journal, apparently his own original words. The specter of death hung over their current location, a pall in the air that frazzled her nerves even further. Who was this phantom that struck so cruelly, then vanished without a trace? Was he truly untouchable? Uncatchable? As elusive as the original one he chose to emulate from over a hundred years ago? She felt ungrounded, indecisive and beat up. Not something she was prepared to deal with. Anna always had a plan, a straight path forward. But she recognized the dark night of the soul in the moment, as terrifying as any she had experienced.

"What?" he asked, giving her an odd look.

She took a few deep breaths in an effort to calm herself, closing her eyes tightly. A sense of wetness on the back of her hand made her lurch away. But it was only a dog, having come up to check her out. The animal's sad and worried eyes watched her intently, needing reassurance. Was this the woman's pet? Sonja and Kelly had a husky dog.

She held out a trembling hand and stroked the silky texture of its fur, needing to comfort the husky as much as herself. "It's okay, boy. We'll get you home." Anna took the dog's abandoned leash and stood up. "I think this is Sonya and Kelly Smith's dog. They live here. I'll take her inside and see to her needs."

"Good idea. I'm calling this in. You going to be okay?"

"No choice." Anna shambled down the alley, the dog's leash firmly clenched in her hand. She'd head around to the front door and avoid the backyard. There would be evidence there she didn't want to disturb.

An owl hooted ominously from a nearby tree, the only sound breaking the silence of the sleeping neighborhood. The husky trotted at her side, seeming comforted by her being there. Animals were so trusting of humans. Though that wasn't entirely true. She'd seen Friday avoid certain people like the plague until he was certain. Of course, he was far more insightful than most. But what had this poor animal witnessed in the victim's final moments? She prayed she'd run away and not been subject to the savagery, especially if it was her owner. Was it Sonja in the backyard? Everything pointed at it, and yet she still clung to some faint hope that Kelly's mom wasn't dead. That Anna hadn't rescued her from Bear only to have her murdered at another's brutal hand.

She was about to knock on the front door when a devastating realization came over Anna. Another woman had also died tonight. Not as hideously attacked as this victim, but she'd have her throat cut if the same pattern was at play and Anna had no reason to believe it wasn't. More importantly, what was she going to say to Kelly? She'd be suspicious of Anna being here with her dog.

Anna was standing there, dithering when the dog gave a sharp bark of warning. Her cell phone chimed and she answered it, grateful for the reprieve, keeping an eye out for trouble.

"How are you feeling?" Zoe asked. Her tone was gruff, unusual for her sister. Not to mention the time of night or more accurately, morning.

Startled by the question, Anna swallowed her pain, needing to try to sound somewhat normal to her sister. She'd know soon enough anyway.

"I'm still standing and on patrol. Why?"

"Food poisoning. I've got it. Cross has it. And tons of other people that were at our event today. Did you eat anything there?"

"No. I ate before we left the house. Remember? I had one of the sandwiches we'd made and a lemonade." The news was startling and unwelcomed. What was going on? The food had been prepared under the best sanitary condition, bought fresh, and stored properly. She gave Zoe's inquiry a quick thought, trying to make sense of it while her mind churned on what she had just witnessed. She swallowed hard against the onslaught of horror, feeling like she was standing on the edge of a precipice. And when she looked downward, it was bottomless. "How about the caterer for the deserts? Maybe the blame lies there?"

"If you're not sick, that could be the case." Zoe sounded relieved. "Are you sure you're okay? You sound off."

She wanted to share the worry, but held her tongue, knowing it would only add to Zoe's bad start to the day. And it was the start of another one, false dawn beginning to lighten one of the darkest nights in Anchor's history on the eastern edge of the distant Denali Mountain, its snowy ridges and peaks firmly fixed in Anna's memory bank. The old mountain had stood silent while humans abused the earth and each other. Did it judge? If not, it should. The mountains were here before them and would outlive them. Humbled by the thought, Anna kept her own counsel. "I just found a dog I'm returning to its owners. I'll call you later."

"Good. I'll check in with the caterers soon as it's a decent hour and try to get to the bottom of this. Oh shit, I gotta go, I'm going to puke again!"

The line went dead. Anna slipped the phone back into her pocket. She wanted to knock on the door, she really did, but found herself slumping down to sit on the bottom step, her arms around the husky dog. A while later the sounds of sirens sliced through the cocoon of silence around the pair, making them both startle. How much time had passed, she couldn't say, but some words ran across her brain now like a tickertape parade, leaving strength in their wake.

Wolf is the pathfinder. They follow the scent and are never sidetracked by emotion as they track their prey.

Anna got to her feet, ready for battle. Or at least to do what had to be done, one step at a time. She rang the doorbell, her heart once more hammering away defiantly in her chest.

FORTY-FIVE

When the door finally opened, a sleepy Kelly emerged, her hair in disarray and her feet bare. She'd pulled a tattered robe around her thin body, her sleep pants covered in a print pattern of cavorting cats, causing Anna to choke up. She looked so young, so vulnerable, so innocent and unaware of the evil that had veered into her path this night.

"Anna, what are you doing here?" she asked, squinting at Anna. The sun had crossed the horizon and was glaring into the young girl's eyes. Then she noticed the husky waiting patiently at Anna's side. "Diva, did you get out again?"

The young girl became aware then of the police cruisers parked on the street. Some had gone around back with the ambulance and Anna could hear voices emulating from the backyard.

"What's going on?"

"Can I come in? Diva needs food and water."

"Aw, sure." Kelly backed up and then closed the door behind Anna and Diva, still hovering at her side, like their shared experience had bonded them. The young girl led the way to the kitchen. "I wonder where Mom is? She's a light sleeper, not like me, and with all this activity..." Kelly's voice trailed off as she caught sight of the expression on Anna's pale face as she turned to face her.

"What is it? Tell me. Is Mom okay?"

"I'm sorry, Kelly. I have bad news."

The girl shook her head violently and put her hands over her ears. "No! Don't tell me. I don't want to hear it."

"Can I get you anything? Some water?" Anna asked, looking around the tiny kitchen. The scent of chocolate still hung in the air, incongruous with the scene happening in real time. The police and medical personnel so close by, not fifty feet from where they stood dealing with her mother's remains. The plate of plastic-wrapped muffins stood testimony to the happy event taking place scant hours ago, now replaced with a horror Anna felt incapable of sharing. But she had to prepare Kelly. The days ahead would be hard, darker than the young girl had ever experienced. Anna felt the burden of guilt descend on her, not having been able to stop this from happening.

"No. I don't need anything from you." Kelly crossed her arms over her chest.

"Kelly, I'm so sorry for your loss. I have no words to tell you how badly I feel."

"How you feel!" The girl was quick to anger. "The great Anna Hale, right! Just go. I want to be alone."

"No, being alone will make it worse. How about I make you some coffee?" Anna ignored her tirade and made herself calm down. Kelly needed her, so much more than she realized. Anna had been there too. Knew this would pass, but it would take time. A lot of time.

Grief always had the upper hand, bending you to her fickle will. But you will get past it. Nothing else for it.

Her fist now pressed to her mouth; Kelly slumped onto a chair. "Is Mom hurt?"

Anna nodded. "She's gone, Kelly. I'm so sorry. She went fast, I'm sure." All the Ripper victims were strangled, rendered dead or unconscious before their throats were cut and the other atrocities inflicted.

"How? Who?"

This was the hardest part, the part shredding her heart with a steel-edged grater. "Looks like she was another victim of the Ripper." The words hung in the air, heavy and stifling. Unretractable.

"No! He's dead. You caught him! You promised! Everyone said."

The young girl swayed on her feet and Anna rushed to her side, gathering her in her arms. The wails of grief penetrated the last of Anna's defenses. Tears trickled down her cheeks, anointing them both.

Loud knocking at the front door brought Anna back to herself. She blinked away the tears and gently sat Kelly down on a chair. "I have to answer it. Someone might need something or have some news."

Diva trailed her down the hallway to the foyer. Anna was beginning to wonder if she and Friday might get along. The dog seemed so lost without Sonja, and Kelly was in no shape to see to her needs. Or maybe Charlie could take her in? She was back at home now; certain the killer was off the streets since Druitt committed suicide.

When Anna opened the door, Josh stood in the opening, his expression weary. "Hey, are you okay?" He gave her a closer scrutiny, obviously noting her reddened eyes.

"Working on it. Any news?"

"Cross is here."

"How's he doing? Zoe said everyone was struck by food poisoning."

"Yeah, seems to be. Not puking or anything. I didn't eat anything so I'm fine. Tom had to go home, hit him hard." The worry lines in Josh's face deepened. "How's Kelly doing?"

Anna sighed, tugging the tie from her hair and redoing her ponytail, shoving in all the pieces that were annoying her. "About what you'd expect. Devastated."

"I think you should take her to your place."

"Sure, if she'll come."

"I'm going to my friend Joy's house." Kelly's voice made Anna spin around.

"You're always welcome to stay with me."

Kelly's mouth pinched tight and she was certain she was holding something back. Anna braced herself for a rant about her inability to catch the killer. Then the girl shook her head. "No. I'm going now." It was then she realized the young girl had a backpack on. "Can you take care of Diva?"

"Of course."

"Kelly, I'm sorry about your mom, but I do have some questions for you before you go," Josh said, his expression pained.

The girl's shoulders drooped.

"It won't take long, I promise. I need to know if you heard anything? Or knew anything about what your mom was doing outside last night?"

Kelly shook her head. "I slept until Anna knocked on the door. Nothing strange at all happened. No weird noises. Nothing. Can I go now?"

"I saw Sonja around midnight," Anna said, glancing at Josh. "She was all dressed up in a pretty blue dress. I mentioned it to her, said how nice she looked. She was baking muffins. Maybe she was meeting someone?"

"Are you saying this is all my mom's fault?" Kelly's voice rose an octave. "Because if you'd done your jobs properly, my mom would still be alive!" And with that, Kelly opened the front door and raced off down the sidewalk, vanishing from view.

"Do we know if there's a second victim yet?" Anna asked, biting her lower lip.

"No, not yet. You should go home and get some rest. Take the dog with you."

"Yeah, I need time to think. How could he do it?" The question tumbled out.

"Who? The killer?"

"No. Druitt. If he was innocent, why would he off himself? Did I do this, Josh? Harass an innocent man? Get him killed?" The heavy burden of guilt fell onto her shoulders like a python around her neck, trying to squeeze the very life out of her.

"No. Quit blaming yourself. It's not going to help. Innocent people don't kill themselves in my experience. He could have stepped up, shouted his innocence to the world." Josh shook his head. "There must be some other reason why he did it."

"Have you checked out his home computer thoroughly? Was he maybe into something else?"

"That's a good question. He died so quickly. It might have escaped closer scrutiny. Everyone thought he was guilty."

"I don't know if I should tell you this, though you might have guessed, but I still have remote access to his work one..." Her voice trailed off. It might be a long shot, but she needed to know. "But if I could have access to his personal one, I could check it out on the oft chance the answer lies within."

"Actually, that's a good idea. There's going to be all sorts of blowback to the department over this."

"You'll bring it to me?"

"No. But I will have our tech guy put it under the microscope. ASAP."

Anna sighed, itching to have the task to do to keep her mind off things. But this would have to do.

"Okay. Call me as soon as you have something."

"You as well, Anna. But get some rest." She was about to speak when he added, "Please, you look all done in."

"Diva, time to go." The dog stood up straighter, obviously prepared to follow Anna.

"Diva?" Josh gave a ghost of a smile. "Friday should find her interesting. Hope you had him fixed."

"Yeah, but I don't know about her. I can only hope they get along okay. Otherwise, I'll need to separate them."

"I'll have someone give you a lift," he said, opening the front door.

"Yeah, I've had enough exercise for one day." They'd walked for hours last night, all in vain. Another woman dead and a body still out there, yet to be found. This case was beyond belief, so confounding it was gutting her.

The hollow feeling continued all the way back to her house in the police cruiser, driven by the constable Josh had asked to see her home.

"Thanks, Mac," she said, getting out of the front seat, instantly followed by Diva.

"Take care, Anna," he said before driving off.

The pair of them trudged up the sidewalk to the front door and let themselves in. Friday appeared, then stood shock still, taking in the sight of a new face, a dog face at that in his home.

"It's okay, Friday, this is Diva. She needs a place to stay for a few days. Her owner, well, she's gone." Why she felt the need to explain things like Friday was human she couldn't say, but usually it worked and things went smoothly. Diva wagged her tail in greeting, like she was saying, *please, don't throw me out. I'll be good.*

A small staring contest ensued. Nobody won, both standing their ground, paws planted, like old-fashioned gun slingers. At least Friday wasn't growling. She'd seen him respond worse to humans he didn't trust.

"Okay guys, I don't have time for this. I'm beat. Maybe we could call a truce? Or I can put Diva into another room? Come on, Diva. I'll put you in a guest room with food and water."

Anna skirted Friday. Diva was careful to stay on the opposite side of her as Friday while they passed by. A low growl ensued, but they made it to the kitchen in one piece. Anna quickly gathered supplies for Diva, then escorted her to a guest room, laying down the items for easy access for the dog.

But Diva began to whine as soon as Anna tried to leave, not wanting to be left alone. Friday waited outside the doorway.

"I'm sorry, girl. I know this sucks. But I can't take a chance somebody might get hurt. Friday is half wolf and he's been with me a long time. Even saved my life once." She crouched down at the dog's side and gave her a hug. Surprisingly, her eyes filled with tears as the young dog licked her face, as if to say, *I understand.*

Friday seemed to have a change of heart, coming into the room to stand near them, offering support. She'd brought Friday home a few hours earlier, feeling it was better for him to be here than out on the streets this night. Looked like she was right. What had poor Diva witnessed in those final moments?

"Are you okay with this?" she asked him, giving him a straightforward look in the eyes.

He gave a soft chuff. When he left the room, then came back with his favorite squeaky toy thirty seconds later and set it down in front of Diva, Anna's bruised heart began to heal.

"Okay, now we rest."

Anna wearily face-planted on the guest room bed. She was fast asleep in seconds.

FORTY-SIX

The annoying ring of her cell phone woke Anna. She groaned and rolled over, struggling to get it out of her pocket and to her ear.

"Hey," she mumbled into it. She checked the time. Almost noon. She'd slept for hours, in a dark hole of sweet nothingness. Friday was awake, watching over her. Diva was still sound asleep, curled up at Anna's side.

"Anna, it's Josh."

Her heart gave a start and she sat up, riveted by his voice underlaid with excitement. "What is it?"

"We found it. Well, the tech guy found it. Druitt was into kiddy porn, that's why he didn't want to be investigated any further."

She let out a long, low breath. "I didn't see that coming. At least it makes sense now."

"So, it means shed the guilt and get back to work. We need your help, now more than ever."

"You got it."

"And brace yourself, the FBI are back and there's a

town meeting scheduled tonight. And Chief Davis sends his regards."

"Chief Davis. Really?"

"I may or may not have leaked the intel that it was your idea to search Druitt's personal computer more thoroughly."

"Thanks." Anna refocused on the case. "Do you think the Ripper knew that about Druitt? Set him up?"

"If so, then the guy's in the know about this town. Someone who lives here and is close to the case. Understands which strings to pull. A killer that clever? Frightening isn't the word for it."

"Not as uncommon as you'd think, though this madman takes it to a whole new level implicating other suspects. He must have planted the deerstalker hat as evidence. A lot of killers like to insert themselves in an investigation. And maybe this unsub is closer to home than we think. Watch your back, Josh. It could even be someone in your department. Remember Karloff?"

"Don't remind me. Lucky he got himself killed or he'd have a lot to answer for. I'd flay him all over again."

"Anything specific you want me to do? Oh shit, I forgot to ask. Sorry, I just woke up, but did you find another body?"

"I didn't want to lead with that, but yeah, we did."

Anna's heart rate jacked up again. "Who?"

"Jennifer Wick."

"The name doesn't ring a bell."

"She was found in Whitechapel, identical killing to the Ripper's supposed quick one before he got more time at the second murder site. She lives in Whitechapel as well, been arrested a few times for prostitution. She was thirty-nine."

"And then there was one," she mused, not realizing she was speaking aloud.

"We have to catch him before that! I have nightmares about what he did to that poor last victim back in 1888. Butchered them beyond recognition. We have to catch him, Anna. I don't think I could live with myself if we don't."

"We *will* catch him. I have no doubt of it." People lie all the times, and sometimes for not as good a reason as reassuring a friend. But damn it, yes, they had to stop the monster before his final immoral act. It couldn't be tolerated, no matter what she had to do, she would stop this if it killed her.

"I hope you're right. I gotta go."

Anna set her phone down and looked at her two furry babies getting along like they were from the same litter, both looking to her to make a signal as to what the deal was. The sight warmed her heart. She hurried to get up. She had a job to do.

FORTY-SEVEN

Anna headed down the hallway to Cross's office, intent on finding answers. As usual the air was thick with disinfectant and other nose assaulting odors that didn't bear mentioning. To date, Cross's intel had taken them exactly nowhere. A fake suspect, no leads, not enough forensics that seemed to help sleuth out the evildoer. Of course he couldn't invent them. But still he needed to step up his game. Was he so enamored of her sister he was letting it hamper him by taking his mind off the case? If that was the deal, she needed to set him straight. They could play footsie later, after the case was solved and a woman's life saved.

"Anna, what are you doing here?" Cross wasn't the only one in his office as she noted when she barged right in. The police chief and an FBI agent were seated across the desk from him. She ignored their inquiring glances and spoke directly to the medical examiner.

"I need to talk to you. Outside. Now."

"I'm in a meeting here. Can't this wait?" Cross was

flustered by her interruption, looking from her to his bosses.

"Anna needs to hear this as well," Chief Davis said, gesturing for her to take a seat. Surprised at the invitation, she advanced into the room and took a chair. Anna recognized Special Agent Jack Decker. She nodded a greeting he returned.

"As I was saying, it's good news. We now have DNA, from one of the victims, Jennifer Wick, that we can compare to anyone we test. And look for facial scratches, that's the most likely place the skin came from—under her fingernails."

Stunned, Anna took a deep breath. *Finally.* Now they had him by the shorties. They could compare the DNA to everyone in town if they wanted, guaranteeing answers. They just needed to finish the process before November ninth, the day of the infamous Mary Kelly murder. If only her lab was in place already. How long would it take to get it up and operational? She knew everyone would pitch in.

"You will have all available services of the FBI at your disposal," Special Agent Decker said, getting up from his seat. "Good work, Cross." The pair shook hands and Decker left the office.

"I want to build a DNA testing lab right here in Anchor," Anna said, turning her focus to the two men left in the room.

"That's an expensive undertaking," Chief Davis said, giving her a closer look of scrutiny. "But we can use all the help we can get. Can it be made functional in time? Cross, what do you think of this idea?"

"Anna and I have already discussed this and I came up with a plan. I need to send the file I've compiled to her. Sorry, Anna, I've been preoccupied." Cross gave her a weak smile of apology. She had to suppress the urge to throttle him. The lab could have already been underway. She knew she was being irrational. The guy had been working hard, no doubt, but if he had time to date her sister, surely he could have gotten to her request sooner.

"I understand. Do you think it's possible to get it up and running in a couple of weeks? I have room at my place to set up a temporary one. Later, I could build a separate lab." The idea was taking shape in her mind. "We've got forty days and forty nights to find this killer before he strikes again." The parallels to the Bible were not lost on her.

"Maybe we can ask Agent Decker to assist us? The FBI must have suppliers? That could speed it up," Chief Davis suggested. "This is a special case. Clear cut, in my opinion. We need resources, and we needed them yesterday."

"Anything. I want to help," Anna said. "What good is money if you can't use to help others? We need to find this monster. Now."

"Good. You'll need deep pockets for this one. I'll talk with him. Good work, Cross."

Anna got up and shook the police chief's hand. "Thank you."

"I'll be in touch, Anna."

Then it was her and Cullen Cross.

"What about the ring? Did he leave any imprints this time?"

Cross nodded. His expression was grim.

"So, what do we do first?"

"I'll send you all the specs right now by email. And if Agent Decker can help grease the wheels, all the better. Hell, with luck, maybe they can even see their way to supplying all our needs."

"Cooperation with the feds. Never thought I'd see the day," Anna said to lighten the atmosphere. Cross looked stressed to her, though that could be the aftereffects of food poisoning, and she needed him onboard to get on with things. Now that they had a direction, a focus, no longer floundering in the dark, needing facts and a plan. Then she remembered what had happened that night, and her stomach rolled over with anguish for the two victims of such terrible atrocities. She would use that to propel her forward, nothing else for it. A wolf howled in her mind. The pack was gathering for the kill.

FORTY-EIGHT

"How's the testing going?" Zoe asked. She'd dropped by Anna's to check in with her sister, saying she had a favor to ask.

"It's going," Anna said, looking up from pouring them each a beer. "No luck yet."

Anna's lab had been assembled and in working order a week ago. Testing had been going on non-stop since. Time pressed at her from every direction. Forty days to solve this mystery, to save a life. Though she had to hand it to all the law agencies, cooperation had been the key to working their way through the backlog of DNA samples that would have swamped the town otherwise. At the town meeting a few weeks back, hundreds of men had stepped forward to have their DNA ruled out.

She handed Zoe a beer and sat down across from her at the kitchen table. Friday and Diva were also both in attendance, bedded down in their separate areas. She had to hand it to them, they'd worked it out better than most people. Kelly hadn't wanted the responsibility and Anna couldn't blame her; she was grieving her mom's death. And she didn't have the heart to hand Diva over to Tia's Place for adoption. Not yet anyway. But Charlie was considering taking her. Anna didn't like to press her, but the sooner she made up her mind, the better. Diva was imprinting on Anna more each day. Friday too.

"How's it going with you and Cross?" Anna asked, pretending nonchalance.

"It's going. Not sure we're compatible. But right now, with so much riding on things, I barely see him so who knows." Zoe picked at the label on her beer bottle, a habit she'd had for years.

"Yeah, it's been a crazy time. Worst summer and fall on record. God, I'm looking forward to New Year's already. This year I swear is worse than when Covid hit. You had a favor to ask?"

"I need to get away. Take a break from all this stress. Women being murdered, someone poisoning food. I mean, what the fuck is going on?" There had been a couple more incidents of food contamination in town since the night Sonja and Jennifer had been murdered. But with all resources geared to finding the Ripper, nothing had been uncovered. Thankfully, no one had died, just been inconvenienced for twenty-four to forty-eight hours.

"You going away with Cross?"

"Yeah, if I can talk Cullen into it."

"I'm sure he could use the break too. Not only is he working at the lab, but he's been putting in overtime with me. He's been a great help. Helped train my lab techs."

"That's another reason I want to spend time with him away from here. My sister speaks well of him."

"I guess I have been rather fussy about who you spend time with. But no apologies. You deserve the best, sis." Anna took a long pull on her beer. She was tired to the core as well, helping out in the lab day and night. "When are you planning to go and where?"

"I wanted it to be this weekend, but I couldn't book us into that picturesque bed-and-breakfast we went to a few years back. Remember the one, Eagle Point Lodge, less than half a day's drive from here. It has to be November seventh. Sorry. But we'll be back on the eighth by lunchtime. It's only one night. And it's the last opportunity to get away before winter settles in and the road to the lodge becomes impassable. Please, sis, I really need this."

Anna gave her sister a look, not needing to mention the date that stood out in infamy, November ninth, the night Mary Kelly was butchered in Miller's Court.

"Everything will be over by then anyway. With everyone getting tested, the killer will be uncovered," Zoe continued in a more confident tone. "Any day now."

"One test at a time." Anna's worry was he was hiding out, refusing to come forward. Though where that could be remained a mystery. Why hadn't the killer been found in the wide net cast already? It defied reason. Either the murderer was a real will o' the wisp which Anna didn't believe in or he was incredibly lucky like the first Ripper. "What's the favor? You said you wanted to ask me something?"

"Yeah, could you persuade Cullen that he's not the only person in the universe that can test DNA? And feed his fish? He's very fussy about his exotics." Zoe rolled her eyes playfully.

It was little enough to ask. "Of course." A part of her was relieved that Zoe wouldn't be here in town if, in the worst-case scenario, the evilest of villains in memory struck again. No. *That can't be allowed to happen. Not if I have to go door to door and beg for more samples right up until November ninth.*

FORTY-NINE

6:30 P.M. NOVEMBER 8—ANCHOR, ALASKA

"This is fucking insane! How the hell has he escaped us? We've tested just about everyone in town and the surrounding area. Where the fuck is he hiding out?" Josh exploded, banging his fist down hard on the table in Anna's basement lab. Another test, another failure. Anna knew his pain. She shared it and then some. At least Zoe was still safely away with Cross, a snowstorm having prevented their traveling home today. They'd decided to be home before the ninth, but in this was better in Anna's opinion, glad her sister was safely out of town. Anna hadn't heard from her since yesterday when she'd called about the weather, the storm apparently hitting the worst at Eagle Point Lodge. But the last terse message was they weren't getting along, fighting about something. It didn't look good for the pair going forward. Well, at least the time away had helped them see things more clearly. Now was the opportunity to find out if they were compatible, not after they'd made a commitment.

She glanced at the clock.

"Oh shit, I was supposed to feed Cross's fish!" She'd call Tom and have him do it but he was back in Nome, visiting family, though he'd promised to be home the following day.

"I'll go with you. I need the fresh air."

"Jill, can you handle things while I go out? I won't be long."

Her dedicated tech looked up from her work, her eyes a piercing green and steady over the mask. "No problem. I had a nap this afternoon. I'm good to go."

"Thanks, I'll be back soon." Anna hoped to keep Jill Livingston on after the crisis had passed. The convenience of having the lab in Anchor far outweighed the cost in her opinion.

Anna grabbed her winter parka and exited the house with Josh and Friday who insisted on coming along. The cold was bitter, cutting to the bone, the storm more than likely having reached blizzard status in the past couple of hours. Good chance it would keep man or beast from moving about tonight. Tom would be hard pressed to make it home tomorrow. She prayed the storm would keep everyone from moving around, that Mother Nature would stop this madman in his tracks.

Anna shivered as the wind picked up, howling its power, throwing ice shards at her like a BB gun at the exposed skin of her face. She bent forward holding the hood of her parka tighter, trying to avoid the onslaught as they hurried to her four-wheel-drive half-ton, clamoring inside.

"Shitty day."

"Not fit for man or beast. Maybe feeding the fish can wait till tomorrow?"

"I promised to make sure they're okay. Cross is fanatical about them. What if the power has gone out at his place or something shut off? He's been so helpful to me. I can't neglect this one small favor."

"Not so small a favor in this storm. But okay, but if we get stuck, you're digging us out this time."

Anna smiled, starting the truck and then driving carefully down the lane to the street. As if Josh would ever let her dig them out alone.

Ten minutes later she pulled into the driveway outside the two-story house Cross had bought near his office.

"Did I tell you that Zoe and Cross were fighting per the last message I got before the storm? Zoe's gone quiet so maybe the outcome was grim."

"Good. I hope they broke up. The guy's not right for our sister. He gives me the creeps."

"I didn't know that. You never said."

"He's good at his job, I'll give him that, and I'm grateful he helped you set up the lab, but otherwise, I think Zoe can do better. Find someone with an actual personality."

"I'm with you there. But then no one's good enough for her, right?" Anna joked. "Okay, let's slug through these snow drifts and get this job done."

The three of them trooped up to Cross's front door and Anna let them in with the spare keys she been given by him. Soon as he was inside, Friday growled a warning, raising the hair on her neck.

"What is it? Do you hear something?" Anna whispered. The three of them stood still, listening in the dimness of the front hallway. But it was hard to hear over the howls of the storm.

Friday gave her a look, as if he wanted to tell her something of great importance. Anna's mouth went dry. What the fuck was going on? Had someone broken in? Was the thief hiding somewhere inside?

But there was no evidence of anything amiss. Then something began to converge in the dimness of the hall, a misty white shadow at first, swirling and collecting finally into a figure of a woman. Tia.

"Tia," Anna breathed the word, her eyes wide open. The figure pointed upward.

She looked at Josh, his eyes as startled and shocked as she knew hers must be. "Do you see her?"

"Yes. We need to follow her."

But the figure vanished as soon as they moved.

Shaken, Anna and Josh pulled their guns. Josh pointed, whispering, "You open the doors and I'll back your play."

Slowly the trio advanced through the house, guns steady between their braced hands, until all the rooms were cleared. They found nothing amiss. Re-holstering her Glock, Anna breathed a sigh of relief.

"I don't know what that was about, but it was damn spooky. Add the storm and I thought we were in a horror movie time warp," Josh said.

Anna's mind went straight to work. They had been warned for some reason. This was no coincidence. What was she missing?

"I want to search every square inch of this place. Tia didn't show up out of the blue for no reason. And Friday agrees with her. I don't take that lightly."

"Neither do I."

They went straight to work, but hours later after a

thorough search they had come up with absolutely nothing.

"I don't know. Maybe we're wasting our time," Josh said, his tone suggesting his exhaustion.

"No. There's something here. Something we're missing."

"But we've looked everywhere. Unless he has a secret compartment somewhere which could take days or even weeks to find, we're out of luck and time."

Think, Anna.

"Who does Cross admire?"

"I have no idea."

"Dexter. From the TV series. The one about the blood splatter guy who took out serial killers. Rather liked him myself. But what if he did the same as the character did? Put the evidence behind a vent?"

Josh looked less tired as he cocked his head. "It's worth a try."

"Cross has no air conditioner like Dexter did, but I saw a vent in the bathroom, one in the kitchen and a few others over the furnace ducts."

"You check the bathroom and kitchen and I'll start on the furnace vents. If we find nothing, then I think we can relax a bit. Chalk it down to a wild goose chase."

She didn't say aloud what she was thinking. How brilliant it would be for the M.E. to be the unsub. He could manipulate evidence, keeping his involvement hidden forever. The more she thought about it, the more convinced Anna was that it was a possibility that Cross was involved. What his possible motive could be escaped her though. But she couldn't allow herself to waste any energy looking past this moment. Too much was riding on it.

She ran back toward the bathroom, her legs filled

with lead, her movements clumsy. An uneasiness had crept into her soul and she fought hard to keep her focus. She tore at the screws holding the vent in place with her Leatherman tool, swearing at them as they seemed to move too slowly, longer screws that necessary for a light-weight vent. Finally it popped free and she held her flashlight up to the entrance, moving it all around to check the insides. Nothing.

She raced to the kitchen, and had the same result. Josh had already removed most of the furnace vents on the main floor with no result. She headed upstairs into the master bedroom, noting how filled up with furniture it was. She walked slowly along the baseboards, checking if maybe a vent was perhaps covered up by a dresser or wardrobe. *Yes.* She caught glimpse of one barely peeking out from behind a dresser. Grunting, she pushed it aside to give her access. Bending down, she worked to loosen the screws and pull it free. To look inside she had to get right down on the floor. Her knees squawked, but she managed the feat.

There was something there. A small metal box. She pulled it out and pried it open. Inside were a few relics. A thick banded brass ring grabbed her attention and she used her Leatherman's nail file to pick it up to avoid leaving fingerprints. Her pulse skittered. The ring had the same design of chain-links that she'd first seen on the Mary Anne Nichols victim copycat, Julie Ann Johnson. The same imprint turning up on all the others as well.

"Josh! Get in here!"

Terror filled Anna, threatening to explode her heart. Zoe was with Cross.

FIFTY

Anna forced away the darkness threatening to overcome her. Now was not the time to succumb. Now was the time for action.

"We have to warn Zoe." Josh pulled out his phone. "Damn, she's not answering. What's the number for the lodge?"

"I have it on my cell."

But Anna's fingers didn't seem to want to obey her command and she struggled for a second calling up the lodge's front desk.

"Good evening, Eagle Point Lodge. How may I help you?"

"I need to connect with room two oh eight. Zoe Pace?"

"One moment please."

Anna couldn't allow herself to think as she waited for the phone to be picked up.

301

Then the sound of her sister's dear voice came onto the open line and her body relaxed, allowing her to refill her lungs with air. "Anna. Why are you calling me on the lodge phone? Aw, shit, with everything that's happened, I forgot to charge my phone."

"Have you been crying?"

"Yeah, Cullen left last night after we had a huge fight, leaving me stranded. I was going to rent a four-by-four today, but the storm's pretty bad here. How's it there?"

"Bad too. Did he say where he was headed?"

"Home, I guess. He didn't share his intentions with me. He left before the storm hit."

"Zoe's safe. Cross left her there." Anna covered the phone for a moment to tell Josh. His expression of relief warmed her. They could both breathe now. Maybe even more important for Josh with his asthma. She noted a slight wheeze to his breathing and it worried her.

"You okay?" she asked.

"Yeah."

"There's been some developments here." Anna quickly filled her in. "If Cross does come back, call the police immediately."

"I had no idea. The fucking monster! To think I spent time with him." A short pause, then Zoe asked, "If he didn't want to hurt me, then who is he going after tonight?"

"I don't know." Anna shook her head, her mind racing. Where was he intending to strike this time? And who?

"We only have a few hours before he could strike again," Josh said as she ended the call with Zoe, mirroring her own thoughts. "We have to figure this out. Now."

Not could, but would. Anna had no doubt that Cross had pulled out of the weekend with Zoe to head back to do his final, foul deed. What he hadn't planned for, was anyone knowing what they knew. Cross was the Jack the Ripper wannabee. Fucking bastard.

FIFTY-ONE

Kelly pulled off her headphones, sensing something off in the house, certain she'd heard an odd noise. A step creaked on the stairs. She shot out of bed, nearly tripping on her backpack.

She grabbed a baseball bat she kept hidden behind her nightstand and crept to the door she'd locked earlier, holding it over her shoulder.

"I've called 9-1-1," she shouted out. Maybe that would be enough? The threat. She kept the bat in place as she awkwardly fished her phone out of her pocket, punching in the number.

"What's your emergency?"

"Someone's in the house. Kelly Smith. Sonja's daughter." She swallowed the grief that immediately overtook her. "I'm locked in my bedroom. I got a baseball bat."

The door suddenly crashed open. She dropped her phone in shock, the bat long forgotten on her shoulder. A man dressed all in white, including a white ski mask, came at her, his hands outstretched. He grabbed her around the throat and squeezed hard. Darkness loomed as he dragged her from the room, helpless to do anything about it. He dragged her down the staircase and into the kitchen, before hauling her out the back door. The world swam around her, her mind spinning dizzily from shock and lack of oxygen. The bite of the icy cold piercing her bare skin woke Kelly up and she began struggling with her assailant to get away.

"Let me go!" she shouted; her voice carried away by the hurricane-force wind.

The asshole in white ignored her, picking her up and throwing her in the back of his van. Then he too climbed in and tied her hands together with a plastic tie before forcing a rag into her mouth.

He jumped out and slammed the door shut. Where was he taking her? Who was this person? Her mind didn't want to go where her suspicions lay. Was this him? The Ripper? The date was right. Why had she moved back home a week ago? She could have stayed with her friend Joy a little longer. Now she was in a terrible fix and had no idea of how to escape.

FIFTY-TWO

"Where to now?" Josh's face was pale in the dash light, his fingers drumming on the dash. They'd been to Kelly Smith's house, and she was gone. The 9-1-1 call meant things were escalating, out of control. They only had one chance left to find the girl in time. The murder was about to happen, any moment, and fear was riding Anna so hard she felt the taste of death in her throat.

"I have to think. Where would he take her? Miller's Court was a rooming house, right. And where was Kelly found when I searched for her? The Yellowbird Motel. That must be it."

Anna yanked the half-ton into gear and took off, making a U-turn and nearly spinning out on the slippery street. To his credit, Josh didn't say "slow down" but held on to the truck frame instead.

"You call Zeke," she said.

Her heart hammering in her throat, they pulled into the parking lot of the Yellowbird before Zeke answered

Josh's call. The vacancy sign was off, meaning Zeke Law had gone to bed.

Then the light went on and the pair of them tumbled out of the truck, headed for the office.

Zeke was talking to Josh on the phone as the pair swept through the door.

"No time. Did a man rent a room tonight? Cullen Cross. Though that's probably not the name he gave you." Anna grabbed Josh's phone and moved close to Zeke, showing him a photo.

"No. Haven't seen anyone like that. I'll grab my coat and keys and we'll take a look." For a man fast sleep, Zeke appeared to be waking up quickly in the emergency.

The three of them headed down the line up of cabins, knocking and then opening any door that wasn't answered. Nothing except a few expletives from the occupants. Had she been wrong? Lost her last chance to rescue Kelly? Sick to her stomach Anna tried to think.

"What about the old cabin George Stubbs and his nephew stayed in out back?" she asked.

"Worth a look," Josh said.

The trio rushed in the direction of the dilapidated old dwelling, stumbling through the deep drifts hampering the way.

"I'll go around back," Josh said in Anna's ear, trying to make himself heard over the fierce storm. Of all nights for an emergency. Worse than fog.

Her cheeks blazing from the frigid temperatures, she pressed onward, praying with all her might with every step. Please, please be here and alive.

When she was certain Josh was in position, she gestured for Zeke to knock on the door, the Glock held between her hands.

"Police, open up!"

Zeke unlocked the door, pushing it open. An unholy scene greeted their eyes. A room encased in plastic, like the TV show *Dexter's* essential killing scene, a man all in white standing in the middle of it. A body lay on a cot pushed up against the wall, outlined by a sheet. The room looked familiar, the plastic having been painted mural-like, resembling something she'd seen in an old photograph. With horror, she recognized what Cross had been trying to recreate: #13 Miller's Court. The location of Mary Kelly's horrific murder.

Was Kelly still alive? She held the gun on Cross who raised his hands up in surrender meaning she couldn't shoot him much as she wanted to. She shouted, "Face down on the floor!"

But instead of doing it, he leaped toward her, pushing her aside. The gun was knocked from her hands. Zeke reacted, jumping on Cross, trying to take him to the ground. Josh came in the door and ended it, grabbing hold of him as well in a bear hug.

"Stop moving, asshole!" Josh said, yanking Cross's arms to secure them behind his back.

Anna rushed to the bed, her hands trembling as she pulled the sheet off. A gag covered Kelly's mouth, but otherwise she looked unharmed, her blue eyes wide open and pleading with her. Anna about collapsed with relief, her head throbbing, a thousand mosquitoes droning on in the worst-case of tinnitus she'd ever experienced. But instead, she held herself together with pure willpower and released the terrified young girl from her bounds. Then hugged Kelly tightly, afraid to ever let go.

FIFTY-THREE

4:00 A.M. NOVEMBER 9—ANCHOR, ALASKA

Josh and Anna sat in her kitchen, having a debriefing over a glass of whiskey. After Josh booked Cross into jail and their statements had been taken, they'd come back to Anna's place by mutual consent.

"I texted Tom about what happened tonight. He was pretty shaken up. Pissed he wasn't here to take Cross down. Not sure Cross would have made it to jail," Anna said, trying to make a lame joke of it all.

"I know how he feels. But Cross will be tortured. Killing him would be to let him off easy. He needs to be vilified, then hung in the town square. He'll be under twenty-four-hour a day suicide watch. No way is he weaseling out of paying the piper, unlike Druitt who left his family to pay the price. He'll be stripped of everything he holds dear. His reputation will be shredded and he'll go down in history as a failed wannabee. That alone will kill him, make his life miserable. He's gone from being revered for his ability to take down criminals in his lab to being a reviled, disgusting criminal. No one falls further than that. No one."

"True," Anna agreed. The liquor warmed her body, added a rosy glow around Josh. As always, he'd been here for her. Always arriving when she needed him the most, ever since they were children growing up next door to each other. "Have I told you lately how much I appreciate you in my life."

"No. Can't say you have of late. But I feel exactly the same. I need an Anna Hale moment every day to make it complete."

"An Anna Hale moment? What is that comprised of?" The drink had loosened her tongue and the words slipped out.

"With my hyperthymesia, I have so many stored in my memory bank of you, it defies reason. But suffice to say they all affect me in some way. Mostly for the good."

"And the best ones?" Why bother asking about the bad ones? She'd always believed humans spend far too much energy dwelling on the bad and not on the good. On moving forward and doing the best they could under any circumstance. Not that she hadn't lapsed, one time in particular stood out in her mind when she was flattened by the Black Rose Killer, but that just made her all the more human. It was the picking yourself up, dusting yourself off, and starting again that counted the most.

"The ones where you thank me with a hug and a kiss."

The words hung between them. Potent. Personal. Perfect.

"I guess I owe you another one," Anna said, getting up from her chair. As she drew closer to Josh his fragrance flooded her. The scent of outdoors, fresh and breezy underlaid by a manly musk. It stirred all her senses as he got to his feet and they embraced. She pulled back after a sweet moment and kissed him full on the lips. "Thank you for being there for me. I don't know how I'd do all this without you." She tasted the whiskey on his lips and licked hers now, enjoying the flavor. Enjoying Josh even more, his strong arms around her holding her tight. He kept her grounded.

"Me neither. You're my rock," he said. "But I'd better go. It's late and you must be exhausted."

She grimaced, reluctant to see him go. "Was a day, wasn't it? Getting the bad guy?"

They broke apart. Josh cleared his throat. "I think we need to channel our energies toward finding out who's been tampering with the food in our town next? No one appears to have a clue. And now that the Ripper case is solved…"

"Yeah, I was thinking that too." Anna moved away and picked up their glasses to rinse, feeling like she'd missed a moment, leaving a sense of longing in its wake. *A wolf can mate, but must stay true to the course, never straying far.*

"I'll pick up Tom tomorrow and we can have a strategy meeting." Josh kissed the back of her head as she stood in front of the sink. "Rest now. You've earned it."

"You too." She turned around and gave him a bright smile she wasn't feeling.

She watched him stride from the room. Friday watched too, then turned his deep golden-brown eyes on her. They were filled with sympathy.

"Yeah, back to being just us, eh boy?"

Diva gave a chuff, as if reminding her she was company too.

"And Diva, of course."

Anna turned out the light, gazing into the backyard with unseeing eyes. Food poisoning? Didn't a cult in some town try it a few years back? She sat back down at the table and rebooted her laptop. She had a new case. Best get at it. What better medicine for lost love than work?

A wolf howled in the distance, its call mournful, before others picked up the chorus. They reminded her she was never truly alone. She had her pack.

ACKNOWLEDGMENTS

I want to thank everyone at Rough Edges Press for their wonderful support, especially Mike Bray, Jake Bray, Rachel Del Grosso, Amy Briggs, Jason Bates, Patience Bramlett, John Buck, Brent Towns, Thonie Hevron, Darrel Sparkman, and all the other authors who blessed me with not only a warm welcome, but a wealth of wonderful stories to read and enjoy!

And to you, dear reader, thanks for taking the time to read and perhaps review with thoughts of sharing my work with others. Absolutely nothing beats word of mouth! And if my story gave you some entertainment or respite while captivating you to another world or touched your heart, that's the best an author can hope for.

A LOOK AT: CITY OF LIES
A HARDBOILED MYSTERY

A Gripping Tale of Identity, Crime, and Survival...

Claire Preston, a script reader for a Hollywood movie studio, has recently lost her mother. Discovering she was adopted as a baby, she goes on a perilous quest for her true identity.

Assisted by her mentor, the seasoned private investigator, Jake Sterling, Claire delves deeper into her past, only to unearth a labyrinth of secrets more daunting than she ever envisioned. Soon, she finds herself in the crosshairs of a ruthless serial killer—an ex-Nazi fugitive evading justice for decades.

As Claire confronts her heritage, grapples with danger, and races against time to evade the clutches of a deadly predator, she finds herself wondering: Is uncovering the truth in a city of lies even possible?

AVAILABLE NOW

ABOUT THE AUTHOR

January Bain is an award-winning author who firmly believes that stories unite us, that good stories help us to discover the commonality of the human experience by supporting values, empathy and understanding. She has had the pleasure of select novels being turned into games, and her work is also available in different languages.

She and her husband live in rural Canada on peaceful acreage where a variety of wildlife comes to visit regularly and expect to be fed and paid attention to.